The Rogue
by Emma V. Leech

Published by: Emma V. Leech.
Cover Art by Victoria Cooper
Copyright (c) Emma V. Leech 2017
ISBN-13: 978-1545172292
ISBN-10: 1545172293
ASIN: B06XF78DKQ

****

All rights reserved. Without limiting the rights under copyright reserved above, no part of this publication may be reproduced, stored in or introduced into a retrieval system, or transmitted, in any form, or by any means (electronic, mechanical, photocopying, recording, or otherwise) without the prior written permission of both the copyright owner and the above publisher of this book. This is a work of fiction. Names, characters, places, brands, media and incidents are either the product of the author's imagination or are used fictitiously. The author acknowledges the trademarked status and trademark owners of various products referenced in this work of fiction, which have been used without permission. The publication/use of these trademarks is not authorized, associated with, or sponsored by the trademark owners. This ebook is licensed for your personal enjoyment only. This ebook may not be re-sold or given away to other people. If you would like to share this book with another person, please purchase an additional copy for each person you share it with.

No identification with actual persons (living or deceased), places, buildings and products is inferred. The Earl of Falmouth was a real person and the family and the house still exist, however this is a work of fiction.

Table of Contents

A Smuggler's Song	1
Chapter 1	2
Chapter 2	11
Chapter 3	21
Chapter 4	27
Chapter 5	34
Chapter 6	45
Chapter 7	52
Chapter 8	57
Chapter 9	66
Chapter 10	71
Chapter 11	77
Chapter 12	83
Chapter 13	89
Chapter 14	97
Chapter 15	104
Chapter 16	109
Chapter 17	115
Chapter 18	122
Chapter 19	128
Chapter 20	135
Chapter 21	140
Chapter 22	145
Chapter 23	152
Chapter 24	159
Chapter 25	162

Chapter 26	168
Chapter 27	175
Chapter 28	182
Chapter 29	188
Chapter 30	197
Chapter 31	204
Chapter 32	209
Chapter 33	215
Chapter 34	220
Chapter 35	228
Chapter 36	235
Chapter 37	241
The Earl's Temptation	250
Prologue	252
Chapter 1	255
Want more Emma?	263
About Me!	264
Other Works by Emma V. Leech	266
Audio Books	269
To Dare a Duke	270
Dare to be Wicked	272
Dying for a Duke	274
The Key to Erebus	276
The Dark Prince	278
Acknowledgements	280

A Smuggler's Song

If you wake at midnight and hear a horse's feet.
Don't go drawing back the blind,
or looking in the street.
Them that ask no questions isn't told a lie.
Watch the wall my darling,
While the Gentlemen go by.

-Rudyard Kipling

Chapter 1

"Wherein our heroine loses a handkerchief and gains more than she bargained for."

Henrietta Morton followed the gaze of her maid as she stared out of the shop window and was unsurprised to see her attention had been taken by a strutting, preening flock of red jackets.

Tutting with impatience, she rolled her eyes. Annie's attention span was limited at the best of times but get her within eyelash-batting distance of a handsome man and you'd lose her entirely.

Though Henri had to admit there was an air of excitement about the men this morning. They seemed alert and full of enthusiasm for something, with the officers shouting orders and the men running to obey them with alacrity. She wondered if the *gentlemen* had been at work last night as they called the smugglers involved in the free trade that was so rife in the area.

Everyone knew to draw their curtains and look the other way when a run was in progress. She prayed that no one got caught. Life was desperately hard here in Cornwall, and it was no wonder people turned to smuggling.

She pursed her lips as Annie fussed with her own mousy brown hair, pinched her already pink cheeks and surreptitiously adjusted her pale, freckled bosoms to greater advantage, obviously hopeful that the men would still be there on their way back home. Ignoring her maid's wistful sigh with a frown, Henri returned her own gaze to the shopkeeper's offerings.

Mr Warren had been most attentive this morning, far more so than ever before, she thought, failing to keep the scowl from her face. He was usually rather short with her, and anxious to get back

The Rogue

to his other customers - the ones who paid. The only reason she dared show her face here now was because her father had finally made good on his outstanding bill. The reason why that bill had been paid was also the reason for her visit, and her unhappiness.

Mr Warren came back again, this time with white silk gloves. The man had been scurrying back and forth with every item and scrap of material he thought might please her for the past hour. She had inspected the finest cloth, sprigged muslin, spotted muslin, striped, checked and embroidered muslin; cambric and kerseymere and enough silk to rig a Man o War. But in fact, nothing could please her, and the acres of white lace laid out before her only filled her with dismay.

She had tried with all her strength not to feel bitter about the situation she now found herself in, but all her hopes and dreams for the future had been shattered, and there was nothing she could do about it.

"Lawd," said her maid with another sigh of longing. "Ain't they pretty?"

Henri tutted and returned her attention to the redcoats, under no illusion that the woman had been speaking of the lace. "Do you think you could keep your mind on the job for just a moment?" she said, looking around and hoping no one else was watching Annie, whose tongue was practically lolling.

"Not while them tight breeches is in full view, no, miss, don't reckon I can."

Henri rolled her eyes and cursed her father. Cursing her father was becoming a daily ritual.

Lord John Morton was an amiable fellow, beloved by all, except those with outstanding bills and currently his daughter. Henri spent most of her time trying to fend off the bailiffs. It was he who had engaged Annie Tripp, a woman of questionable morals and background, to be Henri's lady's maid.

At the impressionable age of thirteen and after the death of her mother, she had been introduced to a far wider world than she had ever imagined by the lurid tales of the woman at her side. Annie had been found in London in the service of one of Lord Morton's friends. Her native London accent and vocabulary was coarse and colourful and spoke vividly of Cheapside where it appeared she had lived since a child. Any further background was vague at best. Rather than bestir himself to find a more suitable prospect for his only child, Lord Morton found Annie was available - her previous charge having been recently married - and instantly engaged her as abigail to Henrietta.

Her suitability or otherwise for such a position seemed not to have troubled him unduly, further than the fact she seemed kind and wouldn't scold Henri too harshly. Of course, it wasn't that her father was uncaring or indeed an unloving parent, in fact he doted on his daughter. He was, however, oblivious to the dangers of the world at large, and specifically those pertaining to a young girl.

Henri had, in fact, navigated those last five years with no visible damage, and would even go so far as to believe Annie had done her much good, opening her eyes to the ways of the world and men in particular. In this at least her father had been forgiven. But she was now to be married to pay his debts, to a man who was considered by her own acquaintances to be the devil himself. This man was possibly even responsible for the death of his own brother; and that she was finding harder to forgive.

She bit her tongue against the barrage of angry words that seemed to be forever crowded in her mouth these past days and tried to find some enthusiasm for the intricate detail on the Honiton lace she held in her hands. It was incredibly fine, with a motif of honey bees dotted around the edges. Wasps would have been more appropriate. She grimaced at the thought and then chided herself for her bitterness. Except it wasn't fair, it was her father's fault they were facing ruin. It was he who had gambled away what little fortune they'd had, and now she was to be sold off to the highest bidder.

The Rogue

She closed her eyes against the prickle of tears that gathered and walked away to the back of the shop on the pretext of looking at the ribbons, leaving Annie to enjoy the view until Henri could regain her composure. She wiped her eyes on her handkerchief and sniffed, allowing herself to indulge in a rare moment of pity.

The shop's back door beckoned. It led out onto the proprietor's garden, and she spent a moment looking out at a rather wonderful view of her own, this time over the fields and countryside and out to the sea. Far more exposed than the southern coast of Cornwall, here on the north coast the little villages huddled against the cliff for protection.

The place had a wild and untamed nature that suited Henri who would often escape for long walks as close to the sheer cliffs as she dared. She would stand for hours with the wind whipping her hair about her face, staring off into the distance and wondering what life might hold on the other side of the world. Annie, always more practical and less romantic, had a different view about these walks, and most especially the shocking state of her petticoats by the time she got home.

But on days like today, she wanted to escape more than ever, perhaps even to run away and not come back. The sea was calm and glittering, the sky a bright and cheerful blue that tempted you into believing spring was just around the corner, though everyone knew well it was far off yet. As always, though, the sea calmed her heart a little and it was with a resigned sigh she turned back, intending to return to Annie and the blasted lace for her veil. But the sudden crash of a door opening and shutting with some force had her spinning around in alarm. The sight that greeted her did nothing to calm her.

It was a man though he seemed to share little resemblance to the fine peacocks parading at the front of the shop. The look of this man spoke of a fierce and wild life, of violence and adventure, and the taking of anything he wanted, when he wanted it. A single, terrifying word screamed in her head the moment she set eyes on him: pirate!

For a moment she was perfectly certain her heart stopped in her chest, only to restart with a crash as a pair of impossibly blue eyes met hers.

He was a large and imposing presence. Tall and broad-shouldered, her eyes fell to take in strong, powerful legs encased in high leather boots. His hair was long and black and fell unruly and untamed around a square jaw. Hooped gold earrings glittered against the thick, dark locks, but it was the black mask painted in a thin band across his eyes that made fear prickle over her skin. The mask was disturbing, pagan somehow, making his eyes glitter with an intensity that would have been unsettling enough in ordinary circumstances.

Another crash of a door sounded from the front of the shop, accompanied by gasps and remonstrations from the clientele as the five-armed militia men that Annie had been admiring entered the small shop. Henri turned with her heart in her throat to see the flash of another red coat heading up through the back garden towards the door. The pirate cursed though quietly, and she could only admire his calm in the circumstances. If he truly was a pirate, he would surely hang.

He looked back to her and she knew this was the moment she should scream. She should shout out to the redcoats that their man was here and to come and get him. He was watching her, those fierce eyes remarkably placid, though it was plain he was waiting for her to react as she should.

For no good reason she could think of, Henri felt a pang of sorrow at the idea of those bright blue eyes being extinguished. In a moment of inexplicable madness, she drew back the curtain that led to a discreet changing area. Her pirate looked at her in surprise for the briefest moment and then wasted no more time in disappearing behind the heavy drapes as the door opened to allow

The Rogue

another red-coated militia man into the small shop. This one, a Lieutenant, bowed to Henri and gave a tight smile.

"Begging your pardon, miss," he said, sounding a little puffed. "I'm Lieutenant Bowcher of St Elizabeth's regiment, Royal Cornwall Militia. May I enquire, did you see anyone pass this way?"

With a calm and somewhat haughty demeanour she didn't entirely understand, she responded. "No, sir, none but my maid, and I cannot imagine it is she who is causing your men to burst in upon civilised people as though you chase Satan from the crypt." Henri gave the lieutenant the benefit of a disgusted look, the one she generally reserved for scolding their fat Labrador when he had been stealing from the kitchens again.

To her consternation it appeared the lieutenant was not quite as easily cowed as the dog, and the man stared back at her with a considering frown before marching off through the shop to demand if anyone else had seen anything.

Henri stood and inspected a truly horrible green ribbon with great interest and trembling fingers and wondered what on earth she was playing at. She was only too aware of the weight of a bright blue gaze upon her from the crack between the curtains and prayed the man would keep his head, stay still, and not prove her a liar.

The lieutenant returned to her, apparently intending to exit the way he'd come, but paused to speak once more. "We are pursuing a very dangerous individual, miss, a pirate in fact. We had word that he had business here and we know he came ashore close by. He's wanted by the crown, and by countries far beyond our own, and his deeds are many and bloody." The man paused for the import of his words to sink in before adding, "Please do let us know if you see or hear of anything that would lead to his capture. And I would suggest you return home with a male escort. It isn't safe for you to walk with just a maid while Captain Savage is on the loose."

"Captain Savage?" she repeated, her voice a little faint.

The lieutenant nodded. "There's a large reward for his capture," he added.

Perversely this last comment made Henri crosser than ever.

"Sir, I hope you do not imply that I would only do my duty as a citizen if I stand to gain some financial reward?" she demanded, drawing herself up as tall as she might.

For a moment the lieutenant looked appalled, and she was gratified to see that his cheeks were a little pink. "Of course not, miss," he said and shook his head. "I meant no offence. If you would please excuse me." And with that he hurried out the door.

Henri glanced around the shop and, satisfied that she was not being observed, she drew back the curtain. She blinked, her breath catching as she was confronted by those blue eyes again and the lieutenant's words rang in her ears.

"The staircase," she whispered, pointing across to the other side of the room. "You can get up to the store room. There is a window on the far side. I think it overlooks the alley. Can you climb down?"

"Aye," he said, his voice soft. "And I won't forget this." He was staring at her and she blinked under the intensity of that blue gaze.

"Y-you must hurry," she stammered, quite unable to tear her gaze away from his, but he just stood there, immobile, as though he was as hypnotised as she was.

When he did move, it was not in the direction she expected. His arm reached out, sliding about her waist and pulling her into the darkness behind the curtain. In some distant part of her brain, she was amazed that she didn't scream. Instead she made a tiny, startled noise of objection, and then uttered not another sound as a pair of warm, soft lips pressed firmly against hers.

The Rogue

For a moment she was frozen, her mind too stunned to react, though her hands were flat against his hard, muscular chest, trying to keep him at a little distance. When at last her shocked intellect did catch up, she was not at all sure she was pleased with it. For instead of pushing him away as she surely ought, her arms reached up, one hand sliding up his neck, fingers tangling in his long, dark hair, which was every bit as soft as she had imagined it might be. He let out a low sound, something akin to a growl which made her skin heat and her heart pound and just as suddenly he released her, but there was regret in his eyes.

"Thank you, darling," he said, amusement tugging at the corners of his mouth. "You've been most ... accommodating." He glanced at where one hand rested lightly upon his broad chest, still clutching the tear-damp handkerchief. He plucked the scrap of lace deftly from between her fingers and held it to his nose, inhaling her scent with a smile before checking the way was clear. The next moment he had crossed the room, heading for the stairs.

Henri looked down as something fell upon her toes. In his rush he had dropped something. A letter.

"Wait!" she called in a hushed voice. He turned for just a second but the sound of voices approaching hastened his tread on the stairs, and he disappeared.

Henri took a deep breath, stuffed the letter into her reticule, and turned in the direction of the voices to see Annie with Mr Warren, the shopkeeper, at her side.

"Oh, what a to do," said Annie, her eyes sparkling with excitement. "They said it 'twas 'im, the Rogue 'imself!"

"Good Lord, we'll likely be murdered in our beds," said the shopkeeper, a dapper little grey-haired man who stood wringing his hands in anxiety.

Henri drew in a sharp breath and hoped they would ascribe her flushed cheeks to the shock of their words, it was true enough. The man was gone, and her madness past, she could only wonder at her moment of insanity. And yet no matter how well she knew it had been sheer folly, she still felt the press of his soft lips against hers with a flush of warmth that heated her cheeks still further.

"Are you quite well, miss?" Annie asked, a curious expression lighting her face now.

Henri cursed her maid's sharp eyes and forced her mouth into some semblance of a smile. "Quite well, Annie, thank you," she replied, sounding a little tart, and stalked away leaving both Annie and Mr Warren looking after her in surprise.

Chapter 2

"Wherein eavesdroppers hear nothing good, a mystery is discovered, and plots hatched."

Henri walked home with what she could only imagine was the air of a brigand. Her eyes sought the shadows and she jumped at the skitter of dead leaves as the wind blew them to dance around her ankles. Annie eyed her curiously, but kept her counsel and said nothing, for which Henri was grateful. But try as she might she could not forget the sound of that low growl, the glitter of those eyes or the intense warmth of the first pair of lips she had ever encountered so closely.

With that thought came the idea she may have allowed a dangerous man to go free. What if someone really did die? It would have been all her doing. She had, however, read the tales told by the adventurous pamphleteer, Mr Charles Batch. He had painted *The Rogue* in the form of Captain Savage as a romantic hero for women to swoon over and men to condemn in public whilst secretly admiring.

Though it appeared the militia had a rather different view of his character. He was known for his dashing good looks and a smooth tongue that could charm the birds from the trees and certainly had no difficulty in liberating merchant ships of cargo and ladies of jewels, money, and sometimes husbands too.

She had once heard - from Annie of course - that he had abducted the wife of a certain Lord Haversham. The lady was en route to America and on capturing his pretty cargo, Captain Savage demanded a huge sum to release her. The monies were duly paid but the wife did not appear. In a fury the husband demanded why his wife had not been returned to him, at which point the charming rogue explained with deep apology that the lady refused to be rescued.

He was reported to have said he might have to pay the husband to take her away again.

Tales of his antics on the Barbary Coast had placed a sum on his head that would keep any man warm and fat for all the winters of his life. For all his charming reputation she wasn't fool enough to believe his life was that of a gentleman. He was a pirate at the end of the day and one who used force to steal from others.

And yet she could not believe the man she had just seen was in any way murderous. She scolded herself internally. How ridiculous, she knew nothing of him and could hardly form an opinion based on a few seconds in a darkened room and a kiss which was hardly the behaviour of a gentleman. She still did not understand why she hadn't screamed and slapped him, which would have been the action of a lady. She could only conclude that she wasn't such a lady as she had once believed. Perhaps Annie's companionship had done more harm than she'd realised after all. She'd certainly given her an interesting vocabulary.

She was so deep in thought she hardly noticed they were outside her own front door, and with horror she recognised the carriage drawn up outside and the coat of arms emblazoned on the door. It belonged to her fiancé.

"Quick!" she hissed to Annie, "round the back way."

As one they ducked beneath the window and scurried round to the servant's entrance.

"What the devil is he doing here?" Henri cursed as they tiptoed indoors through the kitchen, ignoring the cook's tut of disapproval, and made their way to the library. This room was Henri's own personal oasis and, as it was situated next to her father's office, a place where they could attempt to eavesdrop without being seen.

The Rogue

Annie, as she was shorter, stouter and had sharper elbows, reached her position beside the keyhole before Henri, who was forced to fidget with impatience as Annie relayed the relevant information.

"He wants to hasten the nuptials, miss, so ye can be wed before 'e leaves for France," Annie whispered, looking up at her with wide eyes. "Lawd, 'e's only gone an' bought a special licence!"

"What?" Henri imagined the heavy iron of a husband's hold on her person, close about her wrists and ankles. She would be shackled to the cold bastard on the other side of that door even sooner than she had thought. At thirty-six he was far older than her and darkly handsome, but his eyes had as much warmth as a winter sea and there was a cruel turn to his mouth that made her shudder.

It was no secret that all he wanted was someone to supply an heir and a pretty ornament to wear on his arm on occasion. He had no real interest in her at all. His womanising and rakish ways would continue unabated and Henri's freedom, such as it was, would be gone forever. She had already been lectured by her father about the kind of wife this man would expect. Apparently roaming the countryside unescorted and returning looking like she'd been working down the mines was unacceptable.

The injustice and inequality of the situation made her blood simmer beneath her skin. She would be expected to behave, to embroider and give tea parties and speak politely to her husband's guests no matter if she liked them or not. She would be a prisoner, his property to do with as he wished, simply because she was a woman and had no way to fight back. And all the time her worthy husband would continue to lavish grand sums on the likes of the scandalous Mrs Morris. His favourite mistress had just last week set the *ton* on their ears by driving his latest gift to her, a high-perch phaeton with two matching grey horses in violet and silver harness, through Hyde Park at the fashionable hour.

"When?" she asked, hearing the fear in her own voice.

Annie looked up at her and pity shined in her eyes. "Saturday."

Henri swallowed, the cold chill of those imaginary shackles making her shiver. With a sudden wave of empathy she remembered the way the pirate had looked as he saw the redcoat closing in on him. He had sworn low and fierce, but he hadn't panicked; he'd not despaired. Henri gritted her teeth. Well she might not be about to dance with Jack Ketch at the end of a rope, as she'd heard the servants say, but she was facing a lifetime imprisonment which looked damn bleak to her. She wasn't caught yet though. She wouldn't give in to despair, and just maybe there was another way to pay her father's debt.

Henri jolted as she heard movement from the next room as the men exited and she held her breath until the sound of wheels on gravel could be heard drawing her fiancé away outside... for the moment.

Henri crossed the room and reached for a decanter of brandy she kept to hand when her father came to chat with her. She poured herself a measure and downed it before drawing in a shocked breath as a fire lit in her throat and belly. Instead of the recriminations and gasps of horror that most lady's maids would utter on seeing their mistress act in such a manner, Annie merely snatched the decanter from her and picked up another glass.

"Don't hog it, girl, I've 'ad a shock 'n all, ain't I?" Annie muttered as Henri huffed and sat down by the fire.

Taking a deep breath as the inferno in her belly dulled to a warm glow, Henri reached into her reticule and took out the folded piece of paper that her pirate had dropped in his hurry to escape. The seal had been broken and she opened it with care.

L,

Though it seems incredible, the story was true, he lives. It appears, however, that the boy you wished to hear of did not escape after all, indeed he died that night and has been long put to rest. *A body was washed up a couple of weeks later and was identified by a gold ring. It bore the family crest and so there was no doubt in the matter. In the circumstances I think you should meddle no further in the affair, as it is too dangerous, for you more than any. If the truth of the events of that night were to come to light, many would suffer for it. There is already a price on your head but you live yet, so be content.*

I'll be at the Nag's, Wednesday as you wanted, but I implore you to stay clear. The militia is everywhere and you should trust none but your own men.

Your friend.

S

Henri bit her lip as her mind began to turn. Though the contents were cryptic to her, there might be others to whom this letter would give intelligence which her pirate might prefer to keep to himself. She wasn't so cruel as to turn him in, not after having gone to the trouble of saving him, but the fact was this could be information that others might pay for, or that, if pressed, he might pay to keep hidden.

The idea of blackmailing him - and there was little point in trying to pretend she was planning anything else - was appalling. Her stomach clenched in protest at the very idea of it but being forced to spend the rest of her days married to that ... that *fiend*, was not an option either. She folded the letter with care and put it back out of sight before she realised she was being scrutinised.

"What you be plottin', my lady?"

Henri looked up and scowled in response to the shrewd expression on Annie's face.

"Nothing to concern yourself about," she replied, trying to sound haughty to put Annie in her place, which was pointless as it had never worked before. As predicted Annie just put her hands on her ample hips and scowled.

"Don't ye be talkin' at me all *la de da*, like butter wouldn' melt. Them big brown eyes might fool yer father but I got more sense. You've got that look on ye face that means trouble, so ... what's brewin' in that mad brain of yourn?"

Henri huffed at her. Well there was no point in not asking. She needed to know. "Do you know where the Nag's Head is?" she asked, hoping she sounded nonchalant.

Annie's eyebrows hit her hairline and Henri sighed at the futility of trying to put anything at all past the wretched woman.

"The Nag's Head?" Annie shrieked with alarm. "Aye, I know it, but I ain't never set foot in the place, 'tain't safe for a respectable woman, it ain't," she said, crossing her arms over her generous bosom with a disapproving sniff. A sly grin swiftly followed, which was far less surprising and much more in character. "It's full o' smugglers, miss. Oh, aye, the *gentlemen* are the only ones who drink there, though they 'ave the best brandy you ever tasted ..." She stopped mid-sentence and pursed her lips. "Or so I'm told," she added.

Henri rolled her eyes. "Where is it then?" she demanded, watching her perplexed servant with amusement.

"Ye take the old Chapel Road to the Market place, then the alley that leads to the quay, It be down there."

Henri smiled.

"And why would ye be wantin' to go down there may I ask?" Annie demanded.

"That is none of your business," Henri said hoping she sounded authoritative. Annie's eyebrows drew together but she didn't query her any further.

Henri spent the rest of the afternoon avoiding her father and making plans. By the time it had grown dark she had changed her mind about going down to the Nag's Head a dozen or more times. She knew it was dangerous, she knew it was foolish - and she

The Rogue

determined to do it anyway. There was no point in sitting about wringing her hands and wishing the world was kinder. This world wasn't kind and never had been and if she wanted it changed it she'd damn well have to change it herself.

The house was dark and silent when she opened her bedroom door, and the full moon slanted curious patterns across the polished wood floor to the stairs. Bright silver light somehow seemed to amplify every tiny creak of the floorboards and made her anxious journey to the front door fraught with terror. She stopped for a moment on the stairs to compose herself. If she couldn't even make it to the front door without having a fit of the vapours, she wasn't going to get very far at all.

Once outside she took a breath and pulled her cashmere shawl tightly around her shoulders. The evening was icy cold and the sky clear, a heavy frost dusting everything around her with glittering white. Her breath billowed around her face and she tiptoed down the gravel path, quite certain that her father and every servant would be alerted to her night-time activities as both gravel and frozen leaves crunched with incredible volume beneath her feet. She walked with quick determination, keeping to the shadows and ducking into dark corners if she heard anyone approaching.

Henri made it to the Market Square without incident but knew that here she faced the greatest dangers. The alley that Annie had instructed her to take was not in a salubrious part of town and in normal circumstances she wouldn't even have braved it in daylight. She knew well the only kind of women who would be walking there at night *alone* were not the kind she would wish to be mistaken for. But there was nothing else to be done. If she wished to avoid marriage to a man she despised, this was her only option.

She pulled the shawl up over her hair and covered her face, and with her head down hurried into the alley. She quietly thanked her good fortune it was such a bitterly cold night. Everyone with any sense was tucked inside and by the time she stood beside the Nag's Head she could see that the place was packed, even though the windows were fogged up. She hesitated outside, peering in through the steamy glass.

The stench of the alley seemed overpowering against the clear, crisp air of the night. The mingled scents of fish guts, urine and stale ale were already heavy on the air when a large man pushed his way out through the front door of the pub, bringing with him a thick waft of tobacco smoke. Henri clung to the shadows until the man had gone on his way before taking her courage in her hands and reaching for the doorknob.

Once inside, her senses were overcome once more. The perfume of too many people crammed into too tight a space, many of them long unwashed, was spiced with brandy and rum and a heavy pall of smoke. There was a shocked silence as she entered, and she felt a prickle of fear run up and down her spine as the weight of their curious gazes fell upon her.

Scanning the room with desperation she prayed she would see her pirate. Of course it was at this point and rather belatedly that she realised just how foolish that was. He was unlikely to make himself easily seen and sit in full view of all, knowing the militia was after him. Her cheeks burned as catcalls followed her path through the room, with invitations to put a smile on her face and give her a comfy lap to sit on, though the language used to encourage her might even have put Annie to the blush.

Ignoring them with a haughty expression, though she was well aware her cheeks were burning, she fought her way towards a filthy looking bar as the stench of the place became thoroughly overwhelming. Good Lord, had she just ruined herself for nothing more than a fool's errand?

Her gaze fell upon a buxom woman who grinned at her, showing a row of uneven yellow teeth. The strumpet was sitting in some fellow's lap as he openly fondled her bare breasts. Gasping in shock and beginning to realise just how far out of her depth she really was, she began to consider turning around and running for her life, assuming she still could. She cursed her own mutton-headed stupidity and stifled a squeal as a hand reached out and pinched her behind with some enthusiasm. Without thinking she simply reacted and turned to slap the face that belonged to the hand. The deeply tanned and ruddy face seemed unmoved and in fact its owner simply roared with laughter. She noted with dismay that there was no mark of the blow against his cheek even though her hand stung fiercely.

"'Ere, Jay, thisun will warm ye up, I reckon," the big man bellowed, pointing at her as a small rat-faced man beside him leered in response. Jay she presumed.

"Aye, Mousy, reckon she would 'n all."

Henri swallowed down the little bubble of terror that fluttered in her chest before she decided that she'd come this far and she wasn't about to give up. "I wish to see Captain Savage," she said, putting up her chin and ignoring the looks of incredulity that both men were giving her. "I have something he wants," she added, and then regretted that part as the looks became ones of mutual understanding.

"Oh, aye," said the rat-faced man, smirking and looking her up and down. He wetted his lips in a manner that made Henri want to retch. "I'll just bet you 'ave," he muttered with a leer.

Henri fought the blush burning up her neck and glared at the man. "Considering I saw the militia out on the Market Square I would think you might want to take me to him sooner rather than later," she said with as much heat as she could muster. That, of course, was a lie, but lying seemed the least of her problems just at the minute.

The two men frowned with uncertainty, and for a moment she thought they would throw her out or at least question her further. In the end she was alarmed when the big man grabbed her by the wrist and towed her after him. The crowded room parted easily before his bulk and she found herself following him up a narrow and rickety wooden staircase. They continued along a dark corridor until they stood below a hatch in the ceiling. The big man reached up and pounded three times on the opening.

"It's me," he said, the words terse, turning back to look at her with a frown. "There's some woman 'ere to see the Cap'n, says she's got something for 'im."

Henri huffed as the unmistakable sound of men guffawing was heard through the ceiling. And then the hatch was drawn back.

Chapter 3

"Wherein wolves howl, mice growl, and our heroine tries not to bleat."

A pair of highly polished black boots became visible, then long, long legs, followed by a fine pair of muscular thighs in perfectly fitting breeches. The view continued in a pleasing manner as more of the hard, exquisitely sculpted male body appeared through the hatch.

Henri averted her eyes before she could be caught staring but could only echo Annie's earlier sentiments on the matter. Pretty indeed. She looked up as the man jumped down to the floor with the stealth of one who was well used to creeping about in the shadows, and he was quite adept at it despite his size. Her wide eyes once more met a familiar pair of bright blues though this time it was the pirate who looked startled.

"What the devil are you doing here?" he asked, sounding astonished and none too pleased about the matter.

The black mask was gone, but the expression he wore was just as forbidding. For a moment Henri quailed as she realised just how precarious her position now was, but in for a penny …

"I have something that belongs to you," she said, as her heart beat so hard it threatened to escape her rib cage. She swallowed and hoped her fear didn't show in her face.

To her surprise his expression softened, and he took a step towards her and held out his hand. "The letter?" he said, his voice quiet. "There was no need to bring it to me, you have risked much."

She nodded, and guilt filled her heart as she realised he thought she sought to protect him once more. He turned to the burly man beside him. "Go on, Mousy, go back downstairs. I'll deal with this."

Mousy looked back at her, his eyes filled with distrust. He folded his arms, his massive biceps pulling at the fabric of his threadbare shirt. "Lars," he growled what she assumed was the pirate's name. There was worry in his eyes. "She said there be militia in the marketplace."

The pirate looked at her, his expression sharp now. He turned back to Mousy once more and nodded. "Get eyes in the alley and around the Market Square," he said. "I want to know if those bastards so much as look in my direction."

"Aye, Cap'n," the big man growled. Henri flattened herself against the wall as his bulk passed by in the confined space of the corridor and she was left alone with Captain Savage.

He stared at her for a moment and she fought the urge to blush and stammer an apology for disturbing him.

"This way then," he said, moving back down the corridor a little and opening a door. "We can talk in here."

Henri moved to follow him, only to pause on the threshold as she noticed the bed inside the room. She stared at it for a moment, but there was no going back now. With resolution she stepped inside and closed the door behind her. There was really no point in splitting hairs. She was beyond ruined now if she was discovered, bed or no bed.

She scowled as she realised he had seen her discomfort and was smiling at her and looking unbearably smug. His eyes drifted to the bed and back to her and he raised one eyebrow.

"Let's have the letter back first, eh?" he said with a quiet rumble of laughter.

The Rogue

She realised he believed she had come in search of another kiss ... at the very least. Anger and indignation seemed to stiffen her resolve and her backbone, and she looked down at him with all the disdain of her noble birth to one far beneath her. "I don't have it," she said, allowing herself a small smirk at his confusion. "At least," she added with a knowing smile. "Not at the moment."

The air around them seemed to tremble as suspicion flickered to life in his expression. "And why would that be, my lady?" He leaned on the bedpost and she became the subject of his intense scrutiny.

A tremor of unease fluttered in her chest as she interpreted the tone of his voice and the flicker of anger just visible in his eyes.

"Because I believe it is something that has a value, something that perhaps you would be unwilling to have fall into the wrong hands." She was amazed she got the sentence out without stuttering or hearing her voice tremble. Indeed, she sounded perfectly cold-hearted and utterly calculating, which alarmed her almost as much as the fury in his expression.

"Why you little..." He seemed to bite off the end of the sentence, leaving the word he might have uttered hanging in the air between them. Henri blushed but found she couldn't gainsay him. He had every right to be furious.

Taking a step back she noted that his fists were clenched, and she knew she should be terrified. He was no gentleman but a pirate. Heaven alone knew what despicable crimes he was responsible for, and she had come here alone ... and angered him. No one would be the least bit surprised if she was found dead in a back street once they knew what she'd done, and yet she did not believe he would hurt her. Despite his obvious anger he made no move in her direction, and though he muttered foul curses under his breath, he made no threat towards her person.

She wiped her clammy hands on the thick folds of her velvet pelisse and took a breath. "Whatever you may think of me, what I am, sir, is desperate," she said, feeling she owed him some little explanation and sounding breathless now as anger at the situation she had found herself in made her emotional. She spoke carefully, trying to appear calm at least, but she didn't want to blackmail him, no matter he was hardly an innocent.

"I am sorry that your predicament gives me the means to extricate myself from an untenable situation, but the fact remains that it does, and I intend to use that letter in whichever way will serve me best." Her voice quavered, and she clasped her hands together to stop them from trembling, but she held her head up and watched for his response.

He had begun to pace the room as she spoke, only pausing to cast her looks of frustration and anger. "How much?" he growled.

She hesitated before blurting out the sum she knew was owed by her father. "Three thousand, five hundred pounds."

The enormity of the sum seemed to grow exponentially in the shabby surroundings of the inn's bedroom. To her astonishment, however, he didn't rant and curse at her. He laughed. He laughed so hard that his eyes watered, and he clutched helplessly at his chest as he fought for breath.

His amusement endeared him none to Henri, however, who fought the urge to stamp her feet and shout at him to stop. Instead she held herself still and regarded him with quiet dignity until a sharp knock at the door interrupted his mirth.

"Who is it?" he called, his hand straying to the sword at his hip.

"Mousy," bellowed a familiar voice. "Move yer arse, Cap'n, there're redcoats crawlin' the streets and headin' our way."

Henri stifled a gasp of horror as it occurred to her just what that would mean if she was found here.

"Damnation!" she said in unison with the captain who turned to look at her with a grim smile.

The Rogue

"Well I'll be damned for sure, lady," he snarled, crossing the room to her and grasping her by the arm. She took in a sharp breath as he glowered down at her, those vibrant blue eyes full of rage and frustration. "Tell me, is this your doing?" he asked, his voice quieter now. "Did you sell me out? There's a deal more money than that on offer as a reward."

"N-no," she stammered, alarmed both by his proximity and the painful strength with which he was holding on to her. "No, sir, I swear it. I never meant to see you hang. Indeed I cannot be found here, I'll be ruined and this will all have been for naught." She did not need to act to let him see the fear in her eyes; she was sure it was perfectly clear as she blinked back the prickle of tears that threatened to shame her.

He snorted and shook his head but let her go as he crossed to the window to look down on the street. "Forgive me but I can't help but observe that you've made your own bed."

Henri bridled, tears forgotten as her temper rose once again, not that she could dispute the truth of his words, but dammit that was the pot calling the kettle black. "Well, sir, I cannot help but observe that the militia will say much the same thing to you," she hissed, itching to slap his smug, self-satisfied face. "And," she added, wondering if perhaps she sounded just a trifle hysterical. "You can rest assured I will hand them that letter if you don't do all in your power to get me out of here!"

She took a moment to thank God that he didn't appear to have any of the strange and heathen supernatural powers that were sometimes ascribed to men of his ilk who spent much time overseas as the look he gave in return to her words would surely have struck her dead on the spot.

"Oh, I'll get you out of here all right," he said, his voice full of disgust as he strode for the door and once again grasped hold of her arm. He towed her behind him, pausing for just a moment before he opened the door. "And for your information I would have done so without your threat," he murmured, and she caught her breath as the blue in his eyes flashed like a lightning strike. "You might like to remember that *I* am the pirate and cut-throat," he added with a sneer of disdain. "*You* are apparently a lady." He looked her over with such contempt she felt her cheeks heat. "You understand I only mention it as you seem to be acting my part."

She blinked, rapidly, determined that he should not see her crumble, but she had never before been spoken to in such a manner, by such a man, and the shock of it was hard to take while attempting to maintain her equanimity. The problem was quickly solved, however, as she was thrust through the door and instructed to move her damn arse. She complied with as much haste as her skirts would allow and silently cursed every man that ever lived.

Chapter 4

"Wherein our heroine is forced to flee."

Henri thought that if anyone had predicted that she would be running for her life through the town in the middle of the night in the company of pirates and cut-throats she would have believed them quite mad. But she was indeed running through the town in the middle of the night in the company pf pirates and cut-throats, and she became uncomfortably aware that she should look closer to home for madness.

Whatever had possessed her to embark on this ill-fated endeavour could not be firmly brought to mind at this moment. In fact, the shouts of men and the alarming report of gunfire focused the mind quite superbly on the job of keeping alive while all those around ran for their lives.

"This way," Savage yelled over his shoulder as Henri hitched her skirts once more and tried to keep up with him. They were heading down towards the beach and she assumed that there would be a boat waiting. What would befall her after that she could not contemplate. All that mattered at this moment was getting away from the redcoats. She simply could not be discovered, or all would be lost.

She screamed as a soldier appeared from behind a crumbling building and launched himself at Savage. Flattening herself against the wall she watched in horror as the two men fought. The slash of metal against metal seemed to explode in her ears, making her wince and she was utterly unprepared for the violence she was witnessing. Reading about such things in the papers in the comfort of your own home was one thing, seeing it happen before your eyes quite another. Captain Savage was aptly named it seemed to her as he bested his opponent and sent the soldier's sword flying across the cobbles. To her surprise, though, he didn't cut the man down as she'd imagined he would.

"Run you fool," he hissed but the solider, despite the terror on his face, rolled to the side and lunged for the sword. He ran back towards his foe and with terror and repugnance she saw the captain cut him down without a moment's hesitation. She screamed then as blood poured from a wound in the man's side and he slumped to the floor with an appalling cry of pain. The fight wasn't over, though, as another soldier appeared to take the place of the last.

"Run!" he yelled to her and she screamed again as a hand grabbed hold of her arm and Mousy began to pull her down the street. "Get her to the boat!" Savage yelled.

"But ..." she began, pointing as she saw yet another redcoat join the first and the captain turned to meet the new threat.

"Come on!" Mousy roared, pulling her arm so hard she nearly went face down on the slippery cobbles. "Lars will deal with 'em."

As they ran, she looked around, hoping for an opportunity to conceal herself, to be able to slip away quietly once the redcoats had continued in their pursuit of the pirates. But alas cover was in short supply and Mousy's grip on her arm too fierce. A chance to escape both the pirates and militia was far from likely. And so she ran, gasping for breath, quite unused to running at such a pace as ladies were not supposed to exert themselves in such a fashion. Mousy let go of her arm but urged her on as they ran down the stone steps to the shore.

She stumbled as her feet hit the shingle of the beach, the surface slipping beneath the smooth soles of her shoes and she fell, only to be hauled up again by a strong pair of hands.

"Come on," said a rough voice in her ear, and she looked up to see the massive bulk of Mousy looking down at her. "Can't stop now."

The Rogue

The truth of his words was illustrated by the sharp crack of gunfire only too close behind them. She stifled a squeal and allowed Mousy to tow her down the beach. Captain Savage was running towards them at breakneck speed.

"Move dammit!" he yelled, before picking her up, wading into the sea, and throwing her none too gently into the waiting boat.

Moments later and with a screech of gravel and the slap of freezing water against the sides of the small boat, and they were heading out into the fathomless darkness of the sea.

Henri grasped the side of the boat with one hand and clutched her shawl tightly around her with the other, then she closed her eyes and prayed. There was some childish part of her brain that insisted this was just a bad dream, that she wasn't really heading out towards a pirate ship in the middle of the night but asleep in her bed. Sadly, when she dared to crack open an eyelid to see the redcoats arrayed on the beach and disappearing into the distance as they fired at the boat, it became all too real.

Mousy pushed her head down and then jerked in his seat, yelling out, before slumping down in the boat, clutching at his shoulder. Blood oozed out from between his fingers.

"He's hit," she screamed with horror, before pushing up from her seat to move beside the big man whose face was contorted with pain. "Let me see," she demanded, gently trying to prise his large hand away from the wound. "It's clean," she said, inspecting the hole, high on his shoulder. "It's gone clear through the other side. I don't think it's broken anything."

"Maybe so," Mousy grumbled. "But it hurts like a bitch."

Henri was tempted to point out she could still feel the bruise he'd left on her right buttock, but it seemed churlish in the circumstances.

"Thank you," she said, reaching out and squeezing his hand, which was approximately the size of a large ham.

Mousy shrugged and looked sheepish. "S'alright," he muttered, strangely discomfited.

She glanced up to find Captain Savage watching her curiously.

"Is he alright?"

She nodded. "He'll live," she said, wondering if the same could be said of herself. "It will need to be kept clean, do you have a surgeon?"

"Aye," he said, looking away from her. "On The Wicked Wench."

"On the..." she repeated, perplexed until she realised he was speaking of his ship. "Oh."

She looked back to the shore, and the flickering lights of the town twinkling like stars. And they may as well be in the far heavens, she thought, for her chances of reaching them again were about as likely, as the boat pulled her ever further away. "What will you do with me?" she asked, keeping her eyes down and hearing her own voice frail and awkward against the sound of the oars in the water and the men's grunts as they worked themselves hard.

She heard a snort of amusement from the captain and looked up with trepidation.

"I haven't decided yet," he said, though the threat in his tone was quite unmistakable. She swallowed, torn between contrition and holding her nerve. In the end she put up her chin.

"I still have the letter," she said.

In the moonlight his smile took on a wolfish, feral quality that made her skin prickle.

"Oh, but you don't, my lady. You told me yourself you don't have it on you, and now you have no means of contacting anyone who does." Once again Henri was filled with the sudden desire to slap him, he was so damn smug. "And don't bother making out

The Rogue

you left it with someone for safekeeping, for I shan't believe you. No one knows you're here. No one knows you're even away from home. Do they?"

There was amusement in his eyes and she gritted her teeth, damn the man. She began to think she had taken the wrong tack in dealing with Captain Savage. But it was too late now.

Savage turned his back on her and began speaking quietly with the rest of his men. Henri shivered and drew down further into her shawl. She watched with her confidence sinking into her boots as the hull of a large ship appeared in the moonlight.

The faces of men, bleached silver by the moon, appeared over the sides of the ship. Voices drifted over the water and the realisation she was about to become a prisoner suddenly hit home. Finally, and rather too late, she felt most desperately afraid. What had she done?

One thing was for certain, there would be no question of her marrying the damned fiancé now.

"Always look on the bright side, Henri," she muttered to herself.

She gasped as the small boat bumped up against the side of the ship, knocking her sideways. Before she had time to right herself, she squealed with alarm as she was lifted and slung over a strong shoulder like a sack of potatoes.

"Put me down!" she shrieked in fury. "Put me down, you wretch." She kicked and rained down blows on the broad back beneath her hands, to no avail. "You fiend! I am quite capable of climbing a ladder!" she protested though she was completely ignored.

She closed her eyes as her captor began to climb and the sight of the drop made her feel she would quite likely cast up her accounts and vomit.

Once at the top, she was sat on the rail and then given a hearty push and fell with a heavy thud to the deck. She felt quite certain her behind was going to be black and blue in the morning. Righting herself as quickly as she could, she tried to get to her feet with as much dignity as possible.

The rabble hovering all around her lifted lamps to inspect the captain's cargo more closely. She gasped and stumbled back to the rail as she was inspected under the leering gaze of a pirate crew who crowded around her. Her heart lodged somewhere in her throat apparently trying to escape her body as it beat in terror and she wondered what would become of her.

Hard glittering eyes met hers as she took in the swarthy faces of men whose lives were lived as fugitives on the seas, with no laws to constrain them but those of their own making. There was laughter and a number of predictably ribald comments as to the captain's plunder, and how exactly he was going to share it.

The man himself stepped onto the deck and grinned at his crew, accepting their congratulations with laughter. They moved back, making way for him as he walked closer to her. Henri glowered in return and thought every bad word she had ever learnt in her life in his general direction. Having grown up with Annie, the list was quite extensive, and she had every intention of using every single one on him.

"Well then, my lady." Captain Savage walked towards her, took off his hat and bowed with a theatrical flourish. "As you seem to be well aware, I am Captain Lars Savage, and whom do I have the pleasure of addressing?"

Henri brushed down the now damp skirts of her pelisse, glancing around her as her heart thudded too hard, and too fast in her chest. She had once been told that you never show fear when confronted with a vicious dog. She had the feeling the advice would serve her just as well now.

The Rogue

"I am Miss Henrietta Morton," she said, relieved that she didn't stammer. She watched in surprise as the Captain's eyes widened.

"Lord Morton's girl?" he said, clearly astonished.

Henri took a step forward. "You know my father?"

Savage frowned. He seemed vexed with her though she supposed that was understandable. "Of course I don't know your bloody father," he exclaimed. "But I know the name Morton is an old one."

Her attention was taken from the irritated captain, however, by the spectacle of Mousy clambering over the rail. His shirt was now sopping wet, stained with blood and clung to his bulky frame.

"Where's the surgeon?" she demanded, gratitude for Mousy's surprisingly selfless act in protecting her giving her a little courage. "That wound needs to be cauterised."

The look of annoyance on the captain's face grew. "Mousy get yourself below deck and see the butcher. We don't need any nursemaids here, thank you," he snapped at Henri, who closed her mouth, stung by his rebuff.

He stood staring at her for some moments and she couldn't decipher the expression on his face. What the devil was he thinking? The distance between them seemed to shrink as he watched her with the unnerving gaze of a predator. After everything that had happened this evening, Henri began to truly panic. Her breath began to come in short little gasps as the possibilities of just what he was thinking presented themselves to her with stark, cold clarity.

"Jay," he said to the little rat-faced man, without once taking his eyes from her. "Take her to my cabin."

Chapter 5

"Wherein a lamb bares her teeth."

Henri shuddered with revulsion as the rat-faced man leered at her.

"Come on then, my pretty," he said, grasping her wrist. Henri snatched her arm away from him, but he just laughed. She saw his hand move to the pistol at his hip and he tapped it with a finger. "Just as you like, miss, but you'll be coming along with me now, one way or another."

Henri had no choice but to move in the direction in which he gestured. Unused to the sway of the boat she stumbled a little and held the rail to steady herself.

The darkness on deck in the shadowy light thrown by the lamp Ratty carried conspired against her along with the glittering interest of men's eyes in dark corners. She lifted her head high, though her cheeks were burning with humiliation, and she made a point of meeting the eye of every man's gaze she found, though she was trembling so hard they must be able to see it.

If she hoped to shame them, she was disappointed. She found nothing but amusement in their eyes, and other expressions she'd rather not dwell upon.

They weren't allowed to stand idle for long, however, as the captain's voice echoed over the water, yelling instructions that were incomprehensible to her but sent men scurrying into the rigging like monkeys and hauling on lines. Overhead the snap and flap of heavy fabric rent the air as the sails billowed out, vast and ghostly against the night sky as the wind filled them and ropes creaked in protest as the sudden strain pulled them taut.

The Rogue

She followed where Ratty gestured she should go and tried to keep her dignity intact without resorting to tears, for now at least. But horror at the reality of her predicament, made it hard to do anything but put one foot in front of the other and she struggled to stay upright as the ship picked up speed. Ratty opened the door of the cabin and cocked his head, gesturing for her to go in.

It wasn't like she had a choice.

She stepped inside and watched him hang the lamp on a hook before looking around the room. Before she could say anything, she heard the door close behind her and the snick of the key in the lock.

Henri counted herself lucky that he had at least left the lamp. She slumped back against the wall of the cabin, trembling so hard her teeth chattered and holding back tears. Hysterics would not help her though the desire to give in to them was almost overwhelming. What in God's name was she to do?

She looked around herself, wondering if perhaps there was a weapon to be found. From what she could see in the dim light the room was dominated by a large desk, covered with scrolls and maps and a bewildering number of books stacked in neat piles wherever a space allowed.

Along the right-hand wall there was a heavy oak cabinet. The doors had been left open and showed shelves stuffed with more scrolls and books. To her left there was a compact berth, neatly made. A large chest sat at the foot of the bed, which she had no doubt contained the spoils of these men's plunder and would be securely locked, and a number of beautiful gilt-framed paintings hung on the walls.

All in all, the room was surprisingly comfortable and clean, if cold, in the frigid air of the winter's night. She looked around hoping to find a stove to light but there was nothing. Henri shivered, life aboard a ship may be all well and good in the tropics, during an English winter she doubted there was much to recommend it.

Finding a chair, she installed herself behind the great desk, unwilling to make herself more comfortable on the bed. But the sound of the key turning once more had her leaping to her feet.

The captain paused in the doorway, surveying her, and she wished she could see more of his expression. "I'm glad to see you are making yourself at home."

Henri racked her brain wishing she could think of some acerbic comment, but the only words that came to her were pleas that he let her go. She clamped her lips together tightly. She wouldn't be seen to beg, not yet at least. He crossed the room and picked up a little round, long-necked bottle and two glasses, and filled both of them.

"Here," he said, not unkindly, though there was a measuring look in his eyes as he handed her the glass. "It'll warm you up a little."

She took it from him, practically snatching her hand back as their fingers brushed. Unwillingly she remembered a moment earlier in the day when they had touched rather more intimately, remembered the feel of his hard body pressed against hers and the softness of his hair as her fingers had sunk into it. Had it really just been this morning? He chuckled, and she was perfectly sure he knew what she was thinking and was enjoying her discomfort.

"You must get me back," she said, clutching the glass so tight her knuckles whitened. "Before anyone notices I've gone. If you do, I swear I will give you the letter without another word. You can go your way, and I will go mine."

She watched him as he appeared to consider. His eyes glittered in the lamplight, and she could see cold calculation with no warmth or empathy visible. No doubt these were qualities that had made him such a ruthless and successful pirate.

The Rogue

"Why should I do such a thing?" He walked around his desk and she moved away from him, circling to the other side as he sat down, putting his feet up. "You tried to blackmail me." He stared at her, unblinking. "If you were a man, you'd be dead by now."

There was no emotion in his voice, no threat. Somehow that made him all the more terrifying. He was simply stating a fact. She remembered the moment he had cut down the soldier on the streets of her home. It hadn't seemed hard for him to do.

"Yes," she said, her voice too obviously betraying her fear, though she hoped her disgust was just as evident. "You seem quite adept at murder I'll give you that."

He snorted, his face placid. "I gave him the chance to run, he made his choice. Should I have let him kill me?"

"He was just doing his job!" she flung back at him, surprised by the fierceness of her words. At any rate she hadn't swooned that was something at least. Though if things went too far awry perhaps she should try it?

He seemed equally surprised by her rage and smiled at her. "As his job was to kill me, you'll forgive me if I took exception to it."

"He was someone's son!" she said in fury, appalled by his cool humour. "There will be family grieving his loss because of you ... you ... *fiend!*"

His eyes darkened, and she took a breath, stepping back a pace and wondering if she'd gone too far. She'd be a fool to forget the precarious nature of her position.

"I ... am also someone's son, my Lady Morton, in case you perhaps thought I was less than human. Though I'll admit, there would be few to grieve over my mortal remains." There was a sneer in his words and mockery in his eyes though she felt it was more directed at himself than anyone else and wondered at it.

"Yes, a son of a bitch," she cursed him, defiant all over again and then damning her sharp tongue that once again had run away with her before she'd considered the consequences.

The look he gave her chilled her blood and made her vow to watch her mouth.

"Yes," he murmured, his tone sending shivers over her skin. "A *very* good job you are a woman, my *lady.*"

She folded her arms, hoping she looked confident, though in truth she was trying to disguise the fact her hands were trembling. "Then it seems I must be thankful for the fact I have been born a female," she said, not attempting to disguise her contempt. "There is a first time for everything I suppose."

He frowned, his expression curious as he reached for the bottle and poured another measure. "Why would you say that?"

She stared back at him, eyes wide. It never ceased to amaze her that men believed women should be grateful for the accident of their birth. That they should be content to be considered property with no rights of their own, to be given by their fathers to be married off to another man who would own them in turn.

"Why would I not?" His attitude pricked at a grievance that had infuriated her since she was a small child and had first understood the restrictions of her life as a girl. She snorted as his obvious lack of understanding made his frown deepen. "Tell me, why is it you're a pirate? There are many honest ways of working at sea."

He removed his feet from the desk and leaned forward, regarding her with an intense expression. "I have a feeling you're going to tell me," he said.

There was amusement in his eyes and she felt a spark of anger.

"Because you don't like rules and you don't like to be told what to do and when to do it. Because you want to be free."

The Rogue

She watched as he smiled, a slow smile that changed his face. In her fear of the past hours she had forgotten just how handsome he was. That smile reminded her, and she remembered again the moment in the shop when he had pulled her close and kissed her.

"Well you're half right," he said, and she fought the blush she felt rising behind her skin as his eyes travelled over her. "That's not why I became a pirate, but it is why I remain so."

She knew he would not answer the question, so she asked it anyway. "Why then, what drew you to this life if not freedom and adventure?"

He chuckled again, and it was a warm sound that rumbled through her. A good sound, it made her want to make him do it again. It was all too easy to forget her fear in the warmth of that laughter and she realised this was the power he had, that easy, seductive charisma that made abducted wives want to stay with him rather than return to their lives. His long fingers caressed the side of his glass as he considered her.

"Oh no." He shook his head, smiling and rubbed at the stubble on his chin with a calloused hand. Henri looked away, wondering why those hands held her attention so. "I asked first after all," he said, "and you still haven't answered."

She huffed and turned away from him with annoyance. "Yes, I have," she snapped. "If you had only listened."

Henri sipped at her drink, enjoying the warmth that burned in her throat at least and hugged her arms about herself. The freezing temperature was biting now, and she shivered. She was tired, cold to her bones and dismayed by how badly things had gone wrong.

Perhaps the men were right, she should have been happy with her lot. Maybe she should have put her own desires and ambitions aside and been content to sit and sew and paint, to make polite conversation and marry and have children as she was supposed to, fighting it had never bought her anything but trouble and dissatisfaction. She would have been happier if she'd just done as she'd been bid.

She hadn't heard him move, and so his voice when it came directly behind her made her jump.

"You mean to tell me you long for adventure, that you want to be free?"

She turned to find him standing far closer than was comfortable. To her surprise there was no mockery in his tone, and only curiosity in his eyes. She blinked and looked away from him. She was unwilling to tell him she no longer knew what she wanted.

"Doesn't everyone?" she replied, hearing her own despair and knowing the weight of hopelessness was evident in her answer. How many people in the world were truly free, men or women?

He gave a bark of laughter. "No." He gave an emphatic shake of his head and she frowned at him. "Most people do not wish to be free. They like the security of the confines of society. It makes them feel safe. Everything in order and in its place."

For a moment she dared to stare at him, to stare into those cool blue eyes and try to see what it was he truly thought. Again, she saw no condemnation, no scorn for the idea of a woman wanting to be free, independent of a man. He looked interested though she was no fool. That interest was most likely laid in the best way he could profit from her.

She turned her back on him. "Please, take me home."

"I'm afraid that won't be possible." His voice was cool and unyielding, and she turned around to demand he explain and staggered as the ship lurched sideways. Her glass slipped from her hand and smashed to the floor. He grasped hold of her arms, steadying her and tutting in irritation at the broken glass on his cabin floor.

"Where are we going?" she demanded as she realised the movement had been steadily increasing while they spoke.

The Rogue

He grinned at her, and this time the wickedness that was illustrated in the tales of his exploits was only too clear. "Far away from here," he said, showing a row of even white teeth.

Henri tried to wriggle out of the grasp of his hands. "Let me go!" She figured it didn't really matter whether she meant from his hands or off the ship, either way she needed to get away from him, for so many reasons. "Please, you must let me go, surely you do not want to add kidnapping to your list of crimes?" she raged at him.

She gasped as he pulled her closer, one arm snaking around her waist to hold her body flush against him. Putting her hands flat on his chest she pushed him away, but both his grip around her and his chest were hard and immovable.

"You really think I care what they hang me for?" he demanded, his tone just as angry. "If I'm caught, I have enough crimes to condemn me, do you think it matters if I hang for piracy or the kidnapping of Lady Henrietta Morton? Dead is dead."

"The only reason you're not swinging from the end of a rope right at this moment is because I saved you," she said, her voice full of fury as rage outweighed terror. "There was no way out of that shop and you know it. I saved your life, the least you can do is return me to land before you make your escape."

She was uncomfortably aware of his hard body pressed tight against hers, and of just how far she had fallen into his power. She was on a ship bound for God alone knew where, and no one was even aware she was missing.

"Lady, if you had not sought to blackmail me, we would likely never have set eyes on each other again. I was indeed grateful and would have kept the memory of you as something to be cherished. I thought you a delight, a sweet little innocent and was glad to have stolen nothing more from you than a kiss.

It was you who came after me, it was you that tarnished that memory, and it was you who tangled yourself into my life. You said you wanted adventure," he said laughing at her, though he looked just as angry as she was. "It appears you should be careful what you wish for."

"You unfeeling bastard!" she said, flailing her fists and raining down blows on his chest in a rage. "What do you know of my life? I told you I was desperate - it was my only choice. Surely you of all people can understand that? And it only serves to show how desperate I am now that I would willingly return to that life just to get away from you!"

He caught hold of her wrists before she could do any further damage. "Well I'm sorry to disappoint you, but you won't be getting away from me any time soon."

He released her hands and pulled her closer, crushing her against him and pressing his lips against hers. For a moment she was so stunned she couldn't react. When her senses finally returned to her this time however, she decided to make him sorry that he'd been foolish enough to release her hands.

She raked her nails down his neck until he hissed with pain and grasped hold of her hands once again. She then raised her knee with a sharp, angry movement that clearly took him by surprise. He groaned and staggered away from her to lean on his desk, but her moment of triumph was short-lived. To her surprise and fury, he began to laugh.

"Well I suppose I deserve that," he said clutching at the injured part of him with both hands and wincing.

"Damn right," she said, gasping for breath and sparing a moment to thank her foolish, self-centred father for the one sensible thing he'd ever done in hiring Annie to raise her. For it was her lady's maid who had instructed her on the swiftest way of telling a man *no* and making sure he was left in no doubt she meant it.

He got to his feet and her heart thudded in her chest as he crossed to his berth. She watched with trepidation as he pulled a blanket off the bed and moved towards her. He paused, holding up the blanket like a peace offering.

"You're cold," he said, offering the blanket once again.

With reluctance she allowed him to get close enough to lay the blanket across her shoulders. She grasped hold of the corners, putting it tightly around herself and moving as far from him as the confined space of the cabin would allow, stepping carefully around the broken glass.

"Calm yourself, lady. You have my word that no one upon this ship will harm you in any way. Myself included," he added with a wry smile. "However," he added, a steely note in voice. "You must get used to the idea that you are now my guest, and you remain my *guest* at my pleasure. I may change your status to prisoner at any time it pleases me."

Henri gritted her teeth, glaring at him but keeping her counsel. She watched him, like a cat cornered by a ferocious dog. She might be outmatched, but she would use her claws at the slightest provocation. To her consternation he began to move closer to her once more and as she was already pressed tightly into the corner of the room, she found herself with nowhere to go. She tensed, not believing his earlier promises for a moment. He stopped barely inches from her and reached out to curl a lock of her hair around his fingers.

"You liked it when I kissed you before," he said, his voice low and husky.

Henri felt herself grow hot at his accusation, she could do nothing to deny it. He leaned a little closer to whisper in her ear and she could feel the warmth radiating off him.

"You kissed me back."

"I thought I would never see you again," she countered, leaning harder against the freezing wood of the cabin wall and wishing she dared reach for the blade at his hip as he laughed again.

"How very unladylike," he said, apparently delighted. "To only kiss a man you are certain you will never see again."

"I hate you," she said the words with venom, meaning it, and not caring that she sounded childish.

"Good," he said, and she tried hard not to grind her teeth as the insufferable man grinned at her again. "I do like a challenge. And I promise you this..." He leaned down once more, placing his hands on the wall either side of her head, caging her in as his breath fluttered warm against her neck, making her shiver. "By the end of this voyage, you'll be begging me to kiss you."

Before she could think of an adequate retort to his outrageous suggestion, he had turned on his heel and left the cabin, and once more she heard the key turn in the lock.

Chapter 6

"Wherein a pirate finds himself between the devil and the deep blue sea."

Lars sat on the edge of the hammock and regarded his boots with a sigh. The night had not gone as he had hoped, not by a long way. That the militia had come after him with such force had been an unpleasant shock.

His somewhat romanticised and scandalous reputation as a pirate and corsair had always been a source of amusement to him. Suddenly his widespread fame wasn't so funny. Running from the world with his ship and his crew was one thing. Doing it with some ridiculous slip of a girl towed in his wake was quite another. If she was a day over eighteen, he'd eat his hat.

He suddenly felt his own twenty-seven years bear down on him with the weight of centuries.

"Well, you've gone and done it now," said Mousy, echoing his own thoughts.

"If that's the extent of your help, I'll have my rum back thank you," Lars replied, holding his hand out.

Mousy swayed in his hammock and clutched the bottle in his good arm, hugging it to his chest. "Well, there's no need to be like that. I didn't make you bring the blasted woman."

Lars sighed and regarded the big man with impatience. He had known Mousy since he was a small boy. In many ways it was Mousy's fault he was here at all. But he never mentioned that fact. He knew Mousy would never forgive himself anyway, and in truth his lifestyle and reputation as a pirate was not something he did regret.

Although there were others, too many to count.

He took a moment to consider what his life might have otherwise been and grimaced. He'd lived many lifetimes in those years, more than most men would ever have. No, he decided, ignoring the dissenting voice of his conscience, no regrets on that score.

"What was I supposed to do?" he demanded of Mousy, glaring at him. "Leave the damn woman there? She's a lady after all."

He snorted, wondering when he'd become so generous. Ladies didn't generally go around blackmailing pirates unless things had changed greatly in the years of his absence.

"Perhaps," Mousy conceded. "But a woman aboard will cause nothin' but trouble, so what the devil you goin' to do with her now?"

Lars got to his feet and snatched the bottle back from Mousy, holding it to his lips and taking a long drink. He wiped his mouth on the back of his hand.

"Damned if I know," he said. In truth he would have happily put her back on land at the earliest opportunity, but it was far too dangerous. He needed to put as much distance as possible between himself and the English coast as fast as he could. The likelihood that some bounty hunter would get wind of his arrival and decide to profit from it was far too great as it was.

"Perhaps there'll be a reward for 'er?" Mousy suggested, hope lighting his eyes. Lars shook his head and handed him back the bottle.

"Don't hold your breath. The last I heard Lord Morton didn't have a penny to his name." He frowned as he realised this was likely the reason the girl had been trying to blackmail him. Was she in some kind of trouble? Or just trying to pay her father's debts?

The Rogue

That the idea had even entered her head to brave the part of town only frequented by smugglers and the darker side of life staggered him. She had said she was desperate - she must have been to risk that.

He considered the courage it must have taken to enter that tavern alone and confront him. Well the girl had spirit that was for sure, either that or she was in such desperate trouble she would take any risk. He frowned as the possibilities presented themselves.

A man, he realised. It had to be a man who'd driven her to such lengths. The idea made him angry though he wasn't sure why or with whom.

"What's gnawing at your guts?" Mousy asked, watching him with a curious expression. "Ye look like you've chewed on a weevil."

Lars snorted and shook his head. "Nothing," he said and tried to school his expression into something more placid. Whatever trouble the foolish girl had got herself into, it was of no interest to him.

"The kitten's got claws I see," Mousy added, gesturing with the bottle to the scratches down his neck.

"Aye," Lars replied wincing. "And a damn sharp tongue to match."

They sat in silence for a moment, the hammocks swaying in a lulling motion until Mousy spoke again.

"Tol' ye 'twas a bad idea, comin' back ere."

Lars glared at him. "Well you're just full of helpful advice and comfort tonight, my friend."

Shrugging his huge shoulders Mousy stared at the rum bottle with a bleak expression. "Feel responsible," the big man muttered, looking gloomy.

Letting out a breath, Lars looked at him in exasperation. "Not this again! Good God, man. I've had ten years to get used to this way of life and, if I say so myself, I've done a pretty fair job of it, so quit your bellyaching. You didn't put a gun to my head and I've never blamed you, so stop giving yourself more due than you're entitled to take."

He watched as Mousy took a deep drink and shook his head, a sorrowful expression on his face. "Don't change nuthin', this weren't the life ye should 'ave led an' ye know it, well as I do."

"Did the Doc give you Laudanum?" he demanded, and groaned as Mousy nodded, no wonder the stupid bastard was growing maudlin.

"How's your shoulder?" he asked, steering the conversation away from the past and onto safer ground.

Mousy rolled the offending limb experimentally and grimaced. "I'll live," he said with a crooked smile.

Lars nodded. "Be sure that you do. I've got enough trouble without you dying on me." He got to his feet and clapped Mousy heartily on the arm.

The enormous man groaned. "Ah, you black-hearted varlet," he muttered. "I'll get you for that."

"I know," Lars replied with a cheerful grin, before heading back up on deck.

The bitter cold of the November night cut at him as he walked to the rail. After so many years in warmer climes, the ferocity of an English winter came as a shock and brought back memories.

Log fires and crumpets, the tangy salt smell of a seaweed-strewn beach after a gale, of riding out on frosty mornings and returning to a warm, welcoming house, full of love and laughter. Thoughts of a place that had once been his home returned to haunt him. He hadn't thought of that life for a long time, hadn't allowed himself to. What was the point of dwelling on the past?

The Rogue

Particularly when he'd done so much harm to those he'd loved. But now he remembered a place where he'd been happy, happier than he'd realised at the time.

Even in the bright moonlight the jagged edge of the coastline that had once been so familiar to him was hard to make out. He'd been a fool to come back here. There was nothing here for him but ghosts.

Though it seemed at least there was one less than he had believed. For that he was desperately relieved and grateful, and he smiled at the truth of it. The burden of that knowledge had been a weight around his neck and his heart for his whole life. Now it was gone. And yet everything he'd done, everything he'd become, had been because of that knowledge. To know he'd been wrong all this time, that he hadn't been damned after all made it a bitter-sweet feeling that enveloped him. Only his actions since that fateful night had put the noose about his own neck.

He shook his head, raising his face and relishing the cold sting of sea spray against his skin. He'd made his own bed, and there was no one else to blame no matter what Mousy thought. Whatever had befallen him, he alone was responsible, and he would spend the rest of his days as an exile.

It wasn't like there was anything to return to now. He had long since burnt those bridges and besides, he'd had many years to become accustomed to the idea. What was harder was the idea that the life he had made for himself was also over.

Wellington had defeated Napoleon and the war was over. Europe had once more turned its attention to the Barbary corsairs and any fool could see that the pirates were a dying breed.

Ironically, he found he couldn't mourn for many of the men that would suffer. Most had made their fortune in the slave trade, which he had always found abhorrent. But it would no longer be possible to pick off fat American merchant ships, take their cargoes and ransom their more illustrious passengers as had been his own way of working the Mediterranean.

Tripoli, Tunis, Algiers, all were lost to him. Out of bounds unless he wished to find his ship blown from the water and a brief dance with Jack Ketch until his neck was stretched,

Which begged the question. What now?

He had no answer to give. No safe destination, for there was none. It galled him that he had made his reputation on his quick thinking and decisiveness. Now he felt, almost literally, lost at sea.

Mousy was right about one thing, he hadn't been born to this life. He'd been a mutton-headed sap skull, as green as they came and far too soft to survive for long. Those early days had been both the most miserable and the most enlightening of his existence. But in the end, it had been quite literally sink or swim and swim he had.

He'd learned to fight and to curse like the most hardened mariner, and to step up and take a beating, even if he was scared to death. But he'd also learned that his quick tongue and lively sense of humour could diffuse the most difficult situations, and somehow as the years wore on, charm, a shrewd intelligence and plain devilment had got him where he was; The Rogue, captain of a pirate ship and with a price on his head that quite stole his breath.

It was laughable.

Sleep, he decided. He needed to sleep. He'd barely had a moment's rest since land had been sighted on their ill-fated journey here. Now, with the adrenaline of his flight from the militia long since dispersed, he felt weary to his bones. He made his way back to his cabin and was momentarily perplexed as to why his cabin door was locked. And then he remembered the blasted girl. He turned the key in the door with care, trying to make as little noise as possible and entered the cabin.

The lamp was still burning low and the room was still. He waited, expecting any moment to be attacked with some heavy item or at the very least to find himself at the end of Miss Morton's sharp tongue.

With care he touched his fingertips to the deep scratches down his neck and sucked in a breath. But all was quiet. Well she might look as sweet and innocent as a kitten, but the little bitch had claws as Mousy had observed, and he'd do well to remember it too. A sentiment he tried very hard to remind himself of when he crossed the room to find the little minx curled up, asleep on his bed.

He reached for the lamp and held it up, so that the soft, golden light fell across her face. Claws or no claws, she certainly looked like an angel when she slept. Long, thick, dark lashes swept the curve of her cheek, her face surrounded by equally thick, mahogany curls, and her soft, full lips were slightly parted.

For a moment, he allowed himself to remember exactly how soft and yielding her mouth had been the first time they'd met. He remembered the taste of her, the shock in her tawny eyes as she'd given in to him, to her own desire. Need and lust burned in his blood, and he was forcefully reminded of just how long it had been since he'd lain with a woman.

Dammit, but he wanted her.

As if things weren't complicated enough. Still, at least seducing the infuriating Henrietta Morton should allow him some light entertainment during the voyage, even if he currently had no idea what the destination might be.

With a roguish smile he knew suited his reputation to perfection, he eased his way onto the bed. With care not to disturb his sleeping companion, he tucked himself in close behind her. At least she would be warm when she awoke. He chuckled inwardly as he imagined her indignation when she discovered him, and just how furious her expression would be when she greeted him in the morning.

Chapter 7

"Wherein a villain is forced to play the hero."

Alexander Sinclair, the fourth Earl of Falmouth, regarded the woman in front of him with no little scepticism. Despite Lord Morton's assurances that the woman was telling the truth, the truth sounded far too close to some outlandish Gothic novel to have anything other than a passing acquaintance with the real world. And yet, despite the fact that the woman appeared to be quite unsuited to the task of being lady's maid to his future wife, and more at home walking some of the seedier streets near the quay, he felt the fear and anguish in her eyes was indeed genuine. So, she at least *believed* her story to be the truth.

"Let me get this quite straight," he said, keeping his tone cool and clipped and completely devoid of any human emotion.

He abhorred outpourings of emotion of any kind and had been forced to speak to the woman quite severely when she seemed likely to succumb to a fit of hysterics a few moments earlier.

"Miss Morton left the house in the middle of the night, alone, and proceeded to make her way down to The Nag's Head, a notorious spot for smugglers and low-lives," he added. He shook his head once again struck by how unlikely the whole story appeared to be. "You followed her, without making her aware of your presence and watched while she entered the tavern *alone*."

He paused and fixed his icy, grey gaze on the woman. "You made no attempt to stop her or dissuade her from this foolish and possibly fatal endeavour I take it?" he added with contempt.

The disgraceful creature just put her chin up and glared back at him, her arms folded across her ample bosom. "She's a big girl,

The Rogue

knows 'er own mind. 'Twas 'er business, not mine to interfere in." She held his gaze, totally unrepentant.

"If that is the case," Alex said, with growing frustration. "Why the devil were you following her?"

"She's my girl," the woman retorted some asperity, daring to look at him as if *he* had said something out of turn. "I've been with 'er since she was a child, and I love 'er like my own. I wouldn't see any harm to her."

Alex took a deep breath and struggled to keep his temper in check. "And yet, you allow her to walk in to a den of iniquity like the Nag's Head all alone?" he repeated, quite incredulous. "I take it you believed no harm would come to her there?"

Although he had neither raised his voice nor changed his body language, he had no doubt she could see the anger and disgust clearly enough in his eyes.

"Forgive me, *my lord,*" the woman said with a sneer, using his title like it tasted unpleasant in her mouth. "But my Henri's resourceful an' brave, and 'twould be a foolish man who got on the wrong side of 'er." To his astonishment she said the words as though *he* was to blame for everything that had happened. "You just don't know 'er, not like I do."

"And now never likely to!" he said with such froideur and contempt that the brazen abigail had finally crumbled and buried her head in her hands, sobbing.

The girl's father, Lord Morton, who had been dithering ineffectually while this conversation took place, ran to the woman's side and patted her shoulder. "There, there, Annie, Lord Falmouth will bring her back to us, don't you fret."

Henrietta's father was a well-known and despised figure to the earl. The early death of his beloved wife had apparently robbed the man of his heart and his sense and he'd turned to gambling to ease the loss. Sadly, the man had no aptitude and all too predictably found himself without a feather to fly with, mortgaging his family home with selfish lack of regard for his daughter that bordered on criminal.

That the man himself was foolish and hopeless rather than cruel and heartless did little to soften Alex's opinion of him. In the society that he himself kept, Morton was a pitiable creature and it was oft said when he told people with that familiar mournful expression that he'd *lost his dear wife,* one could never be quite sure he hadn't meant at the roulette table.

The ridiculous man looked up at him now with such hope in his eyes that even Alex's cold heart was unable to contradict him. If the rest of the story was true and his daughter really had been kidnapped by the notorious Rogue, she was already beyond saving. Indeed, Alex was moved to hope the girl was already dead, for he could not contemplate what fate awaited her at the hands of a pirate and his crew.

"I will of course do everything I can to return your daughter to you, Lord Morton," he said, knowing it was unlikely he would return with anything more than a coffin, if that.

To his horror Morton embraced him, sobbing upon his shoulder and giving Alex further cause to pity the appalling creature as he noticed the frayed collar of his jacket. "Oh, thank you, thank you, my lord. You are indeed a good man. I will be forever in your debt."

In the circumstances Alex decided not to mention he was already forever in his debt as he had paid off all the man's outstanding bills and forwarded a considerable sum to cover the costs of his impending nuptials to his now missing fiancée.

With a promise to do all in his power, he ejected the pair of them summarily from his office before they could taint his sanctuary with any more of their hysterics.

On the one hand he was furious that his own time and finances would be frittered away on such a pointless exercise. He would not be able to sail before the next tide, by which time the wicked bastard that had taken her would have a good head start, though he had no doubt that his ship was more than capable of outrunning anything else on the seas.

What the foolish chit had been thinking was beyond him though. He hadn't wanted to take a wife at all and it had only been the endless nagging of his elderly aunts about his responsibilities to the family and the need for an heir that had moved him to offer for her.

Alex had only seen Miss Morton in passing and made her acquaintance a handful of times and she had appeared sensible and level-headed, particularly so considering her beauty and her youth.

He could not abide simpering and giggling and had been more than relieved she appeared inclined to neither. His own preferences did not run to seducing innocents, she was far too young and green for his tastes, but he overcame any scruples in that direction by dint of the fact that her father was about to ruin her for good by his own idiotic behaviour.

Miss Morton at least, despite her father's frivolous nature seemed, in his estimation, the kind of independent girl who would be grateful for a house of her own and a husband who was often away to leave her to her own devices, rather than harbouring any foolish romantic notions. But now this! He wondered if she had made some ill-advised assignation to meet a lover. It was the only explanation. It was only good fortune that meant his own ship, The Revenge, was provisioned and ready to sail for France the next day.

On the other hand, his blood quickened at the idea of engaging with The Rogue.

He had read of the man's exploits like everyone else and had to admit to a grudging admiration for him. He appeared extraordinarily courageous and, in his own way, rather honourable. Though if Miss Morton really was on board, it would cause rather a lot of complications as he could hardly wreck the ship and risk her dying at his own hand.

Alex smiled. Whatever was to come it would at least be an adventure and a relief from a growing sense of ennui. After he'd been injured at the battle of Trafalgar, he had promised his dying father that he would take his responsibilities seriously and give up his naval career. As earl, his responsibilities were many and varied and ... interminably dull.

At first, he had simply taken to whoring and drinking too much and spending any free time he could snatch indulging in pleasures that had gained him a reputation that was wholly deserved. Anything to feel alive again. But in the past few years his actions had been rather more dangerous and if he was discovered he would lose everything, the ancient family name would be disgraced, and he may even hang. But bringing a notorious pirate to justice and saving his fiancée in one fell swoop, well that should do his reputation no harm at all.

And, if nothing else ... the coming days were unlikely to be dull.

Chapter 8

"Wherein adventure looms and pirates entice."

Henri awoke with a nagging sense of doom at the back of her mind. Something was wrong. For a moment her brain refused to acknowledge it, preferring to burrow deeper into the warmth of the bed, and she was warm. Warm and surprisingly comfortable considering ... Her eyes flicked open.

Hardly daring to breathe, she remembered her dire situation and realised she was not alone on the bed. The room was icy cold and as her eyes adjusted to the dim light, she saw clouds of her own breath billowing in front of her face. She also became aware of a large, warm body pressed close against hers and the heavy weight of an arm slung over her waist.

She waited, frozen, and quite at a loss as to what to do next.

"Stop panicking," came the sleep-heavy, husky male voice from far too close behind her. "I've been here all night without molesting you, so you needn't look so indignant."

"I'm not looking indignant," she snapped. "Though how you'd know with your eyes shut is beyond me. If you deign to open them, you'll find I'm bloody furious!"

Henri cursed and pushed his arm away before struggling to an upright position which was tricky as he'd left her little room on the narrow bed.

"That is really very uncouth language from a lady," he grumbled as she pushed him farther away.

"How *dare* you!" She kept her voice low, only too aware of the sounds of life on deck and the thin walls between them and the crew as shouts on deck filtered through to her quite audibly. "How dare you get in the same bed as me! I knew you were no gentlemen but truly, you live up to your name with quite startling accuracy."

She huddled into the corner and watched with mounting irritation as he sighed, stretched and rubbed at the stubble on his chin before yawning with enthusiasm, apparently completely unperturbed by her fury.

"Well," he said, with what she imagined he thought was an endearing and sleepy smile. "What did you expect? I gained this reputation for a reason as I'm sure you know."

As his reputation rested rather heavily on the effortless seduction of most of the women he met, she replied to that particular comment with an icy glare.

"Let me get up," she demanded, meeting those cool blue eyes with determination. But to her dismay he ignored her and simply turned onto his side, head resting on his hand as he watched her through heavy-lidded eyes. Henri scowled at him and pressed herself as far away as was possible in the confines of the bed. She wanted to get up more than anything, but she was damned if she was going to climb over him to do it, so she compressed her limbs into the smallest space possible.

"You really ought to be grateful," he said watching her with amusement as she gaped at his words. "You were warm weren't you, when you awoke? Considering the temperature last night that is something of a miracle. You see, I did everything I could to keep you warm and in good health," he said smirking, before reaching out and tracing a finger over her hand. "I would hate you to catch pneumonia," he said, his voice too low and inviting and filled with devilry.

Henri snatched her hand away. "You're all heart," she said, deadpan, glaring at him. "Now. Get. Off. My. Bed," she bit the words off with as much venom as she could manage at this early hour of the morning but to her frustration he didn't budge.

"It may have escaped your notice, sweetheart," he replied with a mocking smile and mischief glittering in his blue eyes. "But this is *my* bed."

Henri gritted her teeth. Never in all her days had she come across a more infuriating and inconsiderate man. By comparison he made her fiancé look like the perfect gentleman.

Her *fiancé*. The word jarred in her mind and she tried to find the resolution she'd had last night. That at least was a problem that would no longer trouble her. Surely that was a good thing as it was what she had set out to do? Though, she'd only really sought to avoid marriage to that one man, not to never be married ... or have a home and family of her own. As much as she railed against her position, those were things she would have liked, if she could have only found a man to love and respect her as she was. She tried to swallow down the misery that welled in her throat as she considered her position.

Even if she ever did find her way back home, which was looking increasingly doubtful, she was ruined. There would never be a match for her now. A night spent in the cabin of a pirate captain was unlikely to make her an alluring prospect as a wife. The enormity of what she'd done and everything she'd lost pressed down on her, taking all the air from the room; she clutched at her chest. Slumping back against the wall she stared across the cabin, not really seeing it. What was she to do?

She sat in silence for a while, quite sunk in misery until she realised she could feel his eyes on her still. Well, let him look, what did she care?

"Come now, Miss Morton, don't look so glum."

She spared a moment to glare at him before turning away in disgust. To her frustration, however, he didn't leave it at that.

"Seriously now, you said you wanted adventure, didn't you? Or was it the safe kind of adventure you were after?" he asked, a faint but unmistakable mocking tone in his voice now. "The kind to be experienced sitting at home sewing, perhaps?"

She turned back to him, her arms folded tightly across her chest. His expression was perfectly placid, just that faint expression of curiosity she had seen in his eyes before. Was he really serious? There was a difference between an adventure and losing everything - your home, your family, your reputation and any hopes for the future - all in one fell swoop.

"It rather depends on what your notion of adventure implies," she snapped at him as fear and misery beckoned, threatening to swallow her whole. "For example, am I likely to survive it?"

She watched with irritation as he grinned at her and then stretched out like an indolent cat, lying out on his back with his arms behind his head. His shirt was undone, and her eyes unwillingly tracked the enticing triangle of tanned skin on show, from the hollow at his neck down to where a scattering of dark hair was visible around his belly button. She had never in her life been this close to a man and as disconcerting and precarious as her position was, it was certainly an education. His skin was smooth and golden, his chest hard and well-defined with muscle. She swallowed and dragged her eyes away with resolution. She was in quite enough trouble as it was.

"Oh, you will survive it," he said, his words followed by a low chuckle that seemed to rumble through the bed. "I promised you no harm would come to you, didn't I? I meant it." He inclined his head to look up at her. "You're free, is that not what you wanted?"

Henri frowned as she considered the implications of his words. That much was true, she supposed. If she'd lost everything, there was nothing left to lose. But then she thought of her father, and his devastation at having lost her. For all his selfishness he really wasn't a bad man, just a weak and foolish one, and as much as she was forever vexed beyond reason at his callous disregard for her future, she knew he loved her dearly at heart. Beyond that he had also lost her worth, as now his outstanding debts would be called in, and he would be forced to sell the house. It was unlikely he would mend his ways, so it was only a matter of time before any proceeds from the house that had been in their family for generations were gone too.

And then there was Annie.

She wondered how Annie was faring. Surprisingly, considering their differences, she loved Annie. Perhaps not like a mother. She frowned thinking on some of the conversations they'd shared, no, certainly not like a mother. But she loved her just the same and knew Annie felt the same about her, despite her lack of maternal instincts.

Henri sighed, there was nothing to be done about that. She would do everything she could to return to them, but she doubted they would thank her for it in the end. Not her father at least, no matter if he was glad to have her back. What on earth was he to do with her? He would be forced to support her still and yet she would cease to have any value to him. She doubted she could even get a position as a governess once people heard what had befallen her. She would just be a burden, another debt to be paid for. Perhaps it was better like this.

But then she realised what options were actually open to her. And the few possibilities she had of making money. She may be lost to polite society, but that did not mean she intended to become a whore. And there was little else that she could do to earn her keep.

"What on earth is going on behind those pretty eyes of yours?" he asked, and she glanced down at him, scowling.

"I'm ruined," she said, hoping her voice and her expression held as much accusation as she felt. Despite the fact that she knew it wasn't entirely his fault. "I may as well be dead. I'm lost to my family and friends, what prospects do I have? How will I live?" she tried and failed to keep the tremor from her voice and then jumped as he moved, wondering what he intended. But he simply sat up beside her with his back against the wall, a little too close, but he made no further move in her direction. She turned to look at him with trepidation, startled to see a fair amount of sympathy in his expression.

"I've sat where you are," he said, his voice low. "I wanted a life of adventure, but I had no idea of the price I would pay in searching it out." He paused, and she imagined she could see the weight of truth in his expression, a wistful tone behind his words. "I lost everything," he added, and then his eyes began to sparkle, and he smiled at her. "But I gained my freedom. And truly, I have no regrets."

She observed him carefully, she didn't entirely believe him, at least not about having no regrets. But she could believe he had lost as much as she had.

"Perhaps," she conceded. "The difference is that you're a man. You can command a ship, you can command respect; no one can *own* you," she spat the last words out, as all the old frustrations tumbled down on top of her again.

The captain frowned at her and for once, after having spoken in such a way in front of a man, she felt it wasn't because he disagreed with her words. She had frightened away too many suitors with her plain speaking, so it was at least refreshing that she hadn't shocked him.

"Oh, I assure you they could," he said, his tone dark and then, after a pause. "Why not?"

"What?" It was her turn to frown now, perplexed. What on earth was he talking about?

She watched as he got to his knees on the bed turning to face her. "There have been women pirates before. I see no reason why you could not do the same."

She blinked, astonished by his words. "You're not serious?" She said as he shrugged, his fingertips rasping at his stubble once more as he considered.

The Rogue

"I don't see why not," he said eventually.

She snorted in disbelief and shook her head. "You're insane."

"Why? Don't you think you're capable?" he said, with a smile tugging at his mouth. "I could teach you all you need know."

Henri gaped at him, truly astonished. "Why?" she demanded. "Why would you help me? Why would you even suggest such a thing?"

He smiled, that slow, confident smile, and once again she was struck by just how handsome this man was.

"Truthfully, I don't know." He shrugged, as though he was as bewildered as she was. But then he looked back at her and she felt there was something honest in his eyes. "Except ... I feel we are kindred spirits, you and I." The look was just as quickly gone to be replaced by a sardonic smile "And besides, I told you I like a challenge. Teaching you to be a pirate? Now that's *got* to be a challenge."

Henri took a deep breath, unsure of what she was feeling. This was madness, surely? And yet ...

She couldn't trust this man, couldn't trust any of his crew. The chances of her arriving at whatever destination he had in mind must be ludicrously low. Yet, he was offering to help her. What other choice did she have? At the very least, she should learn to defend herself.

"Well then?"

She looked back and found he was watching her expectantly, his eyes glittering with excitement. He was serious. He had every intention of teaching her to be a pirate. In truth she had no idea what that actually meant. But she knew it had to mean learning how to use a pistol. That was something she felt an urgent need to understand. He held out his hand to her.

"Do we have a deal?"

She frowned as another idea presented itself and wondered how, considering the mess she was in, she could have been so naïve. Folding her arms, she stared at him, eyes narrowed. "What, *exactly* do you get out of this?"

He grinned and held his hands out, as if he had nothing to hide. "You'll work aboard my ship the same as the rest of the crew. We're a little short-handed right now, so every man - or woman - helps."

She didn't believe a word of it. "And that's all?" she said, one eyebrow raised.

He chuckled again and leant forward on the bed. Henri pressed herself back against the wall as if she hoped to slide between the planks as he moved towards her. He didn't stop until his face was so close, she could feel his warm breath against her skin once more and wished he would keep his distance.

"Well now, Miss Morton," he whispered, his words raising goose bumps. "I think we both know what I would take as my prize for helping you with this endeavour."

She opened her mouth to curse him, but he cut her off, pressing a finger against her lips.

"I will teach you everything you need to know. I will teach you the workings of the ship, how to command men and gain their respect. I will teach you to defend yourself, and to attack another should the need arise. I will teach you everything you need to know to be considered as a man," he said, the promise in his words only illustrating a fraction of the guarantee in his voice. That voice promised so much more. "And if the men truly accept you as one of them, *then* I will teach you all the reasons you should not despise being a woman."

She smacked his hand away.

"I thought as much," she said with disgust.

The Rogue

Shifting her position, Henri drew up one knee, planted her foot against his chest, and pushed hard. The captain flew backwards and landed with a heavy thud, sprawled on the floor of the cabin.

Chapter 9

"Wherein sparks fly."

"Dammit!" he cursed, picking a shard of glass from the palm of his hand.

Henri bit her lip, torn between amusement at having seen him hit the floor in such an ungainly fashion and guilt as she watched blood drip down his arm from the wound on his hand.

"Was that really necessary?" he demanded, showing her the cut as blood fell to the floor with a steady drip, drip that Henri found a little unnerving.

"In the circumstances, yes." Henri folded her arms and looked down her nose at him. She would not feel guilty. He may be pretty to look at, but she knew all too well he was the Devil in a Sunday hat, and she wasn't as green as he might imagine. "You must think me a fool indeed to suggest such a thing. And you can put any thoughts of seducing me far from your mind. I may be ruined but I haven't lost my wits with my reputation. Frankly, based on all I have seen, you are the last man on earth I would consider falling for, even if I simply meant to take a lover."

Warming to her theme she decided to twist the knife a little deeper.

"In fact, I can't imagine how you've gained such a colourful reputation. I can only think that the women you have encountered to date have been a very poor sort indeed and already inclined to sluttish behaviour."

To her satisfaction he seemed quite taken aback by her words which had been spoken with no little force. For a moment she thought she saw a glimmer of some unnamed emotion in his eyes, but it was so quickly replaced by what was obviously dented male pride that she felt no remorse.

"Is that so?"

Something in her stomach did a nervous somersault as so many things seemed to be encompassed in the tone of those three words. They held everything from accusation, the acceptance of a challenge, and a clear promise he would make her eat her words if it was the last thing he did. Belatedly Henri wondered if she had once again mis-stepped and treated him in the wrong manner.

His blue eyes were staring at her with such intensity that she felt her mouth go dry.

"Y-you must see I'm in a perilous situation here, sir," she stammered with as much dignity as she could. "I mean no disrespect, but I will not lose my honour to pay for your help. Just because I've lost all else does not mean I am a cheap amusement."

He snorted at that, looking away from her at last to wrap his bloody palm in a handkerchief.

"Cheap?" he exclaimed, shaking his head. "You expect me to spend hours and days and weeks helping you and get nothing in return. No, lady, indeed you are not cheap."

Henri felt her cheeks burn with fury. Never in her life had she been spoken to in such a fashion and the injustice of her position rankled.

"I do not intend to be a burden upon you for a moment longer than necessary," she said, keeping her voice cold and devoid of emotion for fear she would cry if she stumbled now. "We will part company as soon as you make port and until that time, I will pay my way as I can. I can cook a little if you would send me to the kitchen, or mend clothes, clean your cabin ... I do not care how menial the task. I will earn my keep."

The curiosity was back in his eyes now as he watched her. She raised her chin, holding his gaze, defiant.

"You would prefer to be a skivvy than learn everything I have offered you? Just to keep your maidenhead intact?"

Fury rolled over her at his words. The ignorant, cold-hearted, arrogant bastard.

"Just?" she repeated. The word may have been said quietly but the atmosphere in the tiny cabin was electric as though thunder rolled between them and lightning would strike at any moment. Her chest rose and fell too fast, her heart thundering and she wished she was close enough to attempt to take his dagger, for she would gladly drive a knife into that black heart of his.

With deceptive calm she got to her feet, moving carefully around the broken glass on the floor. He stood also, mirroring her, watching her with careful attention.

"You believe you offer me a boon, don't you? You think you are all charity in offering to teach me your ways?" she sneered. "But it wouldn't matter how much I learnt, it wouldn't matter how well I accomplished everything you taught me. It would change nothing, for the world will change not at all."

She looked at the deepening frown on his face and knew he didn't understand what she meant. Why would he, he was a man.

"For me to gain your men's respect I would need to do far more than match your skills and bravery, your cunning and ruthlessness. I would have to far exceed those qualities before I gained their admiration, for a woman must always fight for every scrap of respect that is handed so easily to a man for the mere sake of his biology. And where your ruthlessness would have you described as fierce and brave and everyone would commend those as admirable traits in a Captain, I would be cursed as being a cold-hearted, sly bitch and everyone would despise me for it," she raged.

In her anger she had crossed the room, stepping closer to him as her temper had risen beyond her control. Now she found she stood so close to him she could see his blue eyes were flecked with

The Rogue

green and was reminded forcefully of the view from her bedroom window on a clear fine day when the sea glittered so enticingly.

Now that her anger had been vented, she didn't know what to do or say and waited for him to retaliate, to return her anger with harsh words of his own. She could see the need to do so burning in his eyes. So, when his hand reached out and traced the curve of her jaw, she jolted with surprise. It was the barest touch as though he wished to gentle down some skittish woodland creature before it ran from him.

She drew in a sharp breath and watched as the anger receded from his eyes, to be replaced with something else she dared not name.

"You are ... magnificent," he breathed, something close to wonder lingering over the words. They seemed to settle in her chest, a warm weight that soothed away all the jagged edges of her fury. She searched his eyes, looking for mockery, for duplicity, but before she was certain there was nothing of the sort to be found, his head lowered, and his lips pressed against hers.

Her mind stalled, caught like a rabbit in a snare, too beyond panic now to even struggle, too lost to know if she wanted to.

His lips were every bit as soft and warm as she had remembered, and his kiss was as gentle and tentative as the touch of his fingers had been. He brushed her mouth once and pulled back a little, enquiring, waiting for her to protest.

Henri waited too but found nothing to say. Perhaps her honour wasn't as precious to her as she had implied, the idea a faint panic that she chose to ignore ... for the moment. He moved closer again to repeat the exercise, twice, three times, and then over and over until she was dizzy. It seemed to her as though each brush of his lips was a drug, the cumulative effect of which was far more devastating when the simplicity of the act was so sweet and apparently innocent.

Again, came the barest touch of his mouth against hers, before moving away, leaving her trembling and wanting more and more with every repetition.

He had not touched her further, had not drawn her into his arms as he had in the dark privacy of the curtained dressing room. His fingertips still lingered at her jaw; a barely there touch that she felt was the only thing keeping her upright.

Finally, he did pull away from her and she looked up at him, too shaken to utter another word.

Those blue eyes were dark with desire, heavy with such need it made her chest ache to know he had felt everything she had, with just as much intensity - that he was just as shaken.

And then, without another word, he turned and left the cabin, slamming the door behind him.

Chapter 10

"Wherein a pirate plots a course."

Lars strode the deck bellowing orders and practically daring any of his men to step out of line as they avoided his eye as best they could. It was perfectly obvious to all aboard that he was in a fine mood to beat the living daylights out of anyone who so much as looked at him wrong.

Frustration simmered in his veins and every sense was on alert and demanding that he return to his cabin this instant and finish what he'd started. He paced the gun deck wondering why on earth he didn't do just that. Why had he cut and run just when things were getting interesting? Because the girl was a damn sight more than just interesting that's why.

Lars stared out across the open sea, watching as the sun climbed, sparkling on the diamond-bright water as it rose into a clear blue sky. Hauling in a lungful of clean, cold air he tried to dispel the lingering desire that fogged his mind and would not allow him to think with any clarity.

He just didn't know what to make of her. In the shop he'd been certain he was a dead man when he'd seen her gaping at him, all wide brown eyes and innocence. He'd been certain she would scream, and the militia would fall on him like crows on carrion. But instead she'd saved him.

He'd felt more of a scoundrel than he ever had in his life when he'd kissed her, but she'd been impossible to resist. The sweetest prize he could ever imagine.

He'd known he would never see her again; a woman like that was beyond anything he could hope for now, but he'd known too that she would haunt his dreams for the rest of his days.

A pirate was hardly the kind of man a respectable woman would aspire to, and the idea of never knowing how those lips would feel against his own had made him feel strangely adrift. So, he had risked her screaming the place down and stolen a kiss. And the astonishment and elation that had coursed through him when she had kissed him back seemed to linger in his blood like a disease, waiting to disarm him and weaken his resolve whenever she chose.

He'd been so tempted to linger that he'd been perilously close to getting caught, as it was he'd only just evaded the red coats. He'd nearly put his neck in a noose for nothing more than a kiss. But the memory of that kiss had haunted his every thought, through each moment of that day until she'd appeared again out of the blue.

He hadn't known what to think when he'd seen her. When he believed she had come to keep him safe he'd been torn between unreasonable joy and fury that she'd endangered herself for a man like him. But he'd been unaccountably angry when she'd tried to blackmail him.

That his sweet little innocent was neither sweet nor innocent had somehow hurt him, as though she'd betrayed him somehow. He snorted at the idea and leaned on the rail, looking down and watching the water slide over the hull as his ship cut a clean line through the waves.

It was obviously ridiculous to think she'd misled him, had made him believe she was as innocent as she'd looked. But he'd wanted to hold the memory of her close, something to warm him when the constant need to keep moving wore him down. For in recent years the hunter had become the hunted and he knew he had little time left before they caught up with him. No one could run forever. No one could always have fortune on their side. Sooner or later the wind would turn, and he'd be out manoeuvred.

And yet now he didn't know what to think.

The fury which she'd turned on him when he'd suggested the idea of paying him for his help with her body, the dignity with which she'd stood up to him and cut him down was astonishing. She was like no woman he had ever met before. She intrigued him and instinctively he knew that was dangerous. He had no place in his life for romantic entanglements. Women were not welcome on board ships for good reason. They caused nothing but trouble, distracted the men and kept their minds from the job.

The best he could do was just as she had suggested and bid her goodbye the moment they made port. Lawrence decided to risk Valencia. He'd had friends there, people he hoped he could still trust. He'd get the lay of the land before he decided what was next.

Perhaps he could escape the noose by becoming a privateer. Poacher turned gamekeeper, he thought with a grimace, not that he had any great love for others of his kind, save those men aboard his ship. The men of his crew he trusted with his life. They had been together for years and he knew them like his own brothers. But the others who called themselves pirates were not like those who had gone before them.

The way of the coast, the brethren and their code, their old ways were long dead and gone and he mourned the loss of the ideal. There was little or no honour among thieves, not any more.

So that was it then, a plan of sorts. He would put her ashore and she would make her way home one way or another. He wondered how she'd fare. Perhaps, with luck, she would find an honourable gentleman who would see her safely home. Or perhaps she'd fall foul of some lecherous bastard who would take advantage of her and kill the spirit that burned so fiercely in those tawny brown eyes.

The idea made something in his chest constrict.

Damn the woman, she would bring him nothing but trouble. He should just go back to the cabin and take what he wanted. She obviously wanted him too, despite her protestations about him being the last man on earth she would ever want.

That had stung, he admitted to himself. He wasn't a fool. He would hardly believe she would want a pirate for a husband and he was certainly not in the market for a wife and never would be. But he knew women desired him, and her vehemence in denying she would ever even consider him, even as a lover, had cut into his pride more than he'd expected.

And then he'd kissed her.

He couldn't say why. She'd raged at him, called him a fool, had made him furious during her tirade, and yet he'd been quite unable to stop himself. And once again, despite everything she'd said, she had responded, willingly, eagerly, and it had taken everything he had to walk away and close the door on her.

She'd been right about one thing, the women who usually warmed his bed were only too easy, more than willing to be seduced by a handsome pirate while their erstwhile husbands raised the money to save them. They usually left with a smile on their faces and both parties well satisfied with the bargain. But she was foolish to think he couldn't seduce her just as easily, as his kiss had proved all too eloquently, and what a delightful pastime, to watch her resolution crumble as she submitted inevitably to his advances.

Tentatively he traced the lines she had scratched down his neck. Perhaps if he took her to bed, he'd feel better? Perhaps then she would cease to be so ... alluring. It was that strange mix of sweet innocence and fierce spirit that was so beguiling after all: the fresh-faced beauty who would dare to walk alone into a smuggler's bar and seek out a pirate. The girl with the wide brown eyes who would stand up to the Rogue himself and give him the sharp side of her tongue.

The Rogue

Yes, perhaps when he'd had her, when she'd been laid open for him, with those little claws in his back and his name on her lips when she came apart, perhaps then he'd break the spell she'd begun to cast.

His attention was taken from the tantalising image by a shout from Mousy. The large man had resumed his duties as quartermaster and was striding towards him.

"We got company, Cap'n."

Lars turned on his heel and scanned the horizon. A tiny speck was just visible, and he snatched the spyglass from Mousy's hand.

"A sloop?" he demanded as he adjusted the glass.

"Aye," Mousy said, his expression grim. "She'll catch us."

"You're sure she's in pursuit?"

Mousy snorted. "There's a chance we're followin' the same course, aye."

Lars shook his head, laughing. "No, I don't believe it either. All right, do what you can to keep her at bay for now and we'll decide when to engage her."

"Aye, Cap'n."

Lars watched as the big man strode away from him. He wasn't surprised they were being followed. He'd expected as much. The price on his head was significant enough now for him to be a target worth pursuing. But the amount of militia men that had come for him meant they'd known not only that he was coming ashore but where to look.

They'd been waiting for him.

An icy finger of doubt trailed down his back. They'd known because someone had told them. The only question was who? The only man there ahead of him, the one who had written the letter, was one of his most trusted men, sent on ahead to get the information he required before he came ashore.

He knew instinctively that he was not the source of this mischief. Which meant the information had to have been sent on before they landed. The last time they made port, perhaps, when he had made his intentions known to the crew.

Which meant someone on his ship intended to profit from betraying him, and he no longer knew who he could trust.

Chapter 11

"Wherein battle lines are drawn."

Henri sat on the bed with a blanket wrapped around her and shivered. She'd never been so cold in all her life, not to mention miserable ... and thoroughly confused. The sound of the slamming door seemed to echo in her ears without cease and she felt utterly bewildered by what had just happened.

What on earth had she been thinking? She'd just finished off telling him he was the last man on earth she would ever contemplate and the next moment she'd wrapped herself around him like ivy round an oak tree.

She put her head in her hands and groaned. Whatever must he think of her. That he'd been the one to break the kiss and leave the room was even more disturbing. He was the Rogue for heaven's sake! Notorious pirate, seducer of women and the furthest thing from a gentleman you should be able to find in all the seven seas. And yet, she had been his for the taking. Her body's desires had far outweighed and trampled over any of the bold and honourable intentions her brain may have happily spouted to him just moments before. One kiss and she'd have thrown it all away and become one of those sluttish women she'd disparaged so cruelly only moments before.

Well, not just one kiss, she amended. It had been many kisses, dozens and dozens of delicious, soft, tender kisses. She shivered again and knew it wasn't the cold to blame. Heat burned beneath her skin as she recalled just how he had made her feel. Dear God in heaven the man was a menace. She was going to have to stay far away from him if she was to have any chance of reaching land with her honour intact.

She looked around the tiny confines of the cabin with dismay and wondered just how many nights she would need to endure. For she doubted very much that he would give up his cabin, and even if he continued to act out of character and play the gentleman, for whatever reason had possessed him, she wasn't at all sure she could continue to be a lady.

Perhaps that was it, she thought wildly. Perhaps they were both possessed by some strange force that had taken hold of them and made them *both* act out of character. So he would play the gentleman and she would play the whore? No! That was not going to happen. She was not going to have her head turned by a handsome face and a wicked smile. She had more backbone than that and she was damn well going to stiffen it.

With this resolution held firmly in her mind she decided she'd best keep busy and began by making the bed and sweeping the broken glass up.

She had just managed to squeeze herself under his desk in pursuit of a last errant shard when the door swung open and her pirate captain strode into the room. She straightened so quickly she banged her head severely on the desk and cursed with an enthusiasm that Annie would have been proud of.

"Forgive me, I didn't mean to startle you."

She glared up, blinking away stars to see concerned blue eyes looking down at her. He reached out a hand and against her better judgement she took it, suppressing the shiver of awareness that prickled over her skin as his warm fingers closed over hers.

"What on earth were you doing?" he asked, amusement and far too much warmth in his expression.

Henri rubbed her head and looked at him with suspicion. "I was clearing up the glass. I told you I'd make myself useful. I meant it."

He nodded, apparently approving. "Thank you, I appreciate it. Especially as I seem to come off the worse for wear whenever we cross swords," he said, waving his bandaged hand as the corners of his mouth tilted up.

Henri's suspicions increased and she refused to acknowledge the fact that he looked adorable when he was trying to be reasonable; like a tiger trying to blend in at a tea party. He gestured to a plate he'd placed on his desk.

"I thought you must be hungry?" To her mortification, Henri's stomach gave a loud and insistent grumble the moment her eyes focused on the plate, bearing bread, cheese and a slightly wrinkled apple. "I thought so." He chuckled.

"Thank you, I could eat something," she said, avoiding his gaze with care and moving to the chair he drew out for her to sit down.

He moved around to the other side of the desk and sat as well, apparently determined to watch her break her fast. Henri ignored him. She was too hungry to be put off her food and too set on not being drawn down dangerous paths again to catch his eye.

They sat in awkward silence for the next ten minutes, or at least Henri found it awkward. Whenever she dared to steal a glance at him he seemed perfectly at ease and tremendously amused when she looked away as fast as she could.

What was the devil playing at now?

"Well then," he said as though they had just left off speaking and not sat in silence for the time it had taken her to eat. "What would you like to do today?"

She frowned, pushing her plate away from her. There had been a suggestive note to his words that she hadn't missed, but she was damned if she was going to acknowledge it. "Oh a stroll around the Vauxhall gardens or perhaps shopping on Bond street," she said with the wave of her hand and a glittering fake laugh before dropping her sarcastic act and scowling at him. "I believe I agreed to make myself useful, so perhaps you would direct me to the kitchen?"

"The galley," he corrected with a patient smile. "Not kitchen, and there's no need to get pettish with me, sweetheart, and furthermore *no,* you didn't agree."

Henri looked at him, puzzled. "What do you mean? You know I did."

The captain sat back and put his feet up on the desk, watching her with that ever present amusement lurking behind his eyes. "No you did not, because to agree to something it must have been suggested to you in the first place, and *I* most certainly did not suggest you work in the galley."

She folded her arms and tutted with annoyance. "Really, must you split hairs? I am well aware of what you suggested and I have told you quite clearly that your offer is unacceptable."

He said nothing for a moment and simply lifted one dark eyebrow. It was enough to make the colour rise on her cheeks. They both knew damn well she was not as clear about his offer as she had intimated. She stood and looked down at him, keeping her voice even and avoiding his eyes.

"Captain Savage, I do not wish to be a burden to you or your crew. Please would you show me to the ... galley, so that I might make myself useful."

"My name is Lars," he said, and she looked back to him in surprise.

"Lars?"

He nodded, smiling at the look on her face.

"But that isn't even a name," she objected. "Is it short for something?"

His smile dipped a little and he shrugged. "Perhaps, or at least it was a long time ago."

"Oh?" Had that been regret in his eyes? Intrigued, she looked at him closely and wondered who he really was, or at least who he'd been. Were people born pirates? Or had fate or circumstance fallen on him just as it had for her. He'd implied as much at least. "What is it short for?"

"It really isn't important," he said, waving a dismissive hand. "But I insist, as we are going to be living together in such ... *close* quarters, that you call me Lars."

The seductive tone was back in his voice and she knew damn well what he was playing at. She stood, squaring her shoulders and glaring down at him, which to her annoyance just seemed to amuse him all the more.

"Captain Savage," she said, her voice as cold as the air that clouded in front of her as she spoke. "Take me to the galley or I shall find it myself."

"Come, Hetty," he said, using a nickname she despised.

"Henri!" she corrected him. "I loathe the name Hetty, though *you* may call me Miss Morton.

He chuckled. "Ah yes, *Henri*. I can see how well that suits you," he said, raising one eyebrow.

Damn the man, mocking her again, but nonetheless her name on his lips sent an illicit thrill down her spine.

"Can we not at least be friends?" he asked as he lifted his feet from the edge of the desk and rose, moving with languid ease but never taking his eyes from hers.

"We are not friends, and I did not give you leave to use my name in such a familiar manner."

Henri froze, rigid with tension as he began to move around the desk. She turned and circled away from him, moving to the side he had just vacated. This was ridiculous, she thought as panic began to scrabble around in her chest like a terrified mouse. Not that she was afraid, she amended to herself, though being afraid in such a situation was quite right and proper. The fact that she wasn't as afraid of him as she was of herself, however, was quite outrageous.

"Do you really wish for me to chase you around the desk?" he asked, with a merry twinkle in his eyes.

Henri glared at him and prayed he would ascribe the flush she could feel colouring her cheeks to anger and not to the fact he'd almost read her thoughts.

"I do not!"

He started to chuckle and then appeared to think better of it and cleared his throat. With all trace of mockery and amusement wiped from his face he looked at her with every expression of kindness and sincerity. "Miss Morton," he said, holding out his hand to her. "Please would you accompany me for a turn about the deck?"

She frowned at him, perplexed by his sudden change of course.

"It is a beautiful day," he added. "The sun is up, and I know a sheltered spot where you may enjoy the sunshine. It will be warmer than this frozen box, I assure you."

The idea of getting out of the cabin and feeling the sun on her face was too alluring to refuse. Plus she would surely be safer out there than in here alone with him.

"That would be ... lovely," she replied, even though she didn't trust the change in his demeanour one little bit. She was perfectly aware that he was simply trying another tack. There was no doubt in her mind that he meant to seduce her, and despite the fact that the idea made her blood thrill in her veins she had no intention of letting him. Let him try to charm her, she thought, gritting her teeth, for in return he would find her as cold and welcoming as the sea beneath them.

With reluctance she allowed him to place her hand on his arm and she followed him outside.

Chapter 12

"Wherein the past appears and mocks the living."

Lars watched Miss Morton as he strolled with her around the deck. His men greeted them with a mixture of good-natured ribaldry and lewd comments and he noted her reaction to each.

"Was the Captain's bed warm enough for ye?" Jay shouted at her across the deck, his sly, rat-like eyes glinting in the bright sunshine. "For if it ain't, I'm at yer service, Miss, should you want a lithesome bed warmer tonight?" he'd added with a leer and a grotesque movement of his thin hips.

Lars smiled as Henri held the man's gaze, unblinking, and then looked him up and down, slowly and with contempt. She looked all the world as though she was assessing a horse and had found it to be a broken-down nag instead of the pure blood as advertised.

"I'd rather the cold embrace of the ocean than suffer your attentions, *sir,* and I will thank you to keep your disgusting comments to yourself."

There was little or no expression in her voice. She sounded bored and totally unimpressed and the men had roared with laughter, leaving Jay looking rather unsettled.

Lars had been struck with ... what he wondered? Pride, he realised with a start. She was alone, friendless and in the hands of men she would no doubt expect the very worst from, but she didn't cower and slink away to hide. She came out with those sharp claws and her tawny eyes flashing with fire and held her ground. The disquieting realisation that he admired her settled in his chest, and it wasn't a comfortable feeling. He didn't want to admire anything but her beauty and the way she would look naked in his bed. Though if they didn't get to warmer waters soon he'd have to settle for feeling his way under a mound of blankets. A pity but beggars couldn't be choosers.

He drew her away from the men and urged her forward until they were standing on the quarter deck.

"What's that?" she asked, breaking him out of the pleasant images that he'd begun to consider, as to what exactly she did look like under all those layers. In an effort to stop his thoughts turning in more disquieting circles, he looked to where she was pointing and saw to his annoyance that the sloop was making good time.

"Mousy!" he yelled and held his hand out for the spy glass as the big man joined him.

He held the glass to his eye and focused it and felt a wave of cold flow over him so intense he knew they must have seen him shiver.

"What?" Mousy demanded. "What is it?"

He couldn't respond. There was ice in his gut and his mind ran in circles. Mousy snatched the glass from his hand and looked to see what the problem was but just frowned.

"The Revenge?" he said, a question in his voice. "That ain't no Navy ship and it ain't the Water Guard. That's a merchant vessel."

Lars nodded. Yes, it was.

It belonged to a vastly prosperous merchant company, and he knew who owned it. A ship made for speed, to move things fast, not in bulk and to his knowledge the company had never actively hunted down pirates. He doubted that had changed. So why? Why would a merchant vessel be on his tail? Why *this* vessel?

He felt like his mind was wading through treacle as he tried to make sense of it and failed. He turned to see Henri studying him. Those tawny eyes were watching him, frank and open, and curious.

He ran a hand through his hair, aware that Mousy was looking at him with concern but ... he just couldn't ... *think*.

"Take evasive action," he said, watching the ship's progression through the water as though he was watching a sand clock, watching the grains slide away his remaining time. He looked away and turned to Mousy. "And whatever you do, do *not* engage."

Mousy looked at him in shock, his mouth falling open in surprise.

"But ... but Cap'n ..."

"But nothing!" he shouted, suddenly furious. "You have your orders."

Lars turned on his heel and walked away, back to his cabin, slamming the door behind him. He paced, trying to clear his head but nothing made any sense. Snatching up a bottle he pulled the cork with his teeth and drank deeply before sitting at his desk. He placed the bottle between his feet and stared down at it, his head in his hands. Was this how he would end? Were the fates so cruel that they would do this to him to satisfy their love of irony?

He looked up as the door opened, fully intending to yell at whoever it was to get the hell out, but his gaze fell upon the anxious figure of Miss Morton. She closed the door and hurried towards him, and to his surprise sank to her knees beside his chair.

"What is it?" she asked.

He frowned, looking at her and feeling even more that the fates were toying with him. Why would she care? Why were her words so soft, and why the devil was she looking at him with such concern?

"Don't worry, Miss Morton," he said, wondering why his voice sounded so dead, he lived yet surely? "I won't let any harm come to you, this is likely an answer to your prayers."

He jolted as a soft, warm hand covered his. "But not yours I think?"

He laughed and pulled his hand away though he wanted nothing more than to grasp it in his and take her to the bed. It would likely be the last thing he did after all.

"Are you afraid?" she asked.

He looked at her sharply. Was she implying that he was a coward? He'd never run from a fight in his life. He'd gained his reputation as a charismatic lover and charmer perhaps, but he'd not lived this long in a brutal world by being afraid of a fight. But it wasn't accusation he saw in her eyes, it was compassion.

"I'm not afraid," he replied, his voice hard.

"Then why did you look like you'd seen a ghost when you saw that ship?"

A mirthless bark of laughter escaped his lips. "Perhaps I had."

He reached down and grasped the bottle at his feet, drinking deeply once more, but to his annoyance she snatched it away from him, stuffed the cork back in and shoved it in the nearest desk drawer.

"If you are to find a way out of whatever predicament you seem to be in, I think you need a clear head. Don't you?" she demanded.

Lars stared at her. Those warm brown eyes were on him with such fierce determination as though she'd decided to save him again and she was damn well going to do it.

"What do you care?" he asked, refusing to believe what he saw there. "I'm not going to escape this one. I can't outrun them and we didn't have time to provision properly, so they can just sit on our tail until we starve to death or the men decide to give me up in return for their freedom, and I have a fair idea which they'll choose."

The Rogue

"But then why don't you fight?" she demanded, and he was quite taken aback by the ferocity behind her words. "Aren't you the Rogue? The stories I read about that man lead me to believe he would never run from a fight!"

"I cannot fire upon The Revenge!" he shouted in frustration and then buried his head in his hands.

He deserved this, he realised, he knew he did. But how the devil was he going to get out of this mess? He couldn't allow The Revenge to blow his men out of the water, and if he didn't take control of the situation and lead them to engage the vessel, they would appoint another captain who would. And he couldn't allow that either. No harm would come to The Revenge, he wouldn't let that happen, not now.

He started as the gentle slide of a hand stroked his hair. It was soothing, calming, and he took a breath as she repeated the motion.

"Who is on that ship?" she asked, her voice quiet.

He glanced up to see those beautiful eyes looking at him as though she really did care, as though she would save him if she could. He felt his heart squeeze in his chest. Well, the fates were really getting their money's worth today, he thought with a bitter smile. *Now* they send him a woman like this when there was damn all he could do about it.

"The past," he whispered. "The past is on that ship, and I cannot do it any more damage than I already have."

She frowned and held out her hand, holding it to his face, her thumb caressing his cheek bone. "You are in quite a fix, aren't you, pirate?"

Despite himself, he laughed. "You could say that." Not daring to move any further for fear she would remove her hand, he stilled. He didn't want her to stop touching him.

Lawrence wanted to sit here and look at those pretty eyes and feel her hand, warm against his cheek. He wanted to pretend that great black spectre on the horizon was nothing more than a storm cloud that would pass by if he was patient. If he kept looking into her eyes.

"Is there anything I can do?" she asked.

Kiss me.

The words were in his head in an instant and he knew she must see it in his eyes but he wouldn't say it. He didn't feel he could. Not now. If he was going to die, whether he was consigned to the depths of the ocean or taken to hang, he would do one good thing before he died. He wouldn't take anything more from this woman than had already been taken.

But then, she moved forward and pressed her lips against his.

Chapter 13

"Wherein fires are lit in a room full of powder."

Henri pulled away and saw her own shock reflected back at her in his eyes. The bright blue had seemed dull, his expression so utterly hopeless that she hadn't known what else to do. She only knew she wanted the insufferable, arrogant pirate back, that all too charming man with the merry blue eyes who made her blood boil and her heart race. She wanted to take away the pain she saw in his eyes and lift off the shadow of the past that hung over him. Henri felt she could almost see it, the weight of it at least, as it bowed his shoulders. And so she had kissed him.

His breath caught at the first press of her lips, an encouraging sign she thought, as she had drawn back, just a little, to brush her lips against his again. She was tentative, not really certain of what she was doing, and only knowing she was mimicking the manner in which he had kissed her before. Had it really only been this morning?

But it was not only shock in his eyes and her heart began to crash with wild abandon as she understood what that meant.

She had read enough romance novels in her life to know she could never be happy being married to a cold and indifferent man who would never love her to distraction. She had wanted to know love and passion, to know what it was to be desired above all else.

Well, her foolish plan may mean she would not experience what it was to be married to a man who loved her, but she knew this man needed her, for the moment at least. And she was likely the biggest fool in the world, but she could no more walk away from him now than she could have let the militia men drag him away to the gallows.

She raised her other hand, holding his face between them and feeling a warmth that spread through her chest as a smile tugged at that gorgeous mouth of his.

"Miss Morton," he said, his voice low, and a familiar thread of amusement behind the words. "You are the most contrary young woman I have ever known, and ..." He shook his head and brushed her cheek with his knuckles. "You never cease to surprise me."

She smiled and blinked, finding her eyes fill at the soft look he gave her. "My name is Henri."

He laughed at that and her heart lifted at the sound.

"Well," he said, taking one of her hands and raising it to his lips. "In that case ... my name is Lawrence." He pressed a kiss to her fingers, his eyes never leaving hers. "And other than Mousy, you are the only person on board who knows that."

She blinked, quite taken aback that he should choose to share something he had taken great pains to keep secret.

"Lawrence," she repeated, smiling. "I like that very much. But I promise you I will never use it in front of your men. You will be Lars until you say otherwise."

"Use it now," he said, his hand closing around hers, and such desperation in his voice that she didn't know how to respond "Please. I want to be Lawrence again, just for a little while at least."

She hesitated, whatever was she to do? She would not see him dead. Whatever he had done, she would not believe he was a bad man. She needed to know exactly what it was aboard that ship that made such guilt burn in his eyes. But he would only tell her that if he trusted her.

She clasped his hand in hers and held it to her cheek, before turning her head and kissing his fingers, one by one.

"Lawrence," she murmured his name against his skin, feeling with delight the shiver that ran over him.

The Rogue

There was a panicked voice screaming in her head, reminding her of how nice young ladies behaved. But then she'd never been that good at being a nice young lady. She had too quick a temper, she was too stubborn and wilful, and she was far too impetuous.

If she was a nice young lady she would have been delighted at being found such a wealthy husband as the Earl of Falmouth. She would not have run to a dubious part of town, alone, at night, in order to blackmail a pirate so she didn't have to.

The voice grew fainter by the moment. His big hand was rough and calloused, and she had imagined how it would feel, sliding over her skin. Oh, good Lord, Henri, *stop*, but she couldn't. She turned his hand over and pressed her mouth to his palm before looking up. His eyes were dark, his breathing ragged, and she knew what she should do, what she wanted to do.

"Kiss me," she said.

He stilled and for a moment she felt as though her heart waited for him to move before it dared to beat again. And then his hand was at her waist, pulling her towards him and she went willingly.

She moved forward on her knees, into the space between his thighs as he pulled her close. One hand clasped her at the small of her back, the other cradling her head. She leaned in, meeting his mouth as his head ducked towards her and this time there was no gentle brushing of lips, this wasn't gentle at all.

His kiss was hard and desperate, and she gasped in surprise as his tongue invaded her mouth. She tensed in his arms, but he persisted, his tongue stroking hers, the warmth of him like being enveloped in a blaze compared to the frigid temperature of the room.

Encouraged by his example she began to imitate his moves as their mouths worked with increasing need. She slipped her hand under his coat until just the thin fabric of his shirt was between them. Reassured to feel his heart was thundering just as hers was she reached up her other hand and slid it around his neck, tangling her fingers in his thick hair and pulling him closer.

Oh God but it felt good. She felt warm for the first time since she had left her home on that freezing night. Except it wasn't just warmth, it was heat, a luxurious burn that blazed just beneath her skin, and the heart of the fire was being kindled somewhere deep inside of her. Every slide of his tongue, his mouth, his hands, added fuel to the fire, and she wanted to burn.

This, she realised, this was what Annie had warned her about. She'd never truly understood the idea that a woman could become so lost in a man's touch she would do anything, risk anything, to be with him, to feel his touch again. But now, now she knew.

Her body was crying out for more, her skin needed to feel his hands against it, and there was a deep and clamouring ache inside her. It demanded his attention, this empty, hollow sensation that only he could fill.

Her hand slid down his hard chest, feeling the taut muscles beneath her fingertips and wishing there was no cloth to keep her from touching the warm flesh beneath. She allowed her hand to drop further, resting on his thick thigh and sliding towards his hip, noting with satisfaction the way her touch increased his desire as he groaned into her mouth.

Confidence growing, she reached for his shirt, snatching at it and pulling it from the confines of his waistband. And then her hands slipped under the neck of the infuriating material and slid over his skin.

He paused, his mouth still so close to hers, but now his eyes were what consumed her, his hot gaze just as intimate as his mouth and tongue had just been. She watched him watch her as her hands explored beneath the shirt.

Beginning at those broad shoulders her hands glided lower, over the strong outlines of his chest. There was a key hung on a lace around his neck and she touched the metal, hot from its continued connection to his skin, absurdly she envied it, so close to his heart. She recommenced her exploration, down over his taut abdomen, finding the trail of coarse hair that tickled her fingertips and led her lower.

He gasped and wrenched her hands away and she almost cried out in alarm that he should stop her now, but then she saw by the look in his eyes he had no intention of them stopping at all.

"Stand up," he demanded, his voice rough.

She did as he asked, almost stumbling and tripping over her own skirts in her eagerness to obey him. With fingers that fumbled at the buttons she shed her pelisse, allowing the deep blue velvet to fall in a crumpled heap on the floor.

"Come here."

If his demanding manner had irritated her before, now it made her breath catch and she climbed onto the chair as he moved her to straddle his lap.

The small voice whispered in her ear, pleading for decency, demanding what she was about, as she imagined she must look like any common whore if someone were to walk in on them now. But then his hands gripped her waist and pulled her down and she gasped as the evidence of his desire was plainly illustrated.

Her skirts had ridden up so there was nothing but the fabric of his trousers between them. She was momentarily pleased that she hadn't given in to the sales lady on a recent shopping trip, who had been trying to sell her the latest fashion in the shape of a shocking pair of bloomers. But then he tilted his hips and rubbed against her, just so, and her breath caught in her throat.

The room was still freezing, she knew it must be, but she didn't feel it. Henri felt nothing but the heat of him, the burn of his flesh under the fabric of his clothes that she wanted to snatch at and tear from his body. She was vaguely aware that she was in the grip of some kind of madness but so far gone that she was beyond caring.

He sought her mouth again and she gave it to him, her breathing coming fast now, and punctuated with sighs and moans and small breathless noises that seemed to inflame him more as his hands slid up her sides to cup her breasts. His fingers caressed her nipples, torturing the tight little nubs of flesh through the cloth of her gown.

Seemingly frustrated by the inconvenience of her dress, he wrenched at the buttons and tugged at the fabric, yanking it apart to expose her breasts, and she gasped as the cold air peaked the tight skin further. And yet that was nothing to the sensation of his hot, wet mouth closing over the tender flesh and suckling her until she cried out.

Her head tipped back, eyes closed as something inside her seemed to contract and the ache intensified. She buried her hands in his hair, pulling his head closer as the sensitive skin between her legs began to throb. She arched and pressed against him harder, seeking relief from the sensation that was driving her to madness. For if this wasn't madness, her all-consuming need for this man, then she did not know what was.

He stopped suddenly, his head resting against her breast, his breathing harsh and she tilted his head, intending to kiss him again when the look in his eyes stopped her.

"Oh, God, Henri," he whispered. "What have you done?"

"What?" she demanded, bewildered, wondering what on earth he meant.

He clung to her, his embrace so fierce she could barely breathe, and then with a ferocious curse he got to his feet, depositing her none too gently in the chair he had just vacated, and crossing the room. Apparently he wanted to put as much distance between them as he could.

"What did I do?" she asked, as colour flooded her cheeks.

She was mortified, humiliated. With fingers that trembled she rearranged her clothing until she was more modestly attired. She felt like a fool and a slut. What could she have done to kill his desire for her so very thoroughly? And yet when he looked on her she could still see that desire in his eyes as though it was a living thing that prowled the room, devouring the distance separating them with hungry bites.

"Nothing ... *everything!*" he exclaimed, running a shaky hand through his hair.

"You d-don't want me?" she asked, not daring to believe the evidence of her own eyes when he stood so very far away from her.

He laughed, a desperate bark of laughter that sounded like he was at his wit's end. Perhaps he was? Was that her fault?

"Of course I want you, you little fool," he ground out, though his words were so angry she wasn't sure she was reassured. "I want you," he repeated. "But I want you enough not to ruin you."

"What?" She stared at him as though he truly had run mad. "What on earth do you mean? I was ruined the moment the militia appeared outside of that Tavern and you well know it!"

He shook his head and met her eyes.

"No. You have a chance now, Henri, and I cannot ... I will not take it from you. I'll not condemn you to a life where you'll have to fight for survival, never mind happiness. I may be beyond help, but you ... For heaven's sake, let me for once in my life do the right thing."

She stared at him, not understanding how he believed she could be saved now, and even more perplexed by the idea that she wasn't sure she wanted him to save her at all.

He walked closer to her and crouched down beside her chair, so that their eyes were level.

"Henri," he said, his voice soft. "The commander on that ship, he's a good and honourable man."

He reached out and took her hand, covering it with his own and the ache in her body seemed to bloom outwards all over again, and yet this time her heart was the source of it.

"He will help you, Henri, I know he will.

Chapter 14

"Wherein a lady may be saved and is none too pleased about it."

Henri frowned. Her brain felt as though the world had been tipped upside down and everything she had understood had been shaken and upended with it. The pirate, the wicked corsair with a reputation for thievery and seduction, was trying to save her. That in itself was ... quite unbelievable. There was a gnawing uncertainty in her heart that told her she didn't really want to be saved ... This fact was shocking, and possibly not so far out of character as she might have wished to believe.

"But then ... if that is true, could he not help you too?"

She watched as Lars ... *Lawrence* shook his head. He smiled but there was an underlying sadness to it she wanted to understand.

"He's a good man, but he can't perform miracles." She saw a shadow enter his eyes and knew the past was stalking him once again. "I'm not sure he'd even want to," he added, as though talking to himself and then, with sudden anxiety in his eyes. "I wouldn't blame him," he said, as if knowing she would and wanting to exonerate the man.

She felt the solid warmth of his hand, as it was still holding hers, and she gave it a slight squeeze, hoping the intimacy of her touch might make him confide in her. "Who is he? Who is he to you?"

He shook his head, and she knew she would not be granted her wish. "Someone I once knew."

She had no opportunity to question him further as there was a bang on the door. He released her hand and a moment later, Mousy stuck his head around the door.

"Ye need to see this, Cap'n."

He was out the door before she could utter another word and she was left alone. She shivered. His departure seemed to have robbed her of the heat he had brought and she felt suddenly cold and sick, and very alone. What was she doing? What in the name of heaven was she doing?

If there really was someone on that ship who could take her back home, back to her life, then she should grab the opportunity with both hands. But even if what he said was true, how was he proposing to get her to him? Henri doubted that the plight of one girl would weigh very heavily on the shoulders of a man who had been sent to hunt down a pirate ship. She could only imagine that whoever was commanding The Revenge had once been his friend. She imagined two young boys and the way life may have conspired to send one on the right path, and one on the wrong. How must it feel to him to see his friend hunting him down to send him to his death?

She felt the slide of ice down her back as it occurred to her just how he might get her to The Revenge. He would give himself up.

Her heart felt as though it had lodged somewhere in her throat and she scrambled up, snatching her pelisse and pulling it on before she ran out of the cabin and on deck to find Lawrence.

She turned and climbed the steps to the quarter deck where he was standing with Mousy.

"She's damn fast," the big man was saying, shaking his head.

Lawrence smiled, and she thought she saw pride in his eyes. "Yes, she is."

"So why the devil hasn't she fired on us?" Mousy demanded and they both watched as Lawrence began to pace. "She's more'n capable of runnin' rings around this ship," Mousy continued as his captain's frown increased. "I've been keepin' 'er at bay but she's jus' shadowin' us. We make a move and she does too but shows no sign of wantin' to take us. Like she jus' wants us to know she's there."

Lawrence suddenly stopped in his tracks and spun around to stare at Henri.

"Why did you come and find me?" he demanded.

Henri started in surprise, taken aback by the fierce tone of his voice.

"Because I need to speak with you, about what you have planned."

He looked perplexed for a moment and then shook his head. "Not now!" he said, clearly impatient. "The other night, when you sought me out at the Nag's Head, why did you come? I know you needed money, but what for?"

Henri flushed, and her eyes drifted to Mousy. Remembering what she'd done was humiliating enough without explaining it in front of anyone else. With a huff of annoyance that seemed to mean he understood her reluctance, he grasped her by the wrist and towed her down the steps, pulling her back into his cabin.

"Explain!" he demanded once he'd shut the door.

She bristled at the tone of his voice. "I really don't think ..."

"Miss Morton," he said, his voice cool and hard, and dispelling any romantic ideas she may have been harbouring that he cared for her. "I have a ship that is quite capable of sending us all to the devil sitting on my doorstep and yet it doesn't seem inclined to engage us. I want to know why that is, and I think it has something to do with you."

She couldn't understand why he would think that when there was a more obvious reason. "But if this man ... your friend commands it, perhaps he wishes to help you after all?"

For a moment he looked perplexed and then he shook his head, all impatience and brusque movements. "He's not my friend, and he thinks I'm dead," he snapped. "No, it's you. It has to be."

Henri opened her mouth and closed it again. "I--I," she stammered as it occurred to her, he might actually be right. She didn't believe for one moment that her fiancé cared a whit about her or her fate, but he might care that something had been taken from him. In the same way as if Lawrence had stolen a fine painting. Perhaps he had somehow discovered her whereabouts and sent someone to retrieve her for him.

"I came to you because my father was marrying me off to a man I despise. But the man in question is very wealthy and had offered to settle all my father's debts as well as giving him a stipend for the rest of his days."

She watched as his face closed off. She had no idea what he was thinking but his stance was rigid, his fists clenched.

"I see," he said. "A very generous offer but then ..." He looked at her, and she thought she saw anger in his eyes. "But then he was buying something very fine indeed."

Henri swallowed. "If my father cannot pay his debts ..." She shrugged, finding she could not continue.

"And this wealthy man," he asked, his tone clipped and cold. "Who was he?"

"Alexander Sinclair." Her voice was barely audible now and she had the impression that some great cloud was gathering over them. "The Earl of Falmouth."

She watched as Lawrence closed his eyes, and she thought he seemed to be in pain.

"Lawrence?" she said.

"Don't," he replied, his eyes snapping open and the blue bright with anger. "Don't call me that. I'm Captain Savage to you, do you hear me?"

The Rogue

She gasped, shocked and hurt by his behaviour but she had no time to demand why he would treat her so as once again Mousy hammered on the door.

"They've signalled, Cap'n, they want the girl, and ... they want you."

Henri's chest grew tight, it was as though all of the air had been sucked out of the room, but Lawrence ... Captain Savage did not seem surprised. He even smiled a little though it was not a happy expression.

"Tell them the terms are acceptable."

"What?" Mousy stared at him, uncomprehending, before storming into the room and slamming the door behind him. "I'll do no such thing! What's wrong with ye?" he demanded. "We've still got a fighting chance! Lord, man, we took the Corona and she 'ad more guns than thisun so you can't be tellin' me ye worrit we're out gunned! What the devil's ailing ye?"

She watched, her chest aching as she saw the pain in Lawrence's eyes.

"It's him, Mousy, it's Alex."

Whoever the earl might be to Lawrence, Mousy seemed to be well aware of the connection. The big man's shoulders slumped. "No," he whispered. "I don't believe it."

"We can't outrun that ship, Mousy," Lawrence said, his voice soft. "And I can't outrun fate. Not anymore. Though I've had a better run than I deserved, thanks to you, but ..."

"Then I'm coming with ye," Mousy said, folding his massive arms and butting in before he could finish the sentence.

Lawrence smiled at him, and it was full of warmth. "I know you would, I know you want to, but the men need you. You must get them away, Mousy, they won't make it without a good Captain.

Mousy shook his head and held out one meaty hand, a finger pointed at Lawrence. "No ... I ..." he began but Lawrence wouldn't listen.

"Dammit, man," Lawrence shouted, growing angry now. He turned away and strode to his desk, tearing open the drawers until he found the bottle she had stashed there earlier. "This is my ship, these are my men," he shouted, pulling the cork and throwing it to the floor. "I'll not go to my fate knowing they're all doomed too, and they will be unless they have someone with the wit to steer them true." He stared at Mousy until the solid man seemed to crumple in on himself and looked at the floor, shaking his head.

"Never thought to see ye go like this."

Lawrence shrugged and offered him the bottle. "Maybe it's for the best."

Mousy frowned and drunk deep, his throat working as he swallowed the liquor. He lowered the bottle and stared at Lawrence. "Maybe ... Maybe 'e can 'elp ye?"

There was a snort of amusement from Lawrence as he took the bottle back. "Even the Earl of Falmouth doesn't have that kind of power, and I wouldn't be at all surprised if he was just as eager to see me hanged, once ... once it all becomes clear." The two men stared at each other. "Go and send the reply."

Mousy hesitated for a moment before touching his forehead with his finger. "Aye, aye, Cap'n."

"Good man." Lawrence smiled at him as his large friend ducked his head and exited the cabin.

Henri sat down in the chair by the desk, her hands clutching at the arms and suddenly unsure if her legs would hold her any longer. She was exhausted and the events of the past two days were so many and so violently different from anything she had experienced in her life before she could hardly believe any of it was real. It was as though she had been plunged into someone else's life and didn't know how she was supposed to act anymore. She put her hand to her temples. Her head was aching and she was overwhelmed. She couldn't bear the idea that Lawrence was going to sacrifice himself to save his men. Surely there had to be another way?

"Is there nothing else to be done?" she asked, looking up at him.

He was standing still, just staring across the room, but she knew he was looking into the past and seeing whatever events had chased him into the life he now led.

"No," he replied. "Nothing." He turned and smiled at her and went to settle himself in the chair on the other side of the desk. "That ship out there is the finest of her kind. She's fast, incredibly manoeuvrable and just ..." To her astonishment he grinned at her. "At least I'll get to sail aboard her for a day or two. I never thought I would." He sat back in his chair, his finger tracing a pattern on the glass of the bottle. "I saw the first designs for her you see. I always told him she would be a beauty."

"Told who?" she asked, watching him with tears pricking behind her eyes.

He turned to her and smiled, and this time there was warmth in the blue.

"My brother, Alexander Sinclair."

Chapter 15

"Wherein a pirate reminisces and reveals the truth."

"Your brother!" she exclaimed. His face had become watchful, and she wondered what he was thinking because she didn't know *what* to think. "Your brother is the Earl of Falmouth?" she said, her voice faint.

"Yes, my brother ... and your fiancé," he said.

She couldn't gauge what he thought about that. His expression was a careful blank and there was no tone to his voice.

"Here," he said, pouring a measure from the bottle into a small glass and sliding it across the desk to her. "Try not to drop it," he added, smiling.

She took it and sipped, wincing at the strong taste but needing the warm burn as it slid down her throat.

"I don't understand why you are so desperate not to marry him," he asked. He wasn't looking at her anymore but had returned to drawing patterns on the glass bottle. "He is the very model of a nobleman, honourable and true ... not to mention wealthy," he added, laughing, though that time she was certain there had been a bitter tone beneath the sound.

"I think," she said, choosing her words with care. "That it has been some years since you have seen your brother."

"What the devil do you mean by that?" he demanded, shifting and leaning forward, his arms crossed on the desk in front of him.

She hesitated, she didn't want to destroy the noble memory he may have cherished of a loving brother, but the man she had known, even so little as she had known him, had not lived up to that description.

"Speak your mind," he shouted, and she jumped in her seat. Anger rose that he would speak to her so, that the soft intimacy of such a short time before had been so easily forgotten.

"Your brother is a rake," she said with disgust. "He is notorious for his womanising, his drinking and cold behaviour and I have seen nothing in him to believe those rumours to be based on anything but the truth."

He stood so suddenly the chair he'd been sat on crashed to the floor, but he didn't seem to notice. "You will take that back!" he shouted.

Henri gasped. "I will not!" she replied as his anger fired hers to greater heights. "Why do you think I would run away from a match to such an *honourable* man?" she demanded of him, slamming the glass down on the desk top in her anger. "I'd wager that you, a pirate, have more honour than that man has ever possessed."

"You don't know a damned thing about him!" he raged. He stared at her, apparently too furious to speak, but eventually he shook his head, holding her gaze. "You don't know him, Henri," he said, and she felt her anger dissolve at the soft way he said her name. "He was ever thus. Alex is older than me, you see, by almost ten years. He would always find a way to take the blame for my endless stupidity and carelessness. I was forever in trouble of one kind or another and he was forever pulling me out of it by my ears. Somehow he always managed to arrange it so they considered him the guilty party and I was the golden son who could do no wrong. Until I made such a mess that even he couldn't save me ... though he almost died trying."

She saw the guilt in his eyes and realised this had been a burden he'd carried for many years.

"I thought I'd killed him," he blurted. "I thought I'd killed him." He leaned against the desk, one hand covering his eyes and Henri ran to him. She righted the chair and moved him to it, making him sit down.

Henri knelt in front of him, as she had earlier that day, and covered his hand with hers.

"That's why I came back." His voice was quiet and he wouldn't look at her, his head bent, his eyes trained on some memory it pained him to recall.

"Only Mousy knows who I am, and I have avoided asking of those I once cared about ever since. They were as dead to me as I was to them, better for them that way. But then, by chance, Mousy heard my father, the earl had died, he'd been ill a long time it seems. I assumed the title would go to our cousin, and then we heard Alex lived. It was like a miracle."

He rubbed his eyes with the heel of his hand. "I came back then. Not because I could change anything. Not to apologise or explain for there are no words for that, and not to try to return to my old life. I knew that was long gone."

Lawrence gave a bitter laugh and her chest ached at the pain in his eyes. "I just wanted to see him with my own eyes, you see. To know he truly lived. All these years I've borne the guilt of it. The knowledge I'd killed that good man, my brother, the one who had always looked out for me. I would have done anything if I could only change that. But I was badly injured that night too, and by the time I was recovered enough to understand what had happened I was half way across the world. There was nothing I could do. I thought I was damned," he whispered. "So what did it matter what I did? How I lived was of no consequence, I didn't intend to do it for long in any case."

She squeezed his hand, willing him to look up.

"You are not damned, Lawrence, and I imagine you never were, but your brother ... he is not the man you remember."

He shook his head, and she could see her words had angered him again. "Maybe I wasn't damned that night but for all that followed ... I have not spent the last ten years of my life well, Henri. I have robbed and held men and women to ransom, for the fun of it as much as for the money," he raged. "I enjoyed the thrill of it, you see, the danger, but it is not the kind of life that goes unpunished." He sighed, and the anger seemed to drain away from him. "And nor should it," he added.

"Lawrence, listen to me. I do not believe the man aboard that ship will help you, brother or no. He's not like you, he's certainly not the man you remember." She drew to mind the brief interviews she had been subjected to before the earl would deign to take her as his wife. She shuddered at the memory. "He's a cold and dangerous man, Lawrence, and he's known for shredding his enemies. Look how he destroyed Lord Heywood two years ago. The man shot himself after your brother took everything from him in a game of cards! He's even rumoured to ...."

She came to a sudden halt as she realised what she was saying.

"To have killed his own brother?" he supplied for her, his voice quiet. "Yes, I heard that one. And now you see how you misjudge him. Alex did believe I was dead after that awful night, and he allowed people to believe he was responsible for it so my father wouldn't bear the shame of knowing his son was killed by the militia for smuggling, for that was what I was about that night. As it was it broke my father's heart." He swallowed and looked up at her. "I don't know what happened to Lord Heywood, but I do know the man was a fool, a bigger one if he tried to gamble against Alex. He never loses."

Henri sat with her mind spinning out of control. Could she really have misjudged the man so badly?

"So, you believe he'll try to save you?" she asked at last.

He frowned, and for a moment he seemed at a loss for an answer. "I truly don't know. The Alex I knew would have done most anything to save me but he believed in honour too, and I think the man I have become ..." He shook his head. "I think he will believe I have earned my fate, Henri. I hope perhaps that will sadden him, but truly, after what I did, I would expect him to send me to the gallows with no regrets."

"No!" she shouted, reaching out and grabbing hold of his arms. She wanted to shake him. "I won't let them hang you, I won't!"

He looked so surprised by her outburst she almost laughed, but his smile when it came took her breath away. He lifted her chin with his knuckle and his eyes on her were so full of warmth she felt the heat as though she was sat by a fire.

"It is good to know there is one who will mourn me a little."

"Oh, Lawrence!" she said, her voice thick, and then she couldn't look at him anymore for her eyes filled with tears. She buried her face in her hands and sobbed.

Chapter 16

"Wherein a pirate faces the past and embraces fate."

Lawrence looked down at the girl at his feet. How on earth had he managed to get her entangled in this almighty mess?

"Hey," he said, putting his hand out and tugging lightly at her wrist, but she wouldn't uncover her face and look at him. He sighed and got up before reaching down and lifting her to her feet.

"There, there, my sweet little minx," he murmured against her hair as he pulled her into his arms. With guilt that stabbed at him with a fine, cold blade, he realised he had no business holding her so. She belonged to Alex, no matter what the foolish child thought.

Henri didn't know his brother like he did. Alex would be a fine husband, he would make sure she had everything she could possibly desire. She would be safe and well and ... damn it all why did the idea of her in Alex's arms make his chest tighten. She was Alex's, he told himself firmly. He'd wronged his brother so much already, he wouldn't compound it by trying to take his fiancée! He'd consign himself to hell before he did any more harm to the brother he'd idolised in his youth. But then, he realised with a grim smile, he'd likely be going there anyway.

His thoughts ground to a halt, though, as he realised she had wrapped one arm around his waist and the other was beneath his coat and rested over his heart. He could feel the heat of her small hand burning through his shirt. He was suddenly aware of the flutter of her breath against his neck, and then the soft brush of her lips against his jaw.

Lawrence closed his eyes, telling himself he would just savour this moment, as it would be the last time he ever held her. But then she kissed him again, this time her lips a little lower. Once more her mouth moved, down his neck, and this time he felt the slightest touch of a warm tongue against his skin, and damn if that didn't make his skin feel stretched too tight and awaken his every desire.

"Don't," he said, but the word didn't sound right, it sounded too much like *oh, God, yes,* when it was followed by a sharp intake of breath as her hand slid down his chest and lingered just below his navel.

Once again her hand slipped under his shirt, her fingers moving over his skin, teasing the flesh so close to his waistband, touching him with feather-soft delicacy, as if she knew she only had to stray a little lower and any shred of control that remained would be unravelled beyond repair.

She pressed her body against him and his hard length pressed into the softness of her belly. He imagined how it would feel if he laid her down, if her legs closed around his hips, pulling him inside her, welcoming him into her heat. Her mouth continued to press hot little kisses against his skin, moving back up his neck as her fingers trailed back and forth, making him shiver with need, the need to lay her down on the bed and lose himself in her, in the unholy longing to make her his alone; though she was anything but his and never could be.

He snatched at her hands, holding her away from him before the little devil could discover how to tempt him further, and thanked heaven she was an innocent as his will power was stretched to its limits. But then he made the mistake of looking down at her. There was such fire in those tawny brown eyes, such demand for his attention. Did she really know what it was she was asking him for?

He wondered if she would look like that for Alex and then squashed the thought before it could turn to anger. He knew how she had looked for him at least, when she had rubbed herself against him, seeking her own pleasure like a sinuous cat. Damn but

The Rogue

he could feel his control slipping further, his desire for her turning from a pleasant ache to a physical pain just thinking about it.

As if reading his mind, she leaned into him harder, pressing her body against his and raising her mouth, inviting him to kiss her. He held her hands still, restraining her, but he was too desperate to deny her. He accepted the invitation she gave, slanting his mouth over hers and devouring the exquisite little moan of desire that escaped her.

The kiss deepened as their tongues danced and parried and the little breathless moan came again, making his blood burn under his skin. Oh God he wanted to hear her moan and squeal and cry out his name as she came apart ... and then he remembered his brother. He pulled away.

"I can't!" he shouted in frustration, his voice rough. He dropped her hands as though she had burned him. Stepping away he turned his back on her, trying not to see the hurt that made those wide, doe eyes glisten. "You belong to Alex."

"Oh!" she shouted, and though he hadn't been looking he was almost sure she'd stamped her foot in rage. "I belong to no man. I will *not* be someone's property!" The next thing he knew she was hitting him with small but well placed blows that rained down upon his back with quite surprising force.

"Henri!" He tried to evade her but as he was unwilling to touch her for fear he would simply give in and take her to his bed, his efforts were thwarted as she followed him about the room, apparently unwilling to give quarter. "Henri, stop that!"

"I won't stop until you stop being such a blithering idiot!" she railed against him in utter fury.

He ducked as she changed tack and his bottle of rum went flying over his head and smashed against the far wall. "Dammit, that wasn't empty!" he raged as the overpowering scent of liquor filled the small cabin. With growing alarm he realised she was scanning the room for another missile and he had no choice but to risk giving her a shake.

"Calm yourself, you damned little hellion!" he shouted, with all the authority of a man well used to commanding a ship of over eighty cut-throats. She seemed singularly unimpressed. Belatedly he realised it may not have been the correct way to address her either as her eyes flashed and she stamped on his toes with all her might.

He hauled in a breath before he sullied her ears with some of his choicer expressions.

"I will not be calm," she shouted, wriggling out of his grasp and pushing him to illustrate her words. "Don't you realise that your brother will never marry me now in any case! I'm ruined, remember?"

"He damn well will," Lawrence growled, even though the very idea of her as Alex's wife made his teeth clench and gave him the strong desire to hit something. "I'll see he does if it's the last thing I do!"

And just like that her rage disappeared, her eyes filled once more and to his dismay her bottom lip trembled, and oh, good God, he had never wanted to kiss a woman more than he did at this moment.

"Henri," he said, keeping his voice soft, and so obviously full of regret it seemed to shred any remaining control she had and she fell against his chest, sobbing.

"I won't marry him, I won't! I won't!" she said through her tears. "I don't belong to him, I never will."

He couldn't just let her sob and do nothing to comfort her and so he gathered her up and held her close. But he couldn't let her have any romantic notions about the future either. It beggared belief that the girl should have any towards him, he thought with a smile. After everything she'd been through, she should be ruing the day he'd been born. But then she was quite unlike anyone he had ever met before. He realised he'd had many regrets in his life, but he thought perhaps not knowing her better would be the very biggest of them all.

"They'll hang me, Henri," he said, and then held her away from him, shaking her a little as she cried harder. "No. Stop that, you must listen to me. I'm not about to go meekly to the noose I swear. If the opportunity comes, I will take it and I'll run. But I'm an outlaw, a wanted man, and this will be the way I will live if I live at all. Even if I was mad enough to want to take a woman into a life like that ..." He took a breath. "You would only slow me down, Henri. I'd likely get caught again and I doubt I'd escape the hangman twice. The chances of me doing it this time are slim enough."

She stopped crying and wiped her eyes, and he frowned as he felt he could hear the wheels turning in her mind. What the devil was she up to now? "Whatever you're thinking, just ... just stop it!"

"Yes, Lawrence." She blinked and looked up at him, tears still tracking down her sweet face and he felt his heart clench. By God, what a pair of brown eyes could do to a man.

Gritting his teeth, he tried hard to forget about his own wishes. "I mean it, Henri, whatever foolish notions you're harbouring, for heaven's sake, put them aside. Surely this little adventure has made you see how easily you can lose everything?"

She nodded, her big brown eyes never leaving his. "Yes, Lawrence," she repeated, her voice quite sincere. "It has."

He sighed, relieved that perhaps he had got his point across, and possibly just a little heartbroken. "Well then ... good."

They both jumped as the door opened and Mousy looked in, his expression grim.

"They're waitin' for the two of ye'."

Lawrence felt something in his gut tighten but he nodded. "We'll be with you in a moment."

Mousy nodded and left the room, closing the door behind him.

"Well, then," Lawrence said, trying to keep his words light. "It looks as though it's time to face the fates, and my brother."

Chapter 17

"Wherein the fates are met bravely, and despair snaps at our heroine's heels."

Henri watched Lawrence and wondered how he could be so calm. She remembered him the same way in the shop. He had to know he was going to be caught and what that meant for him, and yet he had seemed far from panic.

She tried to emulate that calm and wondered if like her he was screaming inside his chest. Her heart was thudding too hard, too fast, and her mind was racing, trying to think of ways she could contrive his escape. For he was right about one thing; this adventure had showed her how easily you could lose everything. A wrong decision, a foolish step on a downward path, and everything fell about in ruins before your eyes.

He pulled out the key she had discovered from under his shirt, and she watched as he removed it and knelt to open the big chest at the foot of his berth.

As she had suspected it was filled with gold and silver and all manner of glittering objects.

Hearing her gasp of surprise he looked up at her and grinned.

"I was a very good pirate," he said with a devilish wink, and she felt her heart squeeze at the idea of all that adventurous spirit, that wicked humour and the merry twinkle in those bright blue eyes being extinguished. She wouldn't let him hang, she swore to herself. No matter what.

He selected a small, blue velvet bag and re-locked the chest before walking back to her.

"This is for you," he said, holding out the bag. "For everything you've suffered, and to ensure that, whatever happens, you will be safe."

She took the little bag from him with fingers that trembled and opened it at his insistence. She poured the contents into the palm of her hand and blinked, momentarily speechless. For there, nestled in her palm, sat seven large, uncut diamonds.

"I pray that you will trust Alex and marry him, for he will do everything in his power to see you happy. But ..." He paused and there was such warmth in his eyes she didn't know how she managed to stand still and listen and not dissolve into hysterics at the unfairness of it all. "I know now just how stubborn you are, so whatever happens, this will keep you provided for and in no one's power. I only ask one thing of you, Henri," he said, his voice low. "Whatever you do with the other six, have one made into something pretty. Wear it when you are happy and remember me. Will you do that?"

She swallowed hard and reminded herself that he wasn't going to hang, she wouldn't allow it. Blinking away tears, she nodded and he smiled and kissed her cheek, returning the diamonds to the bag one by one for her, as her hands were trembling and she seemed unable to move. He looked away as she tucked the jewels securely into her under things and then followed him out the door.

The men yelled and roared and stamped their feet, angry and uncomprehending at the loss of their captain. Lawrence yelled for silence and she looked around at the faces of men who all turned to him, waiting to hear what their captain had to say.

"Quiet, you miserable beggars," he roared, though there was humour in his eyes. "We all know, in this life, that our days are numbered. Well, my number just got called, but my fate is not yet yours. Mousy is your captain now. If the fates allow, I will make my escape and find my way back to you, but if not ..." He swept the hat from his head and opened his arms in a theatrical gesture. "Then toast to your dear, old Captain Savage, and remember that he was the canniest and the best - and without a doubt the prettiest and most loved by our captives!"

There was laughter at that and he grinned at his men, showing Henri all too clearly the character who had been written about in the pamphlets she'd read at home.

"But remember most of all, the spoils he led you to made your fortunes, my fine varlets and scapegallows! And then for the love of God, spread yourselves to the four winds, find a nice fat wife each, and a good living and enjoy a little peace. For if you don't you'll be following me to dance with Jack Ketch, and we all know the steps only too well. Take care of yourself, lads. I'll be seein' ye!"

He turned to Mousy, his expression grave. "The minute I'm on that boat, get clear of here, as far as you can get, and keep this safe." He pressed the key into his hand. "When you hear the news of my death, share it out among the lads."

Mousy's jaw clenched and he put the circle of thin leather around his neck and the key fell beneath his shirt. "I'll keep it 'till ye get back 'ere, an' that's all I'll do," he growled, daring Lawrence to contradict him with a furious glare.

Lawrence huffed out a laugh and nodded, and Henri watched as the two men grasped each other's forearms and embraced briefly.

"Be seein' ye then, Cap'n, I'll take good care o' the Wench while yer gone."

"I know you will," Lawrence said, his voice quiet now.

He looked over the side and Henri followed his gaze. A rope ladder had been slung over the rail and at the bottom waited a small boat. There were four armed men aboard and Henri suddenly noticed the men on deck around her with muskets aimed at those below.

Dizzy with fear, she watched as Lawrence climbed onto the ladder.

"Come then, Miss Morton," he said with a smile, offering his hand as though he was helping her to board a pleasure boat for a Sunday picnic. She took his hand, and managed the rail, finding her feet on the ladder and his reassuring presence behind her, guiding her down into the boat.

Once in the little bobbing gig, she grasped the sides as the sea tilted and rocked them, and the men fell on Lawrence and put him in chains, his arms bound tightly behind his back. There were roars from the deck above and Lawrence yelled himself hoarse, shouting for his men to hold.

"Leave him alone," she shouted in fury. "He's come willingly, he's unarmed, what more do you want?"

The men glared at her in disgust, as though she was quite mad to defend the monster they found themselves in company with, and Lawrence hushed her with a shake of his head.

"They're just doing their job, Miss Morton."

Henri gritted her teeth and saved her anger up. She'd turn it on the right man soon enough, if he didn't do all in his power to help his brother.

She closed her eyes and gripped the sides of the boat as though her life depended on it, quite certain that at any moment they would be tossed like a child's toy, to sink like marbles into the fathomless cold below the thin planks of wood her feet rested on.

It was with relief and no little surprise then that the thud of wood on wood confirmed they'd made the distance between the ships. She looked at Lawrence to see his gaze trained on his ship as she drew away, as far and as fast as it could go, just as he had instructed.

The sun was sinking and the sails all lit up in gold, making it look fanciful and unreal, like something from a mythical tale of

The Rogue

Gods and sea monsters. For a moment she saw the loss in his eyes and then, perceiving he was watched, he blinked and forced a smile.

"You're safe now, be home before you know it," he said with a wink.

Henri scowled at him and he laughed softly before the men hauled him to his feet. They set her to climb first and she made her way, hampered by sodden skirts that wrapped around her ankles and made it heavy work. She made the rail and stood shivering as she found herself confronted by armed men. So many to secure one man, it almost made her laugh. She felt Lawrence would be pleased that his reputation had made them take such measures.

She screamed as the man himself was pushed with force up over the rail. They'd made him climb with his hands bound and he hit the deck with a curse.

"For heaven's sake, are you so timid you must abuse an unarmed man," she raged at the sailor who had pushed him over the rail.

He scowled at her but held his tongue and snapped to attention as the commander approached them. She turned and swallowed a gasp as she saw the Earl of Falmouth stride towards her. He looked her over, those cool grey eyes sharp and assessing. She realised suddenly that she could see the likeness between the men, in their great height, in the breadth of those wide shoulders and that thick black hair. But where Lawrence's gaze held amusement and that merry, wicked twinkle, this man's presence was far colder.

"I am relieved to find you in such good spirits, Miss Morton," he said, his voice as calm and emotionless as she remembered. He reached for her hand and she curtsied, stiff and formal, as he placed a perfunctory kiss on her fingers. "I trust you are no worse for your adventures?"

Henri thought in those words there was perhaps a thread of anger, or was that concern, she couldn't be sure.

She raised her chin. "I have been well treated, my lord, and would suggest you interview your captive in private before you allow your men to abuse him any further. I feel we both have much to tell you."

He frowned at her, clearly perplexed by the demand in her voice, curiosity alight in his eyes.

Lawrence, she noted, had kept his eyes down, his dark hair fallen around his face.

The earl inclined his head a little. "Your wish is my command. Bring the prisoner," he instructed, and then gestured for her to take his arm and she followed him to the captain's cabin.

Though not much larger in size, the earl's cabin was full of polished wood and gleaming brass. It spoke of great wealth and power, and a man who paid attention to details. Suddenly Henri found she hated him more than ever for having all this when Lawrence had lost so much.

The earl turned once Lawrence was brought in, held fast between two men who threw him forward so he fell to his knees on the cabin floor.

"Oh, can't you leave him be!" she exclaimed and ran back to Lawrence, falling to kneel beside him.

"If you'll forgive me for noting it, Miss Morton, you seem unaccountably concerned for the man that kidnapped you," the earl remarked, with a cool and slightly disgusted tone.

She stared up at him in fury, feeling the anger she had been tamping down threatening to finally overspill.

"I do not forgive you, my lord! For he did not kidnap but rescued me from a fate I could not contemplate, and if you open your eyes for a moment I think you will find you have much to forgive yourself for, if you have a heart that can feel any remorse at all."

"Miss Morton," Lawrence said, his voice soft and amused. "Please do not berate him so, he has nothing to reproach himself for I assure you."

"What the devil is the meaning of this?" The earl snapped and then fell silent as Lawrence raised his head.

"Hello, Alex."

Chapter 18

"Wherein ghosts are sent to trouble the living."

For a moment the room was perfectly still, a quiet calm so intense that Henri held her breath for fear of disturbing the silence with something as trivial as breathing.

The earl had gone a deathly shade of white and was staring at Lawrence in disbelief.

"Out!" he shouted suddenly, and the men who had restrained Lawrence looked startled for a brief second before snapping to attention and leaving the room.

The moment hung suspended once more as Lawrence gazed up at his brother, who stood staring, totally still.

When he did move, he turned away and snatched open a drawer in his desk, removing a key. Then he returned, moving behind Lawrence and undoing the restraints. The chains fell to the floor with a clatter and Lawrence stumbled to his feet only to be thrown across the room as the earl drew back his fist and smashed it squarely into his jaw.

Henri screamed and ran to Lawrence who was crumpled against the wall, bleeding from his mouth and looking a little dazed.

"That's for ten years, you bastard!" the earl said, his voice brittle. "Ten years of guilt and misery and regret, for letting our father go to his grave believing he would see you again at last!"

"I'm sorry, Alex."

Lawrence looked up at him, sorrow in his eyes and Henri watched the earl in turn, remembering now, all the reasons she had felt so very afraid of him. That cold, proud exterior that made you believe no emotion could ever touch him, except perhaps for a sharp, clean, slice of anger. And then it all seemed to fall away and he reached down and hauled his brother to his feet and embraced him with such ferocity she expected to hear the crack of ribs.

"Damn you, Lawrence, damn you, of all the things you could have done, you ran off and became a pirate. When you well know it was the thing I always dreamed of."

Lawrence laughed, though his voice was a little unsteady. "I know it, Alex, and I'm sorry for it but ... but I thought I'd killed you, I saw you go down and ..."

"And you never thought to check?" Alex raged, angry all over again now as he turned and walked away from his brother. "You never thought to return and see for yourself?"

Lawrence shrugged. "I heard them cry out that Lord Falmouth was dead, I didn't think much else was required, and even if you weren't dead, which never crossed my mind, I shot you, Alex! How could you ever forgive me?"

"Because you were a green-headed young fool and you never meant to. I got in the way on purpose but I couldn't let you kill a militia man, they would have hanged you and even our father's name wouldn't have saved you then."

"Or now," Lawrence said with a shrug.

Alex rubbed his face with his hand. "Good God, how are we to get out of this?"

"We don't." Lawrence looked at him and shook his head. "I'm Captain Savage and there is nothing to be done, I won't have you risk the family name for me after all I've done. Just hand me over and I'll take my chances, Alex."

Alex looked back at him in disgust at the idea, and Henri wondered if perhaps she had been too hard on him.

"Damn the family name," he raged. "I won't lose my brother twice."

Lawrence gaped at him, obviously astonished that his brother should say such a thing.

"B-but, the family honour, our history should remain untainted - *that* is above all else, no matter what, you *always* said ..."

"And I was a bloody fool!" the earl exclaimed. "Flesh and blood should come before all else, the living are what matter. I should never have been so hard on you, you were just a boy. It was all my fault."

Henri watched this exchange with astonishment though hers seemed to be mild compared to the shock in Lawrence's eyes. He looked dumbstruck.

"I need to think," Alex continued. "For now I will have to allow the men to take you to the hold in chains, though I am sorry for it. However I cannot see what else is to be done for the moment. I will make sure you are not ill-treated but I need time to think of a way out of this."

Lawrence seemed to be trying to say something, but the words wouldn't come. Henri grasped his arm and gave a little squeeze.

"You were right," she said, nodding towards the Earl. "About your brother, now do as he says and let him help you."

Lawrence shook his head and looked back up at him. "If anyone discovers you let me go, there'll be hell to pay, Alex. I can't let you risk it. I won't after all I have done!"

Alex turned on him then, and his anger was something to behold. Henri held her breath as the Earl's rage hit them like a furnace.

"Let me? You won't *let me?* Damn you, Lawrence. I saw the bullets hit you, three bullets! You were bathed in your own blood and I saw you fall into the sea. I have lived and relived that scene in nightmares for a lifetime. Do you seriously think I could live with seeing you hanged? Do you think I can contemplate it and keep my sanity intact? For God knows I feel I've had little grasp on it for the last decade!"

The earl took a breath and she saw the cold demeanour he wore like a cloak slip neatly into place. "You will go now, Captain Savage, while I consider what to do with you. As for you, Miss Morton, you must be tired. I will give you my cabin for the voyage, a meal and someone to assist you will be sent shortly. I believe you will find some of your belongings in that chest," he said, gesturing to a small box at the side of his desk.

He opened the door and shouted, and two men came smartly at his call.

"Take the prisoner below. See he is fed and unharmed, he is to reach the gallows without a mark or you will feel my wrath, do I make myself plain?"

"Aye, aye, Captain."

Henri watched with uncertainty as Lawrence was led away, and Alex's cold eyes met hers.

"Miss Morton," he said by way of taking his leave, and nodded his head, pulling the door closed behind him.

Henri stood there for a moment and then took a breath. She had the strangest feeling that she hadn't actually breathed since the ship she now stood on had been sighted. She walked a little unsteadily to the bed and sat down, suddenly aware of the slightly nauseating motion of the ship, the creak of wood and rigging, and the muffled steps and calls of men both above and below her.

Until this point her mind had been totally consumed with fear, with shock, with wonder - with Lawrence, and her surroundings had all been caught up with that fact. But now she was sat here, still and alone with her thoughts and her surroundings seemed to want her to take note, for try as she might she was struggling to make sense of what had just happened.

The Earl of Falmouth was, indeed, a good man. A man who had been bowed by grief at the loss of his brother. The charismatic pirate captain who she'd come to care for was going, somehow, to be saved from the gallows. Though at this point she could not conceive of how such a thing could be arrived at. But there had been an air about the earl that made her believe he would think of something.

She lay back on the bed and decided she would take a moment to rest before she changed her damp clothes, even though the cold, wet material around her made her shiver. But then she closed her eyes and sleep had begun to beckon when there was a frantic knocking at the door. Frowning she hauled her protesting limbs upright and hastened to answer it.

"Who is it?" she called.

"Henri?" cried an ecstatic voice from behind the wood and Henri was almost bowled off her feet as the generous figure of Annie burst through the door and enveloped her in a hug.

"Oh, Miss Henri!" the lady sobbed, running hands over her Mistress' face and arms, as though ensuring everything was, indeed, in the correct place and quite as it should be. "Are you alright? Did the brute hurt you?"

Henri beamed and hugged her maid with quite as much enthusiasm. "Oh, Annie, I am so glad to see you, you cannot imagine!"

"Whatever were ye thinkin', child?" she scolded, for once in her life overcome with an excess of maternal instinct. "If I hadn't followed ye, oh, Lawd, I dread to think what may 'ave befallen ye!"

"You sent Lord Falmouth?" Henri exclaimed, as all became clear. She frowned as questions crowded in her mind. "Papa? Is he well, is he here?"

Annie shook her head. "No, my lady. Your papa is well, but his lordship insisted he stay home and carry on as usual. No one is to know ye are missin' see. You've gone to stay with a cousin in the north, that way he said, if we found ye, none would be the wiser and yer reputation quite safe."

"Oh." Henri nodded, thoughtful, wondering why this didn't seem to be as much as a relief as perhaps it should be. She had the diamonds, though, she thought. She need not marry the earl now and if Lawrence was freed ...

But she was getting ahead of herself, Lawrence was currently in irons and a long way from freedom.

Annie looked at her young charge and pulled a face. "Look at the state of ye. Now get them wet things off this minute. We'll get ye warm and dry, and ye can tell me what the devil you've been up to. For if I know you, there's mischief brewin' here somewhere."

Henri smiled, reassured by Annie's familiar nagging tone, and allowed herself to be wrangled out of wet cloth and into a warm bed, with tea and crumpets, and a rapt audience to hear tell of her adventure.

Chapter 19

"Wherein truths are told."

Henri forced her unwilling eyelids open and blinked as a shaft of bright sunlight fell across her face. Through the tiny porthole she could see another brilliantly blue sky. Beside her Annie snored, soft huffing sounds that made her smile. Climbing with care, she edged around the curvaceous hills of her maid's slumbering form and exited the bed without so much as a fluttered eyelid from Annie.

Giving it a little shake first, she stepped into a clean petticoat and sighed as Annie's sharp gaze caught her eye.

"An' what are ye about now?" Annie demanded, pulling herself upright and yawning wide with a groan as she hauled herself out of bed.

"Oh, Annie, don't be a simpleton, you know very well I must go and see Lawrence."

Annie folded her arms and gave her an uncharacteristically fierce look.

"Now, listen 'ere, ye said yerself that 'is brother is sworn to see 'im to freedom. Didn't ye?"

Henri opened her mouth to argue as she sensed there would be some reason why she ought not to see Lawrence, and seeing Lawrence was something she felt very strongly about doing, as soon as possible. However Lord Falmouth *had* said that, so she just sighed and nodded.

The Rogue

"An' how is it goin' to look if ye go runnin' down to 'im like 'e's ye lost love or some such with ye fiancée aboard?" Annie gave her a knowing look and Henri stifled a blush.

She hadn't told Annie everything that had happened between her and Lawrence, but her maid had a vivid imagination and she doubted she was far off the truth in divining what had transpired.

"Oh but, Annie, he's all alone and ..."

"And 'e's a big boy is Cap'n Savage. Remember all o' those stories we read about, eh? He's been in worse scrapes an' walked away. Yer pirate is safe enough for now, I reckon, an' yer best off payin' respects to his lordship, after all 'e's done for ye."

Henri pouted as Annie picked out a clean dress and lifted it over her head, quite ignoring her mutinous expression.

"I still don't like him," she muttered, her voice muffled through the thick material of what happened to be her best winter dress in imperial cambric muslin, she noticed and scowled at Annie. "Why have you brought all my best things?"

Annie shrugged. "Because if things had gone bad, ye wouldn't ha' cared what ye wore, if ye'd died ye'd have need ye best fer layin' out. And as it is a lady should always have her looks to fall back on if 'er other plans go awry."

Henri blinked and would have reproached Annie for her matter-of-fact way of speaking of her possible demise, but another more alarming idea came to mind.

"Annie," she said, her voice accusing. "You *like* him!"

Annie shrugged, ignoring her young lady's wide eyes as she turned her around to do up the tiny buttons that ran up her spine and the high neck of the dress.

"Well, 'is lordship's very 'andsome, I'll say that," she admitted, before adding. "And I do like me a commandin' man, an' he's got that in spades. E' says jump and the world hitches its skirts."

"Annie!"

"Ye could do worse n' that is all I'll say."

She prodded Henri towards the chair so she could brush her hair and dress it and Henri was too thunderstruck by such betrayal to protest.

"There's no use in poutin' an' huffin'," Annie mumbled around a mouthful of pins. "What use is yon pirate to ye? If e's anythin' like 'is brother I've no doubt e's dashin' an' easy on the eye, but a man like that will get 'imself strung up sooner or later, no matter if 'e escapes this time around. An' ye can bet 'e'll leave ye with squallin' babes to feed and nothin' to feed em on or to keep ye warm but the memory of him." She leaned down and planted a kiss on Henri's cheek. "It's no way to live, my pretty lass, not for you."

Henri blinked hard and Annie sighed, folding her arms.

"Oh, Miss Henri, what 'ave ye gone an' done?"

Looking away from Annie, who knew her far too well and saw far too much, Henri cleared her throat.

"Nothing at all. I just ..." She sighed. Lawrence had made it perfectly clear that there was no future for them. He wouldn't take her if he had to run, and indeed a life of running and hiding didn't seem very appealing but then never seeing Lawrence again ... "Oh, Annie," she said, her voice full of hopeless regret.

Annie hugged her. "Now, now, none o' that. First things first, ye have to get 'im safe away from the gallows. So go an' see 'is lordship and find what's to be done about it. We'll jus' 'ave to see where the fates take us, won't we?"

Henri sniffed and straightened her spine, while Annie settled her best plum-coloured mantle around her shoulders for her and pinched her cheeks. Henri winced as she was poked at but made no complaint.

"There now, just bite ye lips a little, make 'em nice and rosy."

Rolling her eyes Henri did as she was bid, for there was really no point in arguing.

"Perfect." Annie picked up her dirty linens and packed her other belongings away before heading for the door. "I'll tell his lordship ye wish to see 'im as soon as 'e may."

With annoyance, Henri watched her maid hustle out of the door and wondered where exactly the fates would take them, and if she'd get there with Lawrence.

***

She didn't have long to wait before his lordship deigned to wait upon her. He strode into the room and as always she was left feeling insignificant as he seemed to take up all the available space.

The similarities between the two men were becoming ever clearer, and she took a moment to appreciate the powerful shoulders and arms, and the long, strong legs that showed to such advantage in those tight breeches and black boots they were encased in. But where Lawrence was all devilish smiles and laughing blue eyes, this man still made her shiver. His cool grey eyes cast over her with no apparent reaction as he nodded to her, polite but distant. She curtsied and sat, waiting for him to address her.

"Well, Miss Morton, what is it I can do for you?"

"Have you seen Law ..." she paused, blushing a little at her all too familiar use of his first name and correcting herself, avoiding his eye. "I mean to enquire if you have seen your brother this morning?"

He snorted, apparently amused by her discomfort. "I have seen Lawrence this morning, yes. Yes he is quite well, he has broken his fast and I have made some progress with a plan to free him from the tangle we seem to be in."

"How?" she asked, heart thudding with anticipation.

"I have an estate in Bordeaux, on the southwest coast of France, it was in fact our mother's, the Comtesse de Longueville. As it happens, I had plans to visit and see what, if anything, was left after our friend Bonaparte has ravaged the country. I had people there I could trust, we can both still trust," he amended, adding, "Assuming that any of them still live." This was said lightly, almost callous in tone and she wondered if there was anyone besides his brother that he cared for?

"Once there, I will have Lawrence installed in the cellars beneath the Château. He played there as a boy, there are many tunnels and secret ways in and out of the place. I've no doubt he will make good use of them."

He stood, turned slightly away from her as he spoke, his hands clasped lightly behind his back. He looked every inch an English aristocrat and an extremely forbidding character. She realised she was a little afraid of him and sat up straighter.

"And what then?" she asked, her tone a little more forceful than she had intended, but if the extent of his help was to let Lawrence loose in the French countryside then she was going to have words for his lordship, strong ones.

"And there, Miss Morton, we seem to be at something of an impasse."

"How so?" She turned in her seat, following his movement as he began to walk the room, his face severe with displeasure, his footsteps muted by the thick rug beneath his feet.

"How so?" he repeated. "Because my brother is a stubborn fool, that is why."

He spoke with no little heat and she felt her temper rise on Lawrence's behalf, whatever they had disagreed on, no doubt Lawrence had his reasons.

The earl walked around to his side of the desk and sat down, looking her in the eyes properly for the first time since he'd entered. She quailed a little under that cold grey gaze but she didn't look away.

"I have suggested that Lawrence be found locally by someone who would remember him, that we spread the story he lost his memory as the result of some injury. His scars ought to back that up well enough, and then he would say that he somehow ended up a prisoner of the French. That he has only recently recovered, and now that the war is over, has made his way back to our estate."

She blinked at him.

"B-but, that's perfect!" she exclaimed, excitement bubbling up inside her. "What a marvellous idea!"

Alex nodded, folding one long leg over the other and sighing. "I agree. It is simple enough to be believed but because of the war, hard enough to prove either true or false to be unsurprising if none are able to corroborate. And I know there are those locally loyal to both our family, and most certainly to Lawrence, should the need arise."

"Oh?"

Although Henri was pleased to hear that, a small tremor of doubt assailed her as she wondered who exactly would be so unswervingly loyal to Lawrence and why? She shook herself. That was of no matter, Lawrence needed to be safe, no matter who it took to achieve that. She just hoped it was an old, toothless man and not some pretty young thing who had been in love with him as a child or something horribly romantic of the sort.

"However," Alex said, breaking into her thoughts. "Lawrence is being remarkably stubborn about the whole thing. He refuses to co-operate."

"But why?" she demanded, putting her earlier defence of Lawrence's reasons far aside and wholeheartedly agreeing with the earl.

"Because he believes he is too well known, that someone, somewhere will recognise him as The Rogue and the discovery will destroy the family name."

"And what does he propose as an alternative?" she demanded, feeling quite as furious as Alex had sounded moments before.

"Oh, my brother is full of plans," Alex said, his expression dark. He folded his arms and once more turned the full force of his cold grey eyes on her person. She swallowed. "He has made me promise, upon my honour, to marry you, despite the lengths to which you were apparently willing to go to in order to escape such an unpleasant fate," he said with a sneer as Henri blushed with some force and fervently wished she could join Lawrence in the hold. "He then intends to disappear, never to be seen again."

"No!" she gasped and then shook her head, crossing her arms and meeting his gaze with defiance and not caring a button whether he believed her an ungrateful wretch. "I won't have it. I won't marry you, and I won't let him go!"

For the first time since Lawrence had left the room last night she saw the earl smile, and this time there seemed to be some frail glimmer of warmth in the expression.

"Well, my dear, it appears that finally we have found something on which we can agree. All that remains to be done now is to find a way to persuade my brother of his folly."

Chapter 20

"Wherein Miss Morton agrees to play with fire."

Henri looked at Lawrence's brother across the imposing oak desk and sighed. Why Lawrence, after spending the last decade cultivating a fine reputation as a thief and a rogue, now - at this *particular* moment - felt inclined to be honourable and self-sacrificial was beyond her. It was very bad timing and most irksome, especially when such a simple and effective plan was quite within his grasp.

"So what do we do?" she asked the earl who was sitting with a thoughtful expression, long fingers steepled together. She watched as he pursed his lips, as though contemplating something rather distasteful, before turning back to her.

"Can you act, Miss Morton?"

Henri raised her eyebrows. "Not to my knowledge, though in truth I have never had cause to discover the talent lacking. Why?"

The cool grey eyes looked her over, curious and apparently considering." Because I feel we must indulge in a little play acting, a deception, to convince Lawrence that he would be far better off doing as we wish."

Intrigued, Henri leaned forward over the desk, her arms folded over the polished top. It seemed a most unlikely suggestion from the Earl of Falmouth and she was eager to discover what exactly he was considering. "What manner of deception did you have in mind, my lord?"

"In the circumstances I think you may call me Alex," he replied, though his voice didn't imply that he enjoyed giving her the familiarity of his name.

"In what circumstances?" she asked with apprehension, believing she had a vague idea where this was going.

"In the circumstances of our engagement and the wedding that will take place on our return to England."

"B-but ..."

Alex waved a hand to silence her and glaring, she ground to a halt.

"Miss Morton, *Henrietta* ... if you will allow the familiarity?" Those grey eyes looked at her as though he was bored to death and wanted to get this over with as quickly as possible.

"I prefer Henri," she replied equally stiff and still glaring at him.

"Henri, you were quite right in what you said to Lawrence. He doesn't know me anymore. I am not the man I was when he left." She realised Lawrence must have told him her previous description of the earl's infamous behaviour. A shadow fell over his expression and she could see the weight of guilt that the past years had left upon him. "In truth, I'm not sure I ever was that man, though I did try to be everything I believed was right and proper for the son of an earl. But his death changed everything, it changed me. Before he ... *died*, I was ever conscious of honour and propriety and nothing stood more important in my mind than the family name." He snorted, looking on her with amusement. "And I can see from your incredulous expression how far I have fallen from those lofty heights and just how tarnished that name has become."

Henri felt her cheeks burn and tried to school her face into something less expressive, but tales of the wicked Earl of Falmouth, his gambling and his legion of petticoats were too numerous to hear such confessions without a little scepticism.

"However, you have planted the seed of truth which he will discover is all too real soon enough, and so he will see that I am indeed, as you supposed, the kind of husband it would be better to escape via a pirate ship, rather than face marrying."

"My lord!" she whispered, mortified.

"Come, come, Henri," he said, his mouth twisted into something resembling a smile. "I am not the least bit offended by the truth, and it should play to our advantage, if, as I suspect, my brother has feelings for you himself. He does I take it?"

Henri opened and closed her mouth, quite at a loss for what to say. Alex sighed and looked to the heavens with annoyance.

"If we are to proceed at all, I must insist that you are frank with me. I really have no patience for coy or coquettish behaviour."

Henri huffed but found she still didn't have an answer. Hesitating, she looked down and took a moment to carefully smooth the drapes of her skirts while she tried to formulate an answer.

"I-I believe, that he is a little fond of me, yes, but after all we have known each other such a short time and ... And he went to great pains to make me understand that he would never marry me."

She dared look up and found the grey eyes scrutinising her. "Because he did not wish to or because he was in no position to do so?"

Henri plucked an imaginary piece of lint from her sleeve and wished heartily that she could move the conversation to safer ground. This man really was the limit, to have to discuss such matters as she hardly understood in her own mind in such terms was appalling, and quite improper.

"I do not know," she snapped, quite out of patience with him. "I only know that he believed he would be an outlaw and that the addition of a wife would hinder him such that he would likely be caught again soon enough. Whether that implies that he would like to offer for me if the circumstances were otherwise, or if he sought to let me down gently, I know not."

She sat back in her chair and crossed her arms wishing she had the nerve to throw something at him, for she felt he deserved it far more than Lawrence had.

Whatever it was she had said it seemed to resolve something in the earl's mind.

"Very well then. You will go to Lawrence, and I will make sure you have the privacy to do so. He will likely endeavour, as he did with me, to extract a promise from you to marry me so that your future is secure, and because for some fool notion he believes we will be happy together." They shared a look of equal incredulity and distaste. "Quite," Alex added with an appalled expression which was really most insulting. "So, at first you will protest, and I would suggest, if you do indeed love him, you take the opportunity to tell him so."

Henri blushed scarlet and looked anywhere but at Alex. She had hardly admitted the idea to herself, and even though she suspected it was likely true ... *well really.* She felt his amused grey gaze hover over her but refused to look up so he continued.

"In the end, however, you will accept his argument and agree, and it might be an idea at this moment to make a point in my favour in front of him." Henri looked up at that and was met with the faintest lift of one eyebrow. "Well, surely you can think of *one*?" he said, with a dry tone.

Henri gritted her teeth. She knew as well as he did that he was an extremely handsome man and such a remark should not be hard to find. The idea of deliberately trying to make Lawrence jealous however made her slightly nauseated.

"It's for his own good," he snapped with impatience.

She let out a huff of anger at the ill-mannered, odious man! "Very well," she said with an equally sharp reply.

"Good. Once that is settled we will give him ample opportunity to observe us together. At first it will seem all is quite well between us, with luck just a little jealousy might be enough to shake him from his moral high ground, but if, as I suspect, Lawrence is made of sterner stuff, we may be forced to move onto rather darker tactics."

Henri looked up, alarmed. "Whatever do you mean?"

Alex shrugged. "Simply that we illustrate that I will be an appalling, tyrannical and cold husband who will never love you as you deserve and eventually make your life such a misery you will be condemned to die of a broken heart or shame or ..." He waved his hand, looking faintly disgusted. "Some other mystery illness as tends to happen to ladies of that romantic ilk. Though I hope we will not need to take things quite so far as to endanger your health," he added with a smirk.

Scowling at him, Henri wondered how the devil he knew anything about romance, the man clearly didn't have a romantic bone in his body.

"You're all kindness," she remarked with asperity.

He chuckled at her obvious annoyance. "Well then, you know what to do." She tutted at him as he made a shooing motion and got to her feet, only pausing as his voice followed her to the door. "I take it you do have at least a vague idea of *how* to make love to a man?" he asked her with all the mocking arrogance of a confirmed rake.

She refused to dignify his shocking question with any other answer than a forceful slam of the door, but she heard his laughter follow her quite clearly nonetheless.

Chapter 21

"Wherein the truth and a lie hurt just the same."

Led by one of the earl's men, Henri was taken down into the dark and cramped confines of the hold. A makeshift cell had been formed using the hull and an arrangement of crates and barrels. A metal hoop protruded from an overhead beam, and from this draped a long line of chain. The chain then ran to metal cuffs, and Henri felt her heart contract as she looked upon Lawrence. He sat with his back against the hull on a thin pallet, his head bowed.

He looked up as he heard them approach and his smile made her breath hitch as his blue eyes caught the lamp light.

"Hello, Miss Morton, how very kind of you to call on me," he said, all politeness and good manners, just as though she was calling on an old friend at home.

She swallowed hard and waited for the man who had brought her here to withdraw as Alex had promised he would. Once he was out of sight, and ear-shot, she hurried to Lawrence's side.

"Are you well?" she asked, looking him over for signs of abuse, still a little uneasy at putting her trust in Alex.

He chuckled and nodded. "Aye, don't fret on my account. My brother's men are all terrified of incurring his wrath and they have been instructed to treat me with respect. Do not let the chains trouble you. I have been well fed and handled with kid gloves I assure you. These …" he added, lifting his hands and rattling the chains. "Are just for show, and to keep the crew from becoming too suspicious."

She sighed, feeling a little more secure in the earl's desire to help his brother.

"You see," he said, his voice quiet. "I told you he was a good man."

Henri looked down, frowning. She knew she had to play the part as Alex had instructed but she wasn't quite sure how to go about it. She decided the truth was the easiest path to take.

"He certainly seems to care for you very much," she said, looking up and smiling. "Though, I still find it hard to trust him, he ... he seems such a cold man."

"Truly?" Lawrence replied, obviously surprised. "I cannot see what you do at all. I know when I was a boy people thought him terribly proud and high-handed, but he was never so with me." He shrugged. "Alex was always a stickler for the rules and propriety it's true but then, that's what our father made him. He was always conscious of his inheritance and the importance of being a good earl."

Henri worried at her lip and wondered if she should tell him the truth. He'd find out sooner or later and perhaps it was better he heard it from her.

"What?" he demanded.

"Lawrence," she began, trying to find words that would not anger him unduly. "What I said to you before, about your brother. I know it made you angry and I can see now why that is but ... But those things I said were true. He has a truly dark reputation. He is known as a rake and a scoundrel, he has been named an adulterer and there are rumours about ... well, all sorts of things. I think when he believed you dead, he fell into despair, and he could no longer be the person he was. He is no longer the man of honour you remember," she rushed on, seeing his face darken with anger. "Perhaps he is, in truth, but it is no longer what people believe him to be."

She watched him and held her breath, waiting for his outburst but he said nothing.

"He told me much the same thing," he said, frowning. "And I care not what people believe of him. I have spoken with him and I find him to be the same as he ever was." He looked up at her and reached out, taking her hand and squeezing it gently. "Don't you see, Henri, it is just as it was before. He is doing everything in his power to save me, despite the fact that he is courting great danger in doing so. If the truth of who I am was to get out, if they knew he helped me escape ... If he has as many enemies as you've led me to believe then there is every chance he could hang alongside me if they discover us."

Henri frowned and looked down, his big hand still holding hers and she drew comfort from the contact. She hadn't really considered how big a risk the earl was taking but now she saw he was right. He was putting himself in danger to free his brother. He rose in her estimation considerably for that despite his wretched manners.

"And so you must see ..." he continued, and he reached out his other hand, his knuckle touching her gently under her chin to raise her head towards him. "You must see that I can do nothing more to put him in harm's way?"

She knew he was alluding to the plan Alex had made and frowned with annoyance. "He wants to help you, Lawrence. He wants his brother back."

Lawrence let go of her hand and she heard a heavy sigh and the chink of chains as he moved to sit back against the hull of the ship. "His brother died ten years ago, and there is no saving him now."

Henri folded her arms, scowling at the floor. She didn't have to feign annoyance to go along with Alex's plan. She was damned angry. If Alex wanted to help him why couldn't he just accept it? Alex was a grown man too - he knew the risks.

"He's agreed to marry you as arranged," he said, and she looked at him sharply. He sounded so nonchalant, did he *really* not care at all? She could see nothing in his eyes to suggest that he did. She blinked hard and turned away.

"Well, I don't agree to marry him."

"Henri," he said, the word spoken on a sigh, as though he was addressing a troublesome child. Perhaps that was all she was to him? A nuisance, something to be arranged safe passage through life in order to keep his conscience clear.

"Don't *Henri* me!" she snapped. "You gave me the diamonds so that I didn't have to marry. Well there, I shan't."

She glared at him and crossed her arms, only too aware that she did sound like a troublesome child now, but finding she didn't care. How dare he act as though arranging for her marrying his brother was of no consequence. Had she really meant so little to him? If so he was as much a rake and a scoundrel as the earl for taking advantage of her. How could he have kissed her with such ... Such feeling, if she meant nothing to him? It was too much.

"It's for the best," he said, and his voice was harder now, colder.

"The best for whom?" she demanded, her voice breaking. She got to her feet, too angry to sit beside him any longer "The best for you, you mean?" she said, turning on him in fury. "Then you can walk away and leave us and not feel guilty about it, is that right? No matter that I don't love him, or even like him? No matter that he needs you to stay because losing you broke his heart and changed him irrevocably? No, no." She waved her hand, as though such words were trifles to him. "No, you run along and leave and never give us another thought. Go off and find your men and raid and plunder until you're caught again and hanged, alone with none to care for you!"

She discovered that she was shouting and on the verge of tears so she stopped abruptly and turned her back on him, fighting to keep her composure.

The silence seemed to fill the gloomy space, eating up the noise of the ship, the creak of wood and slap of waves, and the muffled shouts and thuds from the men working above them.

"If you think I would never give you another thought, then you are far from the truth."

His voice was bleak and full of hurt and she turned to see the sorrow in his eyes. Her fierce, burning anger dispersed, as frail as a soap bubble in the face of such misery.

"Oh, Lawrence," she said, choking on his name and running to him. She buried her face against his shoulder and felt his arms come around her, holding her close as she gave in to tears. "Please, please don't go," she begged. "Don't leave us. I can't bear it. I'll never see you again."

He was silent, one hand stroking her hair, and she knew she would never change his mind. He was too afraid of putting them in danger, and so he would leave, and they would never see him again. There was only one thing left she could do.

"Please, Henri. I want to know you're safe, and I want Alex to be happy. He's the only man in the world I trust to look after you, the ... the only one I can bear the idea of you being with at all," he said, and by now his voice was rough and her heart was soothed a little, to know this was hurting him as much as it was her. "And I know you are extraordinary enough to make him happy. You are the best two people in the world, and it would comfort me to know you are content together."

Henri closed her eyes, feeling hot tears stream down her face. Alex had better be right about this, she thought fiercely. Because if this didn't work ... She swallowed hard and raised her head.

"Alright, Lawrence, if it means so much to you, I'll do it. I'll marry your brother."

Chapter 22

"Wherein a pirate tries for honour and discovers a bleak future."

Lawrence looked down at the big brown eyes, full of tears and unhappiness, and felt his heart clench in his chest. He would rather face a hoard of armed cut-throats than endure the hurt in those eyes. It was too much to bear. But he must, it was the only thing he could do for them both. He had caused his brother such harm, and indirectly Henri too. Keeping them safe was all he could do now.

For a moment he dreamed of what might have been. If he hadn't been such a hot-headed fool, defying his brother and running off with Mousy whose father was a smuggler; running tea and rum under the noses of the redcoats and the Water Guard. Mousy had worked in the stables and Alex had strongly objected to their friendship, sure that the older boy would lead him into trouble. As ever, he'd been right.

But Lawrence hadn't seen the harm, neither in his friendship with Mousy nor in his involvement in smuggling. All he could see was that the people around him were starving when he had plenty. The local mines were failing, laying off men all along the county. If they could make money from smuggling then good luck to them, and more than that, it was an adventure.

So he had agreed to go and meet the boats as they brought the load ashore. The life of a smuggler seemed to him a grand thing in any case, much more exciting than lessons and instruction, and learning to behave as a gentleman. Where was the fun in that? And besides he'd lost his ring, gambling with one of the village lads. It was the one that bore the family crest. His father would be furious if he found out and the boy had promised to give it to him, if he helped them on a run. If he wasn't too scared? *As if!* And so he'd gone.

He hadn't realised Alex had been working with the Revenue to protect his father's shipping interests.

And then the militia had arrived on the beach.

He closed his eyes against the memory of that night. If he hadn't been there that night life would have continued. His brother wouldn't have that dark shadow that fell across him now, for Lawrence had seen it just as Henri had, no matter that he denied it.

Perhaps if he hadn't been such a fool, he would have met Miss Morton at one of the local dances, or at a ball given by his father. He would have been entranced by those dancing eyes, enthralled by her wit and sharp mind, and that teasing smile. He would have courted her, tried to win her heart. Perhaps they would have married and lived happily, grown old surrounded by children and grandchildren ...

He forced the images from his mind. There was little point in dwelling on such sentimental nonsense. The past was dead and gone, he had chosen his path and torn apart the futures of others in doing so. Now, at last, there was a chance to make amends. Henri would be well cared for, she would never have to worry about money again, and perhaps she could chase the shadows from his brother's eyes.

And then he looked down again to see her watching him, and he felt as though he'd been laid bare, as if she'd seen it too, everything that might have been. And it hurt.

He didn't think about the right or wrong of it; and wasn't that always his problem, he just did what he felt in his heart and pulled her to him. He pressed his lips against that sweet, soft mouth and felt everything about him pitch and rearrange itself in the rightness of her embrace. She clung to him, her mouth opening to invite him in further and bastard that he was he accepted, with hunger and fire that raged in his blood and threatened to burn him to cinders.

The Rogue

Somehow, though he wanted to remain forever lost in her kiss, he became aware of the sway of lamplight approaching and the heavy tread of a man moving towards them. He let go of her abruptly and found he could no longer meet her eyes.

"You'd best be getting back," he said, hearing his own voice echo, and sound as hollow and dull as an empty casket. "Your fiancé will wonder where you've got to," he added, wondering at himself and the spite he felt at the words, when he alone had done this. He had arranged it all.

He didn't look up as she moved away from him and went to meet his gaoler. But he looked after her as her slim figure receded into the shadows as she walked back to his brother.

As he'd known he would, Alex appeared an hour or so later.

"Well then," Alex said, looking down at him with a resigned expression. "I don't know what you said but she has agreed to marry me."

Lawrence nodded and tried to appear as though he was satisfied with this outcome.

His brother looked at him, clearly unconvinced, and snorted. "You're a damn fool. Can't you see she's in love with you?"

"Well if it's true, I can't help but think she's the foolish one," he replied, avoiding his brother's eye. "A man with a price on his head, no home, no future ... I'll not endow her with all of those worldly goods." He looked up, holding his hands out and smiling. "I'm not such a bastard, you see."

Alex quirked an eyebrow and then settled himself on the edge of a large crate, he gave his brother a shrewd look. "You love her."

Lawrence laughed and rolled his eyes. "Don't be an idiot, she's a sweet girl, that's all, and I like her well enough not to ruin her." He hoped the words sounded plausible because they had a hollow ring to his own ear he couldn't ignore.

"It's not too late to change your mind you know. My plan was perfectly sound. You could remain on mother's estate, assuming it's still there. Before the war I'd been searching for someone with enough vision and intelligence to oversee our interests there and you have certainly proved you have that. Oh and you could also manage the French side of some of the other ... *business arrangements* I have since gained a hand in." There was something to his tone that made Lawrence look up. "I rather think it would suit you," Alex added with a wry smile.

Lawrence looked his older brother over with suspicion.

Outwardly he really looked no different from how he had ten years ago. He was a powerful man in the prime of his life. There was no grey among the thick black hair and he was impeccably dressed as he always had been. It had always amused him how the young bucks among his friends had followed Alex with a slavish devotion he had, at best, ignored and had often been irritated by. But there was indeed a change, a darker air about him, and something Lawrence recognised but couldn't put his finger on. Until it struck him, they were very much alike for all their differences. His eyes narrowed.

"What the devil have you been up to?"

Alex smiled. His expression was placid but knowing and Lawrence frowned.

"Alex?"

His brother stretched his long legs out in front of him, his black boots gleaming in the lamplight.

"You were right, you know, all those years ago." Lawrence watched him as he spoke, confused by the admission, but he saw regret in his brother's eyes. "I should have done more. I should have helped more, instead of blaming the smugglers for breaking the law, instead of helping the militia. I should have looked to the cause, the why of it. You saw that," Alex said, his face grave, and then he smiled and Lawrence recognised the brother he had idolised in his youth. "You always let your heart rule you even then, not like me. I was always so bloody devoted to the rules, to obeying tradition, upholding the laws, even when they made no sense at all, even when they were damned unfair."

Lawrence adjusted his position on the pallet, leaning forward so he could see his brother more clearly in the dim light cast by the lamp. The words were so unlike the man he had known. Alex seemed aware of his thoughts and gave a grim smile.

"I've changed, Lawrence. For good and for bad." He laughed, a dark sound that seemed to roll around in the gloomy cavern of the hull. "Mostly for the worse, in truth, but perhaps there are some things you will approve of?"

Curiosity now had Lawrence galvanised, and he stared at his brother with a strange feeling he knew what he'd done, and he didn't know whether to be proud or howl with sorrow at what he'd done to that honourable man.

"Such as?" he demanded.

"I decided the smugglers were ill-equipped and inadequately led. There were others caught and sent to London to be tried and hanged in the months after ..." He paused and Lawrence felt a sharp pang of guilt at the pain in Alex's eyes as he relived that time. "After you left. You know Jo, one of the men who worked in the gardens? He used to turn a blind eye when we were boys and filched the strawberries, do you remember?" Lawrence felt a lump lodge in his throat and nodded, he remembered. "And young Toby, from the cottages near the church, he was perhaps three years older than you? He'd not been married a year, left his wife with a babe on the way and nothing to support her."

They sat in silence once more as Lawrence brought to mind the faces of those men, and others who had died on the beach that night.

"I couldn't bear it," Alex snarled, his voice full of fury. "They took them to London to try them, and those judges who dished out the sentence, they walked away and dined on capon and roast beef, stuffing their fat faces while those men's families starved and were now utterly hopeless without the menfolk to provide for them. And those amiable creatures, those judges, were the honourable men of the law." The words were spat out with such venom that Lawrence caught his breath. "It made me sick, Lawrence. As far as I knew you'd died on that beach helping those men to feed their families, and I vowed to carry on where you'd left off."

Lawrence blinked and looked on his brother with new eyes.

"My God, Alex, you're a smuggler." He was too stunned to say anything more for a moment and then anger surfaced. "Are you out of your mind?" he demanded, as outrage and pride struggled to reassemble this new vision of the man he'd grown up with. "You're funding a smuggling ring, *on your own doorstep?* You'll be caught, it's ... it's insane!"

Alex folded his arms, looking quite entertained by his younger brother's outburst.

"There speaks The Rogue," he said with dry amusement.

"That was entirely different!" Lawrence countered, narrowing his eyes and hauling on the chain he was bound with to lever himself to his feet. "I had nothing to lose and I was never in the same place for more than a day at a time. You have your home - *our* home! The family name, people who depend on you!"

Alex began to laugh, the deep rumble melding into the sounds of a working ship as Lawrence glared at him.

"And here I was thinking you might be proud of me." His face grew grave once more. "Lawrence, things are far worse than they were even then. Since the war ended the farmers can no longer afford to compete with the low price of imported grain. They are laying men off all around. Many are simply giving up and heading to America to try a new life there. With the mines doing badly too, people are clawing for survival and if I cannot save them by legal means, and believe me I've tried, then I'll do it as they do."

The Rogue

Lawrence sighed and shook his head in defeat. "I am proud of you, dammit. Of course I am. I-I just don't want to lose you all over again." He held out his hands as far as the chains would allow, hoping Alex would understand. "It is a comfort to know you will still be there, that the great house still stands at Tregothnan as it always has, that old Pawly is still putting the fear of God into anyone who dares come to the door, that Mrs Buscombe still makes the best pasties in all of Cornwall, and that the bal maidens are still singing on the dressing floor. Then all is as it ought to be and the world will go on as it should, no matter what mess I have made of my own life."

To his surprise Alex got to his feet with utter rage in his eyes.

"And it would be such a comfort to know you are back among us," he shouted. "That I might see you and talk with you as we once did would be a sight better than knowing you are lost somewhere out in the world where I might never know if you died for real, for there would be no one to tell me of it!"

The two men stared at each other, and Lawrence felt guilt dragging at his heart. If he did as Alex and Henri wanted, he would be putting them in harm's way and if anything happened, he'd never forgive himself, and if he went he would hurt them and break his own heart. He watched as Alex turned and strode away from him without another word. There seemed to be no way forward that would do anybody any good.

Chapter 23

"Wherein parts are played, and neither actors nor audience find pleasure in the performance."

Henri stood on deck. She had passed a restless night listening to Annie snore and the ever present rush of water against the moving ship. She hadn't been able to stop thinking of Lawrence chained below deck.

Tired and dispirited she had risen early, hoping a new day might bring a more hopeful outlook. Indeed it would be a callous heart and soul that failed to find some pleasure in the scene before her. Once more the winter sky was clear and a sharp blue, crisp and defined with cold clarity in the sunlight. The air was clean and pure, imbued with a sweet, icy chill that made it almost painful to breathe and certainly chased any lingering dullness from her tired mind. The sun hadn't long risen and was now climbing in the blue.

She looked up at the sails, full and sleekly fat with the steady breeze that seemed to lay its hand so gently upon them. Everything was so still and quiet, the sails so perfectly distended that there wasn't the faintest ripple to be found in the canvas, the bright white gleaming in the sunlight, as smooth and softly rounded as sculpted marble.

"It is a lovely sight is it not?"

She turned as a deep voice broke the silence and curtsied to the earl as he approached her.

"It is quite breathtaking," she agreed, returning her gaze heavenwards. "And so very high. I feel the mast must be scraping the heavens as we pass, it rides so very proud."

Alex nodded, following her gaze. "Indeed, in fact, that very upper most sail is called the sky sail, so that is an apt enough description."

"You love it here I think?" she said, gesturing vaguely to the expanse of horizon before them. "You and Lawrence both, you live for this freedom."

He nodded and offered her his arm to continue with him as he walked the deck. "Yes, in fact I am discovering we are more alike than perhaps either of us had realised. And certainly as stubborn," he added.

She looked up at him and saw concern in his eyes that was a reflection of her own fears. "We cannot let him go."

"No," he said, his expression grim. "We cannot."

She watched as he returned his gaze to the horizon.

"He has changed too you know," he said, his voice heavy with sadness. "He was always laughing as a boy. Everybody loved him, adored him in fact. Wherever Lawrence went there was laughter and mischief. You see, he was always in trouble of some sort or another, and yet none seemed to think the worse of him because he was always so sorry to have caused trouble, always so ready to make amends that no one ever wanted to scold him." He snorted, shaking his head. "Little devil got away with murder. But now I see such a serious mind behind his eyes and it troubles me. I'm afraid the boy I knew is gone."

She laid her hand on his arm so that he looked down at her.

"He's still there," she said, smiling at him and remembering the merry blue eyes and the wicked smile of the pirate she had first encountered. "I know he is still the same at heart, but he feels such guilt, and he fears any harm coming to us." She sighed as frustration got the better of her once again. "So, he must make us all miserable, himself included, to satisfy his stupid honour."

He looked at her with a measuring glance that made her skin prickle.

"Miss Morton, perhaps I have done you a disservice," he said at length. "I have no doubt any marriage between us would be a disastrous one, but I believe you will suit Lawrence very well."

Henri couldn't help but laugh at his words, so begrudgingly given and none too flattering. She put her hand up to her bonnet as an icy wind tugged at it and made the ribbons dance.

"Oh, it's nothing I am unused to I assure you. I'm not expected to have a thought in my head beyond the next ball and new roses for dancing shoes, so it is hardly surprising. In fact I am astonished that you would own the fact at all, let alone apologise for it."

"Did I apologise?" he asked, one eyebrow raised and the mocking smile firmly in place, and then she saw his gaze catch something beyond her and return to her once more, his smile a little more fixed in place. "Henri, I instructed that Lawrence be brought up for some air and a turn about the deck. He is watching us."

"Oh," she said, as anxiety began to flicker in her heart. "And so ..."

He stepped a little closer to her, holding her gaze. "And so, if we are to proceed with our plan," he said, pitching his voice low for intimacy. "It would be well if we are seen to be ... trying to make the best of things."

He reached out a finger and caressed her cheek and she shivered, fighting the urge to step away from him.

"Yes, I see."

She forced herself to stand in place and saw amusement in Alex's eyes.

"I am obviously more of a monster than even I had assumed. You look positively terrified," he said dryly.

Henri huffed out a breath. "Oh dear," she said, a smile tugging at her mouth. "I'm afraid I am a very poor actress, but I hate deceiving him like this."

Alex moved beside her and, with a hand placed lightly on her back, steered her to stand with him at the rail, looking out over the sparkling blue water. "I have no doubt, but it is our only course unless you have any better suggestions?"

Henri took a deep breath and, praying he knew what he was doing, laid her head against his arm in a familiar manner. "No, Alex, I don't, but I hope we are doing the right thing."

"He's coming," he said quietly and Henri didn't have to affect a look of guilt as Lawrence approached them for her heart was heavy and full of misery. Still she tried to smile at him and hoped sincerely it looked every bit as fake as it felt.

"Good morning, La... Captain Savage," she corrected herself, remembering at the last moment the guard who was walking a little behind him.

"Good morning, Miss Morton," Lawrence replied, and try as she might she couldn't find any expression at all beyond a bland politeness in his eyes or his manner. "And a fine morning it is, especially with a vision as lovely as you to brighten the horizon."

"Very prettily said, sir," Alex said, his expression as carefully blank as his brother's. "I hope you slept well?"

"Like a babe rocked by his mother," Lawrence replied with an expansive gesture, and she recognised the persona of Captain Savage in his manner. She wondered how much of it was show and how much of it was truly Lawrence. From what Alex had said perhaps there was little to discern between the extravagant persona illustrated in the pamphlets of his adventures and the real man. "For a pirate is only ever truly at ease in the arms of the ocean," he added with a broad grin. "And now if you will excuse me, I need to stretch my legs before my man here decides I've had enough excitement for one morning." With a theatrical flourish, Lawrence doffed his hat and bowed, and continued on his way.

"Oh dear," Henri muttered again, before beginning to chew at her lip with anxiety.

"Courage, Henri," Alex said, patting her arm. "Faint heart ne'er won idiotic pirate."

Despite herself she laughed, and then felt horrified all over again as she saw Lawrence swing around, those blue eyes watchful as he looked on the two of them together. Courage indeed.

Alex escorted her back to the cabin where she found Annie engaging in a half-hearted attempt at making the bed.

Henri flopped down in the chair by the desk feeling as worn and jaded as she had on first waking, all the good effects of the morning's sun and fresh air quite negated by her encounter with Lawrence.

"Well what's got you lookin' like you've lost a shillin' an' found a ha'penny?" Annie demanded, easing herself back to an upright position with a groan.

Henri snorted. "That's a remarkably apt turn of phrase," she muttered darkly.

Annie drew in a shocked breath. "I wouldn't be letting Lord Falmouth hear ye refer to 'im as a ha'penny, my lady. Lawks, even your pretty eyes wouldn't be able to flutter ye way out a that remark."

She moved over to Henri and began fussing about, undoing her bonnet ribbons and scolding her for going on deck at all without having her hair properly dressed first.

Henri suffered it in silence and restrained herself from remarking that Annie had been snoring at the time her attentions had been required.

"Alex is perhaps not as dreadful as I first believed," she admitted, once Annie had set to work teasing her hair into something that wouldn't shame either of them. "At least he *does* care for Lawrence if nothing else. But I do hope I'm doing the right thing in putting my trust in him."

She had apprised Annie of her conversation with Alex the night before and now filled her in on this morning's performance.

"Oh, Annie, I felt so awful, and then I felt so damned furious when he didn't seem to notice or care, he didn't even bat an eyelid. I don't know what to do for the best."

Annie snorted and gave Henri a knowing look. "Oh, 'e noticed, miss," she said, smiling. "Don't ye worry. Ye mark my words 'e's sitting down there now, gnashing 'is teeth an' green with envy, but 'e forced you into this so 'e can hardly back down now can 'e?"

Henri groaned. "I don't know whether that makes me feel worse or better," she protested, and then smacked Annie's hand away with a yelp as her maid pulled forcefully on a knot, so hard it made her eyes water.

Quite unapologetic Annie just rolled her eyes and hustled off to rummage in the large carpet bag which seemed overflowing with her own possessions. She emerged a moment later bearing a rather handsome silver flask and a smile. Opening the lid, she took a couple of hearty swigs before handing it to Henri.

"Here, my little duck, have a swallow a that, 'twill make all seem brighter and warmer or my name's not Annie Tripp."

Henri took the flask from her with a sigh and swallowed the uncharitable thought that she wouldn't be the least bit surprised if her name wasn't Annie Tripp. Though she knew the woman had spent most of her life living in Cheapside, in London, before coming to Cornwall to work for Lord Morton, she had never been too keen to give any other information on her parentage or origins further than an oblique *here, there,* and *roundabouts.*

The liquor was fierce and warm, and obviously good quality. "Did this come from home, Annie?" she enquired, surprised if it had that it had lasted this long.

"No, miss," Annie replied with a cheerful grin. "'Tis 'is lordship's, I been filching a bit now 'n then."

Despite everything Henri dissolved into laughter and got to her feet to hug Annie as the shameless maid plucked the flask deftly back from her fingertips. "Oh, Annie, I am so glad you're here."

Annie reached out and pinched Henri's cheek and clucked at her with affection. "No more 'n I am, my girl," she said with a fond smile and then tucked the flask carefully into the crevice afforded by her capacious bosom.

Chapter 24

"Wherein trouble brews and storms gather."

Lawrence braced himself against the hull and stared up at the beam as the ship lurched and bucked. He could hear the snap of canvas as Alex's deep voice yelled to *strike the royals.* They were heading into the Bay of Biscay and the wind was already tossing the ship about like a careless child with a toy.

Guilt layered thicker upon everything he was already feeling as he knew what a risk Alex was taking in sailing into the bay in the winter. Calm and gentle enough in the summer months, from the autumn onward the weather in the bay was treacherous, raging out of nowhere and wrecking ships with ease. He'd done everything he could to dissuade Alex from his course but the pigheaded fool would hear none of it. Lawrence didn't fancy his chances of causing a mutiny, despite the fact that his quartermaster would have repeated every reasonable argument that Lawrence had put forward if he had an ounce of sense.

As Alex never employed fools he could only imagine the man's frustration matched his own over the worm that had got into his captain's head and addled his brains.

The familiar tune of a song the children had sung back home when a storm approached circled in his head, making his skin prickle with foreboding.

"Blow wind, rise storm, ship ashore afore the morn'."

A wreck on the Cornish coast was something to be prayed for and welcomed. It meant goods washed ashore, casks of wine and exotic fare from far-flung places.

For some it was the difference between starvation and survival, so he'd well understood his countrymen's glee and the children's excitement. He'd watched them himself, out on the Lizard, as a ship smashed itself to bits in a raging storm on the treacherous rocks of the peninsula. Being one of the poor bastards on board, though, that was another matter.

He got to his feet and paced as well as the rolling ship would allow, itching to go up on deck and feel the cold, dark heart of the storm closing in around them. Anything rather than remain stuck down here with only the rats or his own thoughts for company, both of which he had become heartily sick of some time ago.

It was two days since he had caught Henri and Alex on deck, looking ... *comfortable* with each other. He gritted his teeth and tried not to think about it. But like a tongue returning to a troublesome tooth, his thoughts inevitably returned a bare moment later.

He had been allowed to walk the deck twice a day since then, and had come across them more than once, talking quietly, their heads together. He had noticed Alex's solicitous attitude, a gentle hand on Henri's arm, the touch of a fingertip to her face and the pretty blush that flushed her cheeks at his attentions. It was all very gentleman-like on his brother's part and perfectly in keeping with the actions of a fiancé getting to know the lady he intends to marry. And Lawrence had never wanted to knock his brother's damn head off more than he had over the past few days.

Jealousy and impotent rage burned through him no matter how hard he tried to tamp the feelings down. He made himself relive every argument with Alex, repeat every reason why he could not stay, why he had to leave, why they should marry and try to make the best of things. Every time he satisfied himself that yes, he was indeed in the right; he had chosen the best course for everyone. There was no doubt in his mind. His heart, however, refused to accept cold, hard logic. His heart was full of envy and misery and he hated himself for hating Alex. He was making the best of the situation after all, trying to put Henri at her ease, trying to make the girl happy. Because of course it would be best all round if she fell in love with Alex. Of course it would. And what wasn't there to love? He was handsome, powerful, incredibly wealthy, not to mention titled ...

His fist connected with one of the barrels that formed the wall of his prison cell and a dull, ringing thud echoed around the confined space as the liquid inside shuddered. He brought his hand away with the knuckles bleeding, but it didn't take the pain from his chest or ease his frustration. With disgust he sat back down on the pallet of his bed and put his head in his hands.

He looked up again at shouts from topside. Moving as far as his chains would allow he strained his ears over the continuous surge of the waves against the hull and the roar of the wind as it gained strength. Alex had called for all hands to shorten sail, and Lawrence could see in his mind's eye the crew battling to bring down the topgallant as the wind tried to snatch it away.

"Damn you, Alex!" he swore and yanked on the chains that held him captive. Pointless as it was he pulled and yanked and turned the air blue with rage and frustration and every filthy curse he could think of.

If not in answer to a prayer, surely in answer to his cursing, one of Alex's men hurried towards him, keys in hand.

"Cap'n said to free ye. All hands on deck," the man shouted over the noise of the storm as thunder cracked overhead.

"About bloody time!" Lawrence yelled back, snatching his hands free and running to find his brother.

Chapter 25

"Wherein bottles and tempers are drained."

Henri covered her ears and prayed to God for deliverance. The shriek of the wind, the groaning of wood under great strain and snap of sails and rigging, was punctuated by shouts and yells from the men on deck. All of this was quite stressful enough but nothing compared to the wailing of Annie.

At first her maid had been stoic, if a little green around the gills, as the storm had gained upon them. At which point Annie had taken to making an earnest attempt to finish anything she might have left in Alex's decanter without the slightest attempt at subterfuge or covering her tracks.

"What will you say when he asks where his rum went?" Henri demanded. "For I shan't cover for you!"

"Miss Henri!" The woman had screeched, clinging onto the bed with one hand and the decanter with the other. "If I survive this voyage, which I bleedin' doubt, I'll take any punishment 'is lordship cares to give for stealin' 'is rum, but for the moment my needs are greater an' it 'tain't doin' no one the slightest bit o' good in that bottle!"

Henri knew her maid of old, and suspected she'd be more likely to say the decanter had smashed in the storm, once she'd drunk it dry, but found little point in trying to wrestle the spirit from her. Especially as it seemed to be calming her nerves. In truth Henri had taken a nip or two herself but found it was only making her increasingly nauseated. She thanked God she hadn't fallen to seasickness before on the journey, for if this was a taste of it, it was miserable indeed.

The Rogue

She squealed as the ship lurched and Alex's chair screeched across the floor and tilted on two legs before smashing itself back on all fours once again.

"Oh, my Lawd," Annie cried. "We're all gonna die!"

Well the rum *had* been calming her nerves in any case. Henri sighed as it now seemed that the wretched woman was blind drunk and hysterical. She briefly considered joining her before thinking how badly Alex and Lawrence would view that kind of behaviour and decided that she would simply have to endure.

"Oh, Annie, do be quiet!" she shouted, joining the woman on the berth and steadying herself as best she could as the boat pitched and lurched.

Annie's lip quivered for a moment before the woman nodded, took a deep breath, smoothed out her skirts with great solemnity… and passed out.

"Well really," Henri muttered, and then was forced to grab hold of both her maid and the decanter before they rolled off the bed and hit the floor. Wedging the decanter between the wall and the mattress, she pulled the cord free from her dressing gown. Muttering oaths as Annie snored, she tied her to the bed as securely as she could manage, braced herself in the corner of the berth and prayed.

She awoke with a start. Her heart pounded with anxiety, breath coming too fast as she looked around her … and found everything utterly still. The quiet was unnerving after the incredible noise of the storm and did nothing to ease her racing heart. The room was in disorder, the chairs lay on their sides, and a bright white light was slanting in through the cabin window. Untying and then climbing over Annie, who groaned and clutched at her head, she ran to the little porthole and looked out.

The sky was white and overcast, and the sea smooth and grey and quite untroubled.

Henri let out a sigh of relief and quickly set about righting the room and tidying herself as best as she could. There was clearly no point in trying to rouse Annie who was making pitiful noises from the bed. Henri poured her a large glass of water and forced it into Annie's hand before making her way on deck.

She found Lawrence standing at the rail, looking at the dark mass of land that was now clearly visible on the horizon. He smiled at her as she approached, and she returned it, noting as she did that he looked tired and worn. With a wave of sadness she also marked that he was back in chains. He lifted his wrists, winking at her.

"No one is taking any chances with port in view. I think they're worried I might try to swim for it."

Henri looked down at the swirling grey waters as the boat cut through the waves and shuddered at the idea.

"Don't even joke about it," she said, feeling chilled by the very idea. It wasn't as icy here as it had been in England, but nonetheless the water must be freezing.

"Oh, I assure you I got quite wet enough last night, I have no desire to do it again," he said, laughing.

Looking at him with concern she reached out her hand. "Oh, Lawrence, your clothes are still wet. You need to change at once before you catch a chill."

He tutted and looked at her with amusement. "Alex is just as wet as I am and he's still on deck. I don't think it likely the men will take well to their prisoner being given a fresh set of dry clothes, not when everyone else is wet and cold and going about their business."

She frowned at him and nodded. She could see his point but was now only concerned that the whole crew would go down with influenza.

"You'll be on the Longueville estate by dinner time," he said, a moment later, and she saw a wistful look in his eyes.

"When was the last time you were there?" she asked.

"When I was fourteen, we came with mother." He looked out over the increasingly green horizon as France came into view. "Father was furious, said it was madness. There was a truce between England and France that year, but he said it couldn't last. He was right of course." He turned to her and grinned. "But mother was determined to see Longueville one last time." His smile faltered. "Of course, none of us knew then she was ill. She died the following spring."

"Oh, Lawrence, I'm so sorry." She covered his hand with her own, but he withdrew his, frowning and looking around to see if anyone had noticed.

"You shouldn't be speaking to me," he said, turning and walking away from her.

Henri looked about and saw no one who was the least bit interested in them. The men looked cold and tired and were going about their work with the methodical concentration of exhaustion.

"How long did you stay?" she asked, following him as he leaned against the rail further along, the chains clattering against the wood as he moved.

He huffed at her but she just returned a placid smile that made it quite clear she wasn't going anywhere.

"Just for the summer," he said.

"Was Alex there?"

He nodded. "He had leave in August, spent the whole month with us. We sailed and fished and swam. It was the best summer." She smiled on seeing the merry blue of his eyes again as he remembered. "You'll love it there, it's a beautiful place, over four hundred years old," he said with enthusiasm. "Well it was," he amended, shrugging. "I don't know how it faired during the war.

But if it still stands ..." He paused and she could see he was picturing the place in his mind. "The gardens and the surrounding countryside are simply stunning, so green and lush, and the house is full of hidden corners and ghosts."

"Ghosts?" she repeated in alarm, before rolling her eyes at him as he laughed at her.

"Well, of course, all the greatest houses have at least one ghost."

She pouted at him, convinced now he was simply teasing her.

"Yes, she is the ghost of Marguerite," he continued. "A pretty young maid who worked for the Comtesse de Longueville sometime in the fifteenth century. The story goes that the Comte seduced her and got her with child. She was in love with him, but he denied the child was anything to do with him and threw her out in a storm. She was heartbroken and managed to sneak back in and hide. The next day when he was away from home, she went to his bedroom, and she cut her own throat."

"Oh my!" Henri stood with her own hand closed protectively around her throat, feeling quite uncertain whether she would like Longueville at all.

Lawrence gave a heavy sigh. "They say you can hear her singing in the corridors on stormy nights." He laughed at the horrified look she was giving him. "Well that's what they say! Though neither Alex nor I have ever heard her," he added.

"Well that is a great comfort, I'm sure," she muttered, shivering.

"I'm sorry, I didn't mean to frighten you." He chuckled, looking thoroughly unrepentant.

"Hmmm." She sniffed and looked away from him before curiosity got the better of her. "What else is there to see?"

She listened, enraptured, as he described the grand old house, the river and the forests, the ancient church and the endless stretches of white sandy beaches where he had played that last hot summer. He talked as though he would show her all of it and then stopped quite abruptly and turned away from her.

"Of course, Alex will show you everything," he said, sounding bored now, though she wasn't fooled for a moment.

"I wish you'd show me, Lawrence," she said, her voice soft, as she laid her hand on his arm. He looked down at it, still for a moment, before shaking her off.

"I won't be there," he said, his voice cold, before shouting at one of Alex's men. "You there, your captain instructed I be taken back to the hold."

And with sorrow forming a lump in her throat she watched as he walked away from her without a backwards glance or another word.

Chapter 26

"Wherein a home is discovered, and our heroine agrees to play dirty."

Lawrence was right of course, she adored Longueville. From the moment the carriage turned the corner onto the long gravelled drive that led to the house she was enraptured.

It was a long, symmetrical, rectangular building three stories high and on each corner stood a round tower. To the left of the great house sat a row of smaller dependences and behind them she could see the church tower. Glorious lawns and topiary lay out around the front of the house with wide gravel paths and a fountain that splashed prettily.

"Well I am relieved to see it still stands at least," Alex said from beside her as the carriage drew up at the house. "But if you would please stay here until I am assured that my men have made a thorough investigation of the place."

Henri nodded and watched as he stepped outside the carriage. He had sent his men on ahead and they had heard nothing to suggest there was any trouble, so Alex had been content to bring her straight to the house.

"Oh, Annie, isn't it beautiful?" she sighed, looking out of the carriage window with pleasure. Annie, who was still suffering the results of excess, made a non-committal sound before returning her head to the side of the carriage and closing her eyes once more.

The night, falling fast and heavy, brought a low mist creeping over the surrounding countryside, but Longueville looked solid and welcoming, and Henri longed to go inside and explore. Of course, then she was struck with sorrow, as she realised what she truly wanted was to see it with Lawrence, who was chained to one of the wagons bringing supplies from the ship.

Henri shivered with melancholy and moved her feet from the hot brick they'd been on as it was now stone cold. Shifting in her seat she strained to look behind her, to see if she could see him but the night was closing in and nothing but dark shapes could be discerned moving about in the gathering gloom.

She could hear shouts from the men as they unloaded, and the glimmer of lamps was flickered past as they moved from place to place. Little by little the house came alive, a warm glow surrounding it as lamps and fires were lit inside, and the sweet scent of wood smoke was redolent on the cold night air.

Henri tapped her feet on the brick to try to bring some feeling back as she could no longer feel her toes and then jumped with alarm as the carriage door swung open.

"Forgive me for keeping you so long in the cold," Alex said, giving her his hand. "We had to be certain there were no unwelcome surprises awaiting us."

"And were there?" she asked, stepping out of the carriage and hearing the soft crunch of gravel beneath her boots.

Alex turned to help Annie down before placing Henri's hand on his arm and guiding her towards the house.

"No," he said, the relief evident in his voice. "I believe we have lost much of the silver but those servants we have left have been with the family all of their lives. They were, and still are, fiercely loyal to our mother who they adored, and so to us. We have been remarkably lucky," he added, and she looked up to see him watching her in the candle light. He paused and looked down at her. "Please do not take this the wrong way as I know it does not signify. I want you to understand that by now I feel quite assured it is Lawrence you care for and that this will change nothing, but I want you to know - if we can only get Lawrence to see sense - I will give him Longueville. So, this ..." He gestured with the lamp he held towards the house. "This would be your home."

Henri felt something in her heart shift. To live *here*, with Lawrence ...

She blinked away tears and smiled up at Alex. "I feel I owe you an apology also," she said, remembering how he had admitted to having misjudged her a few days before. "I know you have done everything you can for Lawrence and ... I am sorry for the things I have believed about you."

"Oh, don't be," he exclaimed, and the cold eyes glittered with mockery. "I assure you it was all perfectly true."

And with that he led her into the house.

An impromptu supper was supplied of fresh bread and cheese and cold meat while servants scurried about the great house like anxious mice, full of alarm and falling over themselves to please.

"Is there no ... resentment towards us?" Henri asked, pitching her voice as low as she could. She had seen no anger or disgust in the eyes of those she had seen so far but still, they had been at war such a short time ago.

Alex shrugged and shook his head. "I had a long talk with Madame and Monsieur Bertaud, happily they have always looked on Lawrence and myself as being as French as our mother. Father rarely ever came here," he added, picking up an apple from a pretty blue and white porcelain bowl in front of them, and cutting off a neat slice. "She said our mother always treated everyone fairly and as we have always followed her lead since she left us they saw no reason not to continue here, where they have been happy and fortunate. Those who might have caused trouble have long since gone, headed to the city to find work." She saw a frown cross his brow. "They have been lucky here, I think. The vineyards are of value, but Longueville is not a huge estate nor widely known, and I think that has kept much trouble from our doors."

He smiled at her obvious lack of understanding.

The Rogue

"Mother died once the war had resumed, but so far as anyone knew she still lived, and the estate was held in her name not father's. The vines here are still young and the war has not allowed us to make the most of exploiting them so ..." He shrugged, his mouth quirking upwards a little. "They did not realise the value of what is here and so overlooked something of a gem."

"Do you think that would be an inducement for Lawrence to stay?" she asked.

"I don't know," he said, and he sounded weary. She realised then he hadn't slept at all as the storm had been upon them all last night.

"You must be exhausted," she said, stifling a yawn of her own. "And I find I am also rather tired," she added and then sighed as she wondered where Lawrence would be chained for the night. Alex seemed to read the concern in her expression with great accuracy.

"I've spoken rather candidly with Madame and Monsieur Bertaud," he said, his voice little more than a whisper. "I've explained our dilemma with my pigheaded brother, and they have assured us of the loyalty and the willingness to help of all the staff that remains on the estate. Happily, it is the same here as at home and he was always their favourite." He gave her the benefit of a rare and somewhat rueful smile. "For the moment I have been obliged to keep the men on the ship here, however, and so Lawrence is indeed chained in the cellars beneath us as I said he would be. But in the morning, they will return to The Revenge and we can stop pretending he is our prisoner. I hope to persuade him to remain here, at least for a few days and ..." He gave her a hard look. "And during that time, one way or another, Henri, you *must* induce him to stay, for good."

Henri nodded, her hands twisting together beneath the table as she imagined what it would be like if she had to say goodbye to him, the idea of watching him walk away, knowing she would never see him again. She swallowed hard and looked down at her plate before the tears that threatened to consume her began to fall.

"Henri."

Henri looked up to find Alex's grey eyes upon her and shivered. She could see a steel core in those eyes, the heart of a man who could be ruthless and cold-hearted if the need arose.

"May I be frank with you?"

She nodded, as unease rippled down her spine. "Yes, of course."

Alex looked at her, apparently choosing his words with care. "My brother is an honourable man, Henri, but ... he *is* a man, like any other."

Henri frowned, perplexed and feeling more anxious than ever.

"I am in no doubt of either your feelings for him or ... your character," he said, and she felt her heart pick up a little more as she wondered what exactly he meant by that remark. "I am also certain of the regard in which he holds you." He gave a grim smile. "That much has become obvious, the poor bastard can hardly look at me anymore. If I didn't know him better, I might fear for my life." He gave Henri a pitying look, who was by now extremely alarmed and wondering where this was going. "My dear girl, he's so jealous I can see the desire to murder me in his eyes."

She gasped and then found she was laughing as he in turn snorted at her delight on hearing this information.

"There is no need to look quite so gleeful at the idea of my cold corpse at his feet," he muttered. "Anyway, the point I am trying to make is ..." He smirked and obviously decided he had to spell it out as his next words shocked her to her core. "Henri, he wants you in his bed. No matter he feels he can't have you, he wants you more than anything."

Henri felt the blush creep up her neck and settle to blaze upon her cheeks. This was not an appropriate conversation to be having with her fiancé - *about his brother*. But nonetheless she wanted to know what he was getting at.

"And so?" she said faintly and then felt her blush increase as Alex's eyebrows rose to the heavens.

"And so," he repeated, with clear impatience. "And so, you must seduce him!"

"Oh," she said, though her voice sounded faint and rather a long way off. Her mind had drifted back to the night in the cabin, to the feel of Lawrence's hot mouth closing around her breast, the evidence of his desire hard between her legs. She felt suddenly breathless and everything below her navel seemed to clench with an aching desire to run to Lawrence this moment and do exactly what Alex suggested.

She started as Alex sighed and spoke again. "Do you think you can manage that?" he demanded, scowling at her and clearly doubting her abilities.

Mortified, both by what she had been thinking in his presence and the idea he thought her incapable of seduction, she returned his scowl with one of her own.

"I think I might be able to manage it," she snapped, gaining herself a look of amusement and watching as he fought not to smile at her annoyance. He cleared his throat.

"Well then ... good. Because if you can, I feel there is no way Lawrence will leave." He frowned then. "And if he tries to pass you back off to me after using you in such a way, then ... Well then I shall have to take things into my own hands," he said, with such an icy tone that Henri felt quite alarmed.

No, she would have to do this herself. She would use every method in her power to make sure the blasted man stayed here, with her, where he belonged.

With that in mind she made her excuses, only too eager to be free of the earl's presence after *that* conversation and hurried off to find the one woman whose advice she most desperately needed.

Chapter 27

"Wherein our heroine desires to play the temptress."

To both her chagrin and delight, Alex had not seemed to be in any doubt of her willingness to give up her virtue and entrap Lawrence into marriage. To that end he had already sent to Bordeaux, before she'd even set foot on land, to instruct the very finest gowns, shoes and jewels be made available for her the very next morning to aid her in her seduction. She wasn't sure at this point whether to be grateful, or deeply insulted that he believed she needed such a great deal of help in the matter.

And so, it was after another rather restless night, with her mind turning over some of Annie's rather alarming words of advice, that Henri surveyed this vast and generous bounty with her the next morning.

"What price honour," she muttered as Annie gaped, trailing her hand over the rich materials. Velvet, sarsnet, lustring silks and fine muslins were arrayed before them in pretty pastel tones and crisp, perfect white, although her eye was drawn immediately to the white as it was a colour she would have never countenanced before. Only the very rich could afford to wear white. It was so very hard to keep clean and was dreadfully impractical, something she had never had the luxury of being. Annie too, was seduced by the snowy silk, holding it up against Henri with a sigh.

"Oh, this is so lovely, my lady."

Henri could hardly disagree, but it was an evening gown, not a day dress and so hardly appropriate for this morning. She scowled at Annie who rolled her eyes.

"I thought you wanted to seduce 'im, propriety be damned!" Annie mocked.

"There are limits," Henri muttered, watching as her frustrated maid then picked a very beautiful white muslin which would have been perfect. Henri considered it and sighed. Somehow, in the circumstances, she could not but feel the purity of the colour was in very bad taste, and so she turned her back on it and plucked a gown of pale blue muslin from the dazzling array before them and an iris blue silk fichu. It reminded her very much of the colour of Lawrence's eyes. And so, decision made, she went about her toilette under Annie's strict command, who surveyed her mistress with something comparable to the eye of a general surveying battle lines.

By the time Henri had been primped into something that passed muster as far as Annie was concerned, she was feeling way out of her depth. Far too late for breakfast, and far too nervous to attempt to eat in any case, she made her way around the great house and looked about with interest.

The place was undergoing a rapid transformation as servants whipped off dust covers and tried to recapture the glory of the old days before the war had turned their lives upside down. Every fire in the place had been lit, and Henri was discomforted when she realised this was probably for her benefit. After all a seduction was so much more comfortable if you weren't shivering and covered with goose-flesh.

Once again Henri found herself feeling quite out of countenance with Alex. On the one hand she was grateful, as the sheer material of her gown was not fit to withstand the chill weather that was clearly visible outside the windows, and she was showing so much décolletage she was certain she'd catch pneumonia if the temperature dropped anywhere below tropical.

On the other, it made her extremely self-conscious that he was even thinking about it at all, let alone making plans to help her, and she wondered if he felt he'd hired himself a courtesan.

The Rogue

She met the man himself, as he left the breakfast room and was heartened to see him stop in his tracks, one eyebrow lifting in what she hoped was approval.

"Well, well, Miss Morton, I do believe my brother will be hard put to do anything other than whatever you command," he said, his voice low and filled with amusement.

He walked forward and took her hand, raising it to his lips, his eyes lingering on the low neckline with obvious approval.

"I commend the dressmaker and will take back the oaths I swore on receiving his bill," he added, with just the slightest twitch of his lips. "I should tell you also that Lawrence has agreed, with little grace, to stay until after my birthday at the end of January. So, you have ten days in which to accomplish a satisfactory conclusion to this ... affair."

Before Henri could make any attempt at a reply which was likely to have been pithy and short, they were both startled by the opening of a door, and the appearance of Lawrence. He paused in the doorway, and his jaw tightened, just a little, as he took in the scene before him.

Alex turned back to her, away from Lawrence and, giving her a smirk she assumed was his idea of encouragement, announced his intention to be gone for the day.

"I have much to attend to so do make yourself at home. I'm sure my brother will be glad to give you a tour of the place," he added with a careless tone as he strode out of the house.

They heard the slam of the front door and were suddenly very much alone.

Henri cleared her throat. Lawrence had been staring after his brother with an expression she couldn't decipher but which made her nervous.

"You look very fine," she said, meaning it as she looked him over. His piratical image had been replaced, for which she was sorry as he had looked a dashing and romantic figure, but she couldn't fault the new look either. Gleaming black Hessian's were matched with fitted buckskin trousers and a dark blue coat that moulded to his broad shoulders and highlighted an embroidered silk waistcoat and a snowy white shirt and cravat beneath.

He shrugged, his face still troubled. "My brother thinks of everything it seems," he said, his tone as dark as his face.

She swallowed, unsettled by his obvious bad humour. "I do miss the earrings though," she said, reaching out and moving to touch the place where they would have been. He moved a step back, so suddenly it was as though she'd burned him, and she dropped her hand, feeling foolish and not knowing what to say. Lawrence, however, seemed aware of having hurt her, and his bad temper diminished a little.

"You look ... lovely, Miss Morton," he offered, though the smile he gave did not appear to reach his eyes.

"Thank you," she said, wishing suddenly they were back on his ship. How foolish, to be desperate to escape a situation one moment, and the next to find you would do anything to have it back again.

The silence stretched between them, and she half expected him to make an excuse and leave her standing, so great seemed his discomfort. But then he appeared to remember his manners.

"Would you like to see the house?"

"Oh, yes please." She accepted with alacrity and took his proffered arm as he led her down the wide hallway. With real enthusiasm she followed him from room to room, expressing appreciation for all the beauty and charm of the old house and delighting in every story he recited, every history of an object or painting that came before them. Until they were standing before a portrait of the last Comtesse de Longueville.

The Rogue

"She was very beautiful," she said, looking up at sparkling blue eyes that were a perfect match to those belonging to the man beside her.

He smiled and nodded gazing on the painting with a fond expression. "You would have liked her very much I think."

"I'm sure I would."

They stood in what had been the comtesse's bedroom, and despite the fact there was a very inviting and comfortable-looking bed taking up a great deal of the space, Henri felt uneasy at making an attempt at seducing Lawrence while his mother looked down on them; even if she had the slightest idea of how exactly she was supposed to go about it in the first place. She sighed inwardly and walked to the window that overlooked the front of the house.

At least his forbidding demeanour had lessened as they had toured the house. His natural amiability seemed to struggle to remain in dudgeon, and little by little he became his usual animated self as he had regaled her with stories of mischief he'd made as a boy.

"Come, I want to show you something," he said, grabbing her by the hand and towing her from the room. She ran behind him, exclaiming as her shoes slid over the parquet floor, until they reached the end of the corridor. There were portraits all along the walls of the wide stretch that ran the entire length of the house and gave onto the landing in the middle and the bedrooms on both sides of either end. There was laughter in his eyes as she looked around her. They were at the very end, with nowhere further to go. She raised her eyebrows at him, wondering what he was smiling at.

"What do you think of this fine fellow?" he asked at length, drawing her attention to a full height painting of a rather solemn and bad-tempered looking man, who glared down at them, bewigged and bespectacled, with an air of deep disapproval.

"I ..." she hesitated, unwilling to insult a worthy ancestor.

"Terrifying, isn't he?" he asked her, clearly trying not to laugh.

"Well, he is a little forbidding, yes." She frowned up at him perplexed. "Who is he?"

"Damned if I know," Lawrence said, shaking his head. "But he's been awfully good to the family."

"Oh? How so?"

He grinned at her and strode a few paces back down the corridor. "You remember how I showed you each tower has its own staircase and you can only access them from the ground floor?"

"Yes?" she replied, laughing at his mysterious enthusiasm.

"Ah-ha," he replied, tapping the side of his nose and returning to the painting. "Look."

With the air of a magician producing a rabbit, he moved to one of four ornate gold bosses that seemed to be part of the gilded frame and pulled. To her astonishment the painting swung forward to reveal a hidden door.

She squealed with glee and practically bounced on the spot. "Oh, how Gothic! It's like something from The Mysteries of Udolpho," she exclaimed. "Can we go in?"

Lawrence chuckled. "I knew you'd like it, and of course we must go in! Wait here while I fetch a lamp."

He came back a moment later and led the way up a narrow curving staircase. At the top was a tiny round room. It was simply furnished with a chair - a blanket draped over one arm, a table, an oil lamp and a stack of books. There was a tiny slot of a window which gave a little light and a truncated view of the gardens below.

"They say this is where poor Marguerite hid after the wicked count threw her out into the storm."

"Oh, Lawrence, please say you're teasing me?" she whispered as a shiver ran down her spine.

The Rogue

He shrugged, putting the lamp down on the table, and moved to look through the little window. "I don't know, but that's what everyone says, and it's certainly saved a neck or two since in times of trouble," he said, his voice softer now.

The atmosphere had changed somehow, and his previous dark demeanour seemed to be making an appearance. No, she thought, I won't let you do this, and I won't let you go. She took a step closer to him, and not having far to go in the confined space found herself right by his side. He turned, suddenly aware of her proximity, and paused as he discovered her so close to him.

The moment seemed to freeze between them and he stared down at her but made no move in either direction. His eyes never left hers, though, and she felt her heart thud in her chest. *Please, Lawrence, please*, she begged inwardly but he didn't move.

Well, if he wouldn't, she must. Taking courage in her hands she reached up on her toes and pressed her mouth to his. For the barest second he didn't react and she thought perhaps she had miscalculated, perhaps she had been totally wrong. Perhaps ... and then his arms went around her; and he swept her into a fierce embrace.

Chapter 28

"Wherein hearts are touched as surely as flesh."

 His kiss seared her, burned her from the inside out and she wanted nothing more than to step into the inferno. This time she knew what to expect, was ready for him when his tongue demanded entry and she willingly submitted. She reached her arms up around his neck and arched into him, feeling his hands on her, one sliding down her back to cup her bottom and pull her closer, the other stroking the column of her neck. His touch was at once tender and furious, and he held her as though she was precious, as though he wanted to caress and worship every part of her with care. Yet his kiss was fierce and hungry and threatened to take them quickly into dangerous waters.

 She reminded herself that this was where she needed to go when her courage might have failed her. If she wanted to keep him here, to keep him safe where he belonged, then she had to forget everything she'd been taught, she had to forget she'd been raised a lady and make him want to stay - here with her - with every means she had at her disposal. With that in mind her hand fell, sliding down over his chest to caress the hard length of him that was only too easy to find in the fitted breeches.

 His breath caught and held as her hand pressed against him and she felt suddenly powerful as he pulled back a little and she saw the look in his eyes. There was such need there, such heat; there was the inferno she had desired. She moved her hand, stroking him through the buckskin and he closed his eyes and groaned. Her breath caught, her eyes on his face as her hand caressed him, watching the expressions of pleasure as they crossed his face, wanting him to need her so much he couldn't refuse her.

The Rogue

"Oh, God, Henri, you're killing me." The words were harsh and ragged, and she smiled, leaning forward to press a kiss against his neck.

No, she thought to herself, *I'm saving you.*

"No ... no, I--I can't," he groaned, and she found herself suddenly chilled as he released her, taking the heat of him away as he went.

She shivered, clutching her arms around herself and feeling foolish. She'd picked the one room in which there was no fire to aid her seduction, how ironic. Not that she thought a warmer temperature would have helped her with this pigheaded man.

He'd picked up the lamp. "Come," he said, his voice dull. "I expect they're waiting to serve the luncheon."

This wasn't over, she thought, glaring at him as he gestured for her to return down the stairs, not by a long chalk.

He avoided showing her the rest of the bedrooms on the way back and she took a little comfort from the fact that it might be he didn't trust her, or himself, in the vicinity of a bed. He declined to eat with her and so she was left alone, picking at a simple repast of bread, cheese and cold meat with little enthusiasm.

It was growing dark by the time Alex returned to the house. She had curled up in a chair by the library fire after taking some time to select a book from the vast array that stacked the shelves. Unsurprisingly many had been in French, and although her French was adequate for speaking, she had no desire to struggle through pages of text, so she'd been relieved to find a comprehensive selection of titles in English.

She looked up, getting to her feet and bobbing a curtsey as Alex entered the room.

"My lord."

Alex sighed with irritation. "Oh do, for the love of God, let the formalities go. Really, I have no patience with them."

"As you wish," she replied, irked by his sharp tone and taking her seat again. "I trust you had a good day?"

He watched her as he unlocked a beautiful wooden Tantalus and retrieved one of the crystal decanters within, pouring a generous measure.

He declined to answer but gave her a shrewd look. "By your demeanour and the fact you are here alone, am I to take it you've not had a successful day?"

Henri blushed, grateful that the light in the library was muted as she hadn't yet lit all the lamps. "No, sir," she replied, with as much froideur as she could manage. The nerve of the man, how dare he ask such questions!

He snorted and poured another glass and walked over to give it to her before occupying the other available seat by the fire. "Come, Henri, no need to be coy. We both know what hangs on your success." He grimaced at his unintended pun. "How did it go?" he asked. "And for God's sake don't be shy, I would help you if I could."

Henri looked at him, utterly mortified. What on earth did the man expect her to say?

He snorted and sat back in his chair. "Very well, I will ask questions and you simply nod or shake your head."

She huffed and rolled her eyes, taking a large sip of the drink he'd provided.

"Did you kiss him at least?"

She nodded, avoiding his gaze.

"And he responded?"

Her smile betrayed her, and he laughed. "Well, thank God for that, I was beginning to think we were not actually related." Henri tutted at him and he gave a heavy sigh. "I take it that his honour got the better of him and he forced himself to walk away?"

"Something like that," she muttered, staring down into the crystal glass. Perhaps it was her, perhaps she just wasn't enough to tempt him?

She dared to look up and found Alex considering her.

"Don't look so down-hearted. I think you've had a successful enough first day. But you cannot afford to let any opportunity slide. You must seek him out, touch him whenever you can, even if it is just a brush of your fingers over his, your hand on his shoulder. Find his eyes, even if you are not alone, make sure he can read what it is you want there. You must smile at him and make him realise *exactly* what it is you are thinking about. You must use all the ammunition at your disposal, Henri, and every opportunity to deploy it. I know you dislike behaving in this manner, but we all use whatever weapons are at hand when the need arises and like it or not, sex is a powerful motivator."

He got to his feet, leaving her with her cheeks flushed.

"Speaking of which I'm going to dress for dinner. Choose your weapon with care, my dear," he said, clearly enjoying her discomfort as he smirked at her. "Your next battleground awaits."

Henri cursed under her breath as he left her and made her own way back to her room to dress. Annie was waiting for her and she drew her maid to the armoire and the rows of lovely dresses.

"Well then, Annie," she said, frowning at the display of silks and muslins. "What here is most likely to topple this idiotic man's defences and give me the victory I need?"

Without hesitation Annie reached for the white silk she'd picked earlier that morning.

"Perhaps this time, ye'll heed my advice, my lady," she said, one eyebrow raised.

Henri sighed and nodded. "You win, Annie. I am entirely in your hands."

***

A short while later, Henri stood in front of the full-length mirror, feeling thoroughly scandalised.

"Oh, Annie, I can't!" she said, turning this way and that and looking at her own reflection, torn between disbelief she could look so very lovely and shock at the idea of dining alone with two men, neither of whom she was married to dressed like ... like ...

Words failed her.

"Ye can an' ye will," Annie said, drying her hands after having spent some time damping down the fine silk so it clung to every intimate curve.

"But you can see ..." she waved her hand to encompass pretty much everything, as the very fine *unmentionables* did little to hide what the dress was putting on display. Not to mention the fact that the bust was cut so low Henri didn't dare take a deep breath for fear of spilling out of it. "I cannot imagine what the staff must think of me!" she wailed, covering her flushed cheeks with her hands.

"Oh, I reckon ye can, miss," Annie muttered, chuckling to herself.

"Oh, Annie! How can you laugh at me so?"

Annie turned back to her, clearly making a valiant effort to rearrange her face ... and failing miserably.

"Oh, I'm sorry, my little duck," she clucked, patting Henri's hot cheek with a cool hand. "But if ye want to marry that young man, well ... like 'is lordship said, you've got to use every weapon at ye disposal." She looked her mistress over with satisfaction and nodded. "And a fine arsenal ye 'ave too, if ye ask me."

"Oh, Annie!" Henri covered her mouth with her hand and giggled despite herself. "You are awful," she scolded, though Annie just poked her tongue out at her.

"Now then," Annie instructed, gathering up discarded clothes as she went. "You remember everythin' I tol' ye?"

The Rogue

"I assure you the images are seared onto my brain," Henri murmured, still feeling shocked to her bones at the instructions Annie had given her on how to seduce her reluctant pirate.

"Well then," Annie said with a sigh. "Short of goin' an' doin' the job for ye' ... an' I'm quite willin' to give it a go," she added, waggling her eyebrows. "Then I've done all I can for ye."

Henri snorted and moved to give Annie a hug. "You are utterly beyond the pale, Annie, and I thank the heavens for it." She released her maid and walked to the door. "Well then, to arms," she said, turning and grinning at Annie. "And let battle commence!"

Chapter 29

"Wherein no quarter is given."

Lawrence sat by the fire in his brother's office, brooding. He knew damn well what Alex was up to. Trying to use poor, sweet, Henri as his bait, to get Lawrence caught on a hook he couldn't wriggle free of. It was ... it was *unforgivable*, and so far from the kind of behaviour he would have expected of his older brother that Lawrence could only finally admit defeat on one matter. Alex had changed.

The idea that Alex would not only allow, but actively encourage Henri to deploy such tactics, when he knew that she was quite an innocent, well it ... it beggared belief! And he had obviously been aiding and abetting her, for else, where on earth had that dress come from which she'd worn today? He'd damn near lost his mind when he'd seen his brother kissing her hand and blatantly admiring the view from his vantage point. But of course, if Alex and Henri failed to get him on the hook, Alex would be forced to marry the girl. And he'd be doing a great deal more than admiring the view once she was his wife.

The idea made him want to kill something with his bare hands. One thing was for sure, if he didn't stay, he would never be able to return in case he killed his own brother. He scowled into his glass, his mind filled with jealousy and rage, before draining it and reaching for a refill. He paused with his hand on the decanter as he realised that might not be the best idea. One thing he was sure hadn't changed. Alex hated to lose and rarely did, and he had no doubt at all that he would have encouraged poor, sweet Henri to up the ante.

The Rogue

He closed his eyes and swallowed a groan as he remembered her in the hidden tower room. The taste of her, the feel of her in his arms, her hand as it caressed him so intimately. He bit back a curse and forced the image from his mind as he found his breeches becoming uncomfortably tight. He got to his feet and began to pace, reliving as many unpleasant and repulsive memories as he could bring to mind in an effort to dispel the lingering effects of the tantalising Miss Morton.

"Ah, here you are," said the deep voice of his brother as he entered the room. "I don't know about you, but I'm famished. I can't wait to see what Madame Bertaud has rustled up for us now she's had a bit of notice. The woman was always a superb cook if memory serves."

"Well you're in a very fine mood," Lawrence remarked, feeling every bone in his body tense as his temper took a worse turn. How dare Alex be so damned cheery when he was doing everything in his power to help Henri drive him out of his right mind?

As if on cue, the woman herself appeared in the doorway and any comment either men might have made apparently died on their lips.

Lawrence was speechless. He tried to find something to say, words of outrage perhaps? A demand that Miss Morton retrace her steps this very moment and go and put something on more suitable for an unmarried woman. That she go and put *something* on! But he couldn't. The words wouldn't come.

For standing in the doorway was not a woman of flesh and blood, it simply couldn't be. She was a goddess, an ancient deity stepped out from the veil between worlds, there was no other explanation. Lawrence had never seen a woman look so lovely and never had he wanted one as badly.

The white silk dress was so very fine that the light from the corridor behind her shone through, illuminating everything that the dress itself didn't highlight by clinging lovingly to her every curve. The soft white emphasised her creamy skin, the delicate pink of cheeks and lips, and the dark mass of her hair that was arranged around her face, with artless curls that framed that sweet heart-shaped face and those huge brown eyes. Those eyes that fell upon him with such warmth, and hope, and desire.

Oh, dear God, he was a dead man. For he didn't know how he would be able to refuse her anything, and if he stayed, he would bring a world of trouble to her door, and for that he would never forgive himself.

Shaking himself from his reverie he dragged his unwilling eyes away to look at his brother and found with fury he was every bit under this siren's spell as he was.

"Alex!" he snapped, to which his brother looked to him with surprise. "Shall we go through?" he practically growled, moving forward to take Henri's arm before Alex had the chance to.

"Good evening, Lawrence," Henri said, her voice quiet, though he was fairly certain there was a thread of amusement underneath that soft tone. Her hand was light upon his arm and he refused to look down at her for fear of getting ensnared in those eyes.

He gritted his teeth and managed to get them into the dining room and Henri seated so that at least some of her was obscured beneath the table. Once he'd taken his own seat, he discovered this helped very little at all as he was directly opposite her and everything he could still see only served to make his mind wander to consider everything he couldn't.

Henri, of course, was doing everything she could to make matters worse. Whenever he looked at her, she was watching him, with such a seductive light in her eyes he ached with the need to show her exactly what it was she was asking him for.

He wondered, by now approaching a state he could only describe as frantic, if someone had schooled her for tonight's performance or if it was just natural talent. And then she scandalised him further by picking up an asparagus spear with delicate fingers, and closing those luscious pink lips around it, all the time looking at him with such clear intent of what she was really thinking about, that he found himself grow hard, right there at the table. He clenched his fists in his lap and forced himself to look at his plate, the servants and nowhere else.

It was going to be a bloody long night.

By the time the dessert was served Lawrence was at his wit's end. Alex had obviously decided that being married to the vision by his side would not be such a bad idea after all and had turned on the charm. He had flirted outrageously and in a manner totally unfit for a lady of good character, but to Lawrence's horror, Henri had not only allowed it but responded in kind.

Of course, he could have mitigated the situation by being equally charming and flirtatious, but jealousy had tied his tongue, rage had made him dare not speak for fear of calling his brother out, and pity at his own situation made him sink further into despair. So, by the time a crystal dish of syllabub was placed in front of him he had become a glowering and unhappy presence at the table, in stark contrast to their laughter and frivolity.

"Well, Lawrence, what do you say?"

"What?" he snapped, torn out of his dark thoughts and then recalling himself as Alex raised an eyebrow at him. "I beg your pardon," he said, with little grace. "I was not attending the conversation."

"You don't say?" Alex murmured, idly tracing a pattern on the damask table cloth. He leaned back in his chair regarding his younger brother with undisguised amusement glittering in those cool grey eyes. "Well forgive me for interrupting your thoughts with our idle chatter, but I had suggested you take Miss Morton riding tomorrow, out to the ruined abbey. It appears, like many young ladies, Henri has a love of the Gothic and the macabre, and as sadly I am to be away from home all day, the pleasure of the outing must fall to you."

Lawrence gritted his teeth. "No, I'm afraid that won't be possible," he said, thinking of nothing further but the need to spite Alex and his damn scheming. Turning Lawrence's beautiful girl to his own devices and dressing her up and teaching her to act like a courtesan was beyond anything he would have believed of his own brother. Well, damn him, he couldn't play if Lawrence was no longer here.

"Why ever not?" There was a dark and challenging tone to Alex's question which didn't escape him but there was nothing else to be done. He had to get away, get away from both of them before he was too entangled to ever be able to leave.

"Because I won't be here. I intend to be on my way at first light."

There was silence at the table with the exception of a soft gasp from Henri, and he found he couldn't meet her eyes. It was for the best. The words kept circling over and over in his head but the more he heard them the less sense they seemed to make.

"I see," Alex said. There was no inflexion in his voice and the room seemed utterly still.

Finally, Alex broke the silence once more, placing his napkin on the table and getting to his feet.

"In that case I will bid you a good evening so that you may take your leave of Miss Morton now, as I imagine you will not wish to disturb her at such an unfashionable hour of the morning. I, however, will see you before you go, Lawrence."

This last was said with a tone that brooked no argument and Lawrence was forced to nod his acceptance. He wished he had the nerve to follow Alex out of the room without another word, but he couldn't treat Henri in such a way. It would be unforgivable.

The Rogue

The door closed quietly, and he was left facing her. With difficulty he forced himself to look up and meet her eyes, only to find her staring down at her untouched dessert. He had the uncomfortable suspicion she might be crying.

"Henri," he said, his voice soft, bracing himself for tears as she looked up at him, and totally wrong footed when he discovered the fury of a goddess in her eyes.

"You damned coward!" she said, eyes blazing with rage. She got to her feet and began to walk away from him without another word.

"Henri!"

For some fool reason his brain would not accept that this was the moment he required, it gave him the ability to be able to leave her, and what's more to leave her angry with him. If he did that, he would allow her to hate him, instead of mourning the loss of something she might have had. She could be happy then, happy here, with Alex. If he was really as honourable as all that, he should take this chance and thank God for it. So why was he running after her?

"Henri, please ... wait."

She paused by the door and turned back to him.

"Why?" she demanded. "To wave you off with a tearful smile and a kiss for luck?" she said, sneering at him. "Well I shan't, so don't hold your breath!" She glared at him, defiance and anger in every fibre, shaming him. "I would have done anything to keep you here with me," she said, tears sparkling in her eyes now. "I would have risked anything, everything to keep you, to have you love me, but if you don't have the guts ..."

He could stand no more, and he could not stand by and have her believe he didn't love her, that he was too much of a coward to give her his heart, even though he knew there was truth in her words. He had to make her see that it was killing him, but he had to go.

Lawrence moved, and the kiss stopped her tirade in its tracks effectively enough, and the way he touched her, the desperation that she must be able to sense in the way his hands clutched at her, the way his arms crushed her against him, the way his mouth devoured hers with a hunger that could never be sated; surely all of this must illustrate how badly he wanted to stay here with her? And yet now he was caught, just as Alex had known he would be when he forced Henri to play this game, for he couldn't stop.

He hoped to God Alex had the sense to send the staff to bed but found he couldn't spare another thought before his mind was wholly occupied with the woman in his arms.

The silk of the dress was at once cool and slippery and warm as the heat of her body blazed through it. He pressed against her and a feeling of triumph, of having won something precious and unique persisted as she marched into him, making little desperate sounds as she tore at his clothes. Could he really not have this? Wasn't there a way?

Reality reasserted itself and he paused, his forehead pressed against hers, their breath fluttering together.

"Don't you dare, Lawrence," she warned him, tears glittering in her eyes. "Don't you dare."

He gave a laugh born somewhere between incredulity and despair. "Oh, God, Henri, what do I do?"

"Stay," she said, tugging at his jacket. "Stay and be with me. Tell me it's what you want?"

He reached out his hand to cup her face and looked down at her with too much emotion in his heart, it seemed bruised and fragile, overfilled with everything he felt for her.

"I want to stay," he whispered, hearing the truth of it himself. The first time he had allowed himself to own the fact. "But, Henri, what if someone recognises me? What if my enemies track me down here, or the militia come after me? At best the family would never survive the scandal, and at worst ..."

The Rogue

He closed his eyes, too horrified by the idea of finding men who counted him as an enemy to be repaid in blood, *here*, in this place where he had dared to consider being happy, where he had, for just a moment, allowed himself to imagine what life might be like, with her.

For the first time in his life the idea of a home, a wife, perhaps even children, wasn't something he rejected without consideration because it was something he could never have. He'd always been able to dismiss it before because he had never been able to imagine it. But now he could. Now he could see what life would be like ... and he wanted it.

He had always assumed he would die at sea, going down with his ship or bested by a faster swordsman or a better shot. He'd been lucky so far, but his life was too dangerous for that luck to hold forever. But what if that dangerous life couldn't be shrugged off, what if he brought it here and Henri paid the price for it?

He opened his eyes as her hands cupped his face. "Lawrence," she said, and he looked down at her, seeing such love in her expression he thought his heart would break at the idea of leaving her. "You have to stay."

He shook his head, wanting so badly to agree to it that the ache was a physical pain far worse than any injury he could remember sustaining. Three bullets had stopped him in his tracks ten years ago, but he couldn't recall the pain of those wounds being anything like the pain of leaving this woman behind for good.

"I won't put you at risk, Henri." He stroked her face, hoping she could see how badly he wanted to stay, because if he tried to put it into words he was going to crumble. "I would never forgive myself if ... if anything happened to you."

She gave an impatient huff of annoyance and smacked him, the flat of her hand hitting his chest with frustration. "No, Lawrence. You have to stay because if you don't, I promise you that I will follow you. I will leave everyone behind and follow you wherever you go, and I will do it alone, with none to protect me, and *then*, if something happens to me you will know it is your fault because you didn't stay!"

She was staring at him, fury and triumph glittering in her eyes and he knew damn well she meant every word and the little wretch would do it in a heartbeat.

"You're blackmailing me!" he growled, incredulous.

Her fury seemed to fall away now that she knew she had him cornered and she blinked up at him, the picture of innocence, her lips pursed together in a small pout that made desire burn in his blood with the need to kiss her.

"Yes," she said eventually, nodding. "I mean, I didn't manage it properly the first time I tried it, but this time ..." She arched an eyebrow at him. "I think I've got the hang of it."

"And if I gag you and tie you to a chair and make my escape now, no one will know until morning. You'd never find me!" he threatened, even though he knew he'd never do it.

She shrugged as if it was of little concern. "Perhaps not, but you know I'll try to ... that I'll be all alone and ..." She gave a heavy sigh.

"Damn you, Henri!" he exclaimed, running a hand through his hair in exasperation. "I have never in my life known a more infuriating, manipulative ..." He stopped in his tracks and sighed as he looked down at her and those big brown eyes. "Oh, dammit to hell," he said, giving up all hope of ever getting away from her, or even pretending he could ever have wanted to. Instead he pulled her tight and kissed her.

Chapter 30

"Wherein explorations are made, and a great deal of ground covered, with much delight."

Surely, he could not run now, Henri thought, although rational thoughts were rather hard to pursue with any enthusiasm as Lawrence kissed a path down her neck. But this was not a moment for taking chances. She had to make it so that he couldn't find a way to wriggle out of this, in case somewhere in that stubborn head of his he came to believe she hadn't meant what she'd said, or that if faced with the reality of following him alone, courage would fail her.

He wanted to stay that much he had admitted, and she believed him. How much of it was because of her, and how much that he simply wanted his life back she couldn't be certain of, not yet, but she intended to find out.

"Lawrence," she breathed his name against his mouth but then put her fingers against his lips before he could claim another kiss. "Come with me."

He frowned at her as she moved away from him and opened the door, but she was going to take both of their fates in her hands, and whatever came of it would be on her head. She knew the risks he had illustrated were genuinely something to fear, but she also knew it was a risk she was willing to take. Taking his hand, she led him through the silent house, praying no one would see them and spook him into changing his mind.

The door to her bedroom opened without so much as a creak to give them away. Henri sent Annie a heartfelt, if silent, word of thanks as she looked around and found the room serene and tidy, with just enough lamplight to cast the room with a warm and intimate glow.

The fire added to the warmth, crackling merrily and heating the air further, though she felt she really didn't need the help. Her skin was burning with anticipation, with the need to be touched, and the desire to try the thing that Annie had mentioned earlier too.

She had seen the look in Lawrence's eyes when she'd decided to give him a hint at dinner. It had taken every ounce of courage she possessed to pick up that asparagus but had been so worth it for the confidence his reaction had given her. She had almost laughed out loud at his expression and was very relieved Alex had been thoughtfully studying his plate. Yes, she felt he would certainly like that and was eager to test the theory.

She turned to find him closing the door behind him and removing a pistol from his jacket to lay it carefully on the bedside table, a reminder perhaps of the seriousness of his concerns. But then he looked at her and suddenly she was in no doubt that he was going to stay. There was a possessive light in his eyes that made her breath hitch as he walked towards her, and continued to move, circling her, his expression one that left her in no doubt of his intentions.

"A very lovely dress, Miss Morton," he said, his voice low as he walked to stand behind her.

"Thank you, sir," she said, smiling and biting her lip at his formal tone.

His hands slid around her waist, pulling her back against him so that she could feel the hard heat of his erection pressed between the clef of her bottom. She sighed and tilted her head back to lean against his shoulder. With one hand he tilted her head a little sideways, so that his mouth was almost against hers, and she could feel his breath fast and uneven against her lips.

"But if you ever wear this in front of anyone but me, I shall be forced to kill every man that lays eyes on you, do I make myself clear?"

She smiled up at him, eyes glittering with amusement. "I shall make sure to only wear it in front of people I despise then."

He growled, a low noise in his throat that sounded just a little desperate before his mouth closed over hers. His hand tugged at the shoulders of the dress, forcing it down to expose her breasts and he cupped them both, calloused fingers rubbing over the tender flesh, pinching her nipples and making her cry out in surprise at the delicious mixture of pleasure and pain that coursed through her. She turned in his arms, wanting to touch him in return, and setting her fingers to the task of undoing his cravat, unbuttoning his waistcoat and shedding the far too many layers that kept them apart.

"Off, take it off!" she said, tugging at his linen shirt and ignoring the pleased amusement in his eyes at her impatience.

She held her breath as he removed the offending article, pulling it up and over his head, and it was a moment or two before she remembered to breathe once again. The tanned chest she had tried hard to ignore the first morning she had awoken with him beside her on the ship now had her undivided attention. She placed her hands flat on the upper part of his chest and allowed her hands to smooth over him. Over the curve of muscle, pausing for a moment to tweak the darker circles of skin that puckered at her touch. She smiled at the way his breath hitched, pleased that he reacted as she had when he'd touched her. Her hands moved to the scars he bore, scars of the bullets that had almost taken his life all those years ago.

Henri felt a shiver at the idea she might never have known him and leaned forward to press her lips to each in turn. First his upper left shoulder, then to the right of his chest, and then, moving lower, she kissed his left side and the ragged scar where the bullet had torn his skin. She kissed each with a reverence that she felt in her heart and hoped to convey to him with her touch. And then her attention wandered, lips and fingers trailing to his stomach and the scattering of dark hair that disappeared beneath his waistband.

She sank to her knees and moved to the buttons on his breeches, undoing them, one by one, hearing the quality of his breathing change. Looking up she found his eyes on her, intense and with that same look she had seen at the dinner table. Pleased by that slightly febrile glint in his eyes she allowed the material to fall open and turned her attention to the part of him she had only been able to guess at from Annie's indelicate advice and her own limited explorations of him before now.

She looked up at the murmured curse he gave as she touched him but was far too consumed with curiosity to pay it much heed. Instead she returned her attention to the strange combination of hard strength, encased in satiny skin.

Her fingers trailed over him and dallied at the tip, finding it glistening and wet. She wondered if this was further evidence of his desire and looked up to find his eyes dark with wanting. Holding that dark gaze, she leaned in a little and touched him with her tongue, finding the salt and musk and that remarkably silky skin something she wished to explore further. He closed his eyes, his hands fisted at his sides and she smiled, pleased that she appeared to be on the right track, for torment was a part of this, if Annie was to be believed, and Henri was inclined to do just that.

She leaned in once more and licked, trailing her tongue from hilt to tip in one long, lingering sweep, and gloried in the deep, heartfelt groan of pleasure that issued forth as a result. The sound of his pleasure, the look of undiluted ecstasy on his face, tugged at something inside of her, something raw and primal and desperately powerful. With growing confidence only matched by a hunger that burned in her blood and made her skin ache she held him still, closed her mouth over the glossy head and caressed him with her tongue.

The Rogue

The curse that escaped him might have alarmed her, might have made her believe she'd hurt him, if it wasn't for the hand that sank into her hair, holding her in place, and the way he spoke her name a moment later. "Henri, oh God, Henri ..."

She smiled around him and continued in her efforts, lavishing attention on him with tongue and lips and the occasional teasing scrape of her teeth. Until he stilled her with a desperate cry.

"Stop, for the love of God!"

She was hauled unceremoniously to her feet and pulled into his arms, his mouth demanding, frantic hands tearing at the delicate buttons of her dress until she stood in nothing but a thin shift. At this point his remaining patience appeared to be gone for good as he lifted her and laid her on the bed, pausing only to kick off breeches and boots with muttered oaths until he was quite wonderfully, gloriously naked and prowling over the bed towards her.

"Well, Miss Morton, I hope you are happy?" he growled, and her breath caught at the look in his eyes as he crawled over her. "It seems you have me where you so clearly wanted me."

She bit her lip and raised an eyebrow. "Well ... not quite yet, sir," she said, blinking at him with what she hoped was an innocent expression. "But I do believe we are getting there."

He gave a bark of laughter before silencing them both with a searing kiss that scattered any remaining ability for clever remarks.

Thought of any kind vanished completely as his lips continued on their path, mapping the lines of her body with delicious pauses at points of interest, as he lavished his attention on one breast and then the other. She arched beneath him, revelling in the feeling of his skin against hers, the heat of his mouth on her, those rough hands caressing as he explored her tender flesh.

Henri wondered at her own surprise as he continued down, kissing his way down her body until he parted the soft curls at the apex of her thighs, spreading her open to him. She had enjoyed bestowing her attentions on him, using her mouth to bring him pleasure, but it simply hadn't crossed her mind that ...

The sound that escaped her throat was like nothing she had heard before. It sounded wild and wanton and illustrated perfectly just how she felt. She felt the soft huff of a chuckle against her overheated skin, and then he pushed her legs wider apart and she found she was only too willing to comply.

She writhed as he held her still with strong arms that allowed her no escape, should she be foolish enough to want to. His tongue explored and laved her, his mouth taking turns to suck at the delicate flesh before returning his tongue to its devilish work. And just when she thought there was nothing that could surpass his wonderfully wicked tongue and the torment it gave; his fingers joined the attack on her sanity and caressed her from the inside. And suddenly there was nothing else, nowhere else to go and a great unnamed force overtook her, power building around the centre of his attentions, enticing, tugging and pulling her into some decadent void, body and soul, until she held her breath, aware of some new precipice she lingered on.

And then she fell. Falling as the world shattered, any grip on reality flew apart and she heard his name on her lips in some distant place, but she was lost and wanted no return, adrift in a sensuous sea where nothing but this mattered.

She came back to herself in increments, blinking, dazed in the soft light of the bedroom, her limbs molten and too heavy to lift. Her eyes fastened on the very male, exceptionally smug man lying by her side. She gave a small huff of amusement at his expression and allowed him to preen. She couldn't help but feel he deserved it.

"Goodness," she murmured, barely able to summon the energy to speak aloud.

A deep chuckle rumbled through the bed and a finger touched her mouth, and then it trailed slowly and surely down her neck, between the valley of her breasts, and irresistibly on to recently charted but still unfamiliar territory.

"Miss Morton, I find I am bound to point out to you that goodness had little to do with it."

She giggled as his curious fingers teased the soft line of skin at the top of her thigh. "That's as may be," she replied, trying to scowl and failing. "But I swear if you ever call me Miss Morton again, I shall hit you."

With a grin he moved, insinuating himself in the space between her legs and dipping his head to steal a kiss.

"Well, I find that suits my plans after all," he said, his voice low, and his eyes intent on hers. "As I intend to change your name to Sinclair with all due haste." And then he silenced any words of triumph or joy she might have uttered by claiming her mouth with his own.

Chapter 31

"Wherein many things are taken."

Well he had made his bed, he thought, looking down at the lovely creature beneath him with awe; and what an enchanting place it was. How it could ever have entered his head that he had the will or the resolve to walk away from Henri was something he couldn't quite comprehend. He simply wasn't that honourable, and he thanked God for that fact.

For if he had left her, he knew the idea of her about in the world without him, with his brother in her bed instead of him, would have driven him to madness or an early grave. But as it was, she was here, and so was he, and the delight to be derived from that fact already far exceeded all his expectations.

She was at turns eager and shy, wanton and curious and so earnestly committed to giving and receiving his pleasure that he was quite undone. He loved her and could think of nothing beyond the need to make her his own, in all ways.

Lawrence could even bear the idea of Alex's self-righteous expression when he discovered their victory, and the ragging he was bound to endure from his elder sibling for years to come with equanimity. He didn't care for anything but teaching his soon to be wife everything she could possibly need to know in answer to the question in her eyes.

She moved beneath him and he slid between the slick heat of her thighs, only too eager to show her what came next. The way she had shattered under his touch moments earlier, the way she had said his name, the sound of her pleasure, all of it still lingered in his mind, and he found himself needing to hear it again and again. He moved, finding the entry to the fierce heat of her and readying her with gentle fingers, caressing and opening as he had before. She sighed and then gasped, her breathing uneven and her heart clearly racing.

"Do you trust me?" he asked, kissing her as sweetly as she deserved to be kissed.

She opened her eyes, dark and hazy with desire and filling him with such need it took everything he had not to just give in and sink into her.

"Swear you'll never leave me," she whispered, her hands gripping his shoulders, her legs wound about his hips.

"If I had any honour, I would leave," he replied, on a groan as she tilted her hips towards him, rubbing against him until it stretched his sanity to breaking. "But I cannot. I couldn't leave you tonight and now ... I never will, I swear it."

And with that he gave in, sheathing himself inside her and only pausing when she cried out, clinging to him as he took everything she offered. He hushed her with gentle words, murmuring promises that it was only for a moment, kissing her until her tension fell away. She looked up at him then and smiled, hand reaching out to touch his cheek, those soft brown eyes so trusting in him he felt overwhelmed by it.

"I love you," he said.

For the briefest of seconds old instincts kicked in and he wondered what the hell he was about, giving her such power over his heart. But then he saw the answer to any doubt in her eyes, and knew that, for once, he had said and done the right thing.

"I love you," he repeated, with more surety this time as he showed her how to move with him and how to seek and find their pleasure together. Lust and a primitive desire to lay claim battled against the need to please her, to school her gently. His own needs raged, threatening to overwhelm him but something within him, something that cared for more than his own desire stayed his hunger and he found the will to hold back.

He found the strength to savour rather than devour, and his prize was the spell she cast as she clung to him. Her slim fingers grasped at his flesh, her head flung back, dark hair all undone and cascading over the pillows as her climax took her and drew him with her, soaring and tumbling into the heavens where nothing but the most exquisite pleasure could exist.

***

The early fingers of daylight teased their way around the bedroom curtains and Lawrence sighed, a sigh of deep, boneless contentment. He turned his head a little and smiled at the sight of the woman beside him. Asleep he could look his fill, without those all too seeing eyes delving into his soul. She saw far too much of him, he thought, and then chuckled to himself. Whatever there was to be seen she had been given a thorough viewing of last night. He had opened his heart and his soul to this woman, and all the regrets and anxieties he had expected to be plagued with on waking, simply weren't there. He could not find it in himself to regret it. None of it. Not for a moment.

As if aware of his train of thought, Henri murmured in her sleep and snuggled closer. *Well this is a first*, he thought, quite unable to keep the smile from his lips. Usually if he found himself beside a female form in the early hours, he was up and out of the bed with as much haste as he could manage. But today, he found no such desire. Today the rest of the world could go to hell.

At some point he needed to make arrangements for their betrothal but ... well another hour or so really wouldn't make the slightest difference. The staff may be scandalised, but all would be forgotten once she was safely wed.

With such pleasant thoughts murmuring through his increasingly drowsy brain, it was perhaps only years of life as an outlaw that drew him forcefully back to consciousness. He stilled, ears straining, every muscle taut. Nothing but the soft huff of Henri's breath against his shoulder, the chatter of birds beyond the window and the occasional sound of servants moving about their daily chores could be heard.

And yet ...

With the practised ease of one used to creeping in shadows he slid from the bed and pulled on breeches and boots. He reached for the pistol he always kept close, even when he slept, and walked to the window. With a fingertip he pulled the curtain back and watched the garden through a crack in the shutters.

All was still. A crisp white frost covered the grass, the trees and buildings, everything coated in a sparkling rime of white ice. But nothing moved. He held his place, anxiety gnawing at his guts. Something was wrong.

Lawrence had only ever once not trusted his instincts that something was not as it should be, and he'd paid the price with three bullets. It was a mistake he would never make again. Better to live long and be considered a paranoid fool than die by ignoring that little prickle of alarm that raised the hairs on the back of his neck.

And there it was. Behind the wall that separated the garden from the orchard beyond, a cloud of breath on the freezing morning air.

"Damnation!" With as much speed as he could manage, he ran to the bed, waking Henri with regret by covering her mouth with his hand. "Hush, love," he murmured. "I think there are men outside for me, whether they are militia or pirates I know not, but they are not friendly."

He withdrew his hand as her eyes widened with alarm and understanding.

"What shall we do?"

"Get dressed and find Annie and stay away from the windows. Gather all the women and children and take them to the hidden tower room. You remember how it opens?"

He sighed with relief as she nodded and smiled at her, proud of her calm manner in the face of such an event.

"I'm going to rouse Alex and find what men we have about the place. Keep everyone calm if you can, Henri. The longer they think we are unaware the more chance we have."

He didn't add that their chances were slim to none. For no matter if it were militia or pirates, they would have come in numbers. To his knowledge there was him, Alex and possibly three other men in the house. Their only hope was that they could keep them at bay long enough for someone to sound the alarm and help to arrive. He kissed her, pulling her to him and holding her close, filling the moment with everything he felt for her.

He let her go but she reached up, grasping his arm.

"I love you, Lawrence," she said, fear glittering in her eyes. "Please be careful."

He nodded and turned away, racing to find his brother. Rage at the men outside filled his heart. Just once in his life he'd had a chance for something real and good. A life where he could be the kind of man he now realised he wanted to be. A husband and father, instead of some desperately romantic and roguish figure that in reality hid the truth, that his life was hollow and lonely and doomed to meet a violent and ignominious end.

It had all been within his grasp, and he was damned if he would let anyone take it from him. Guilt fell about his shoulders in the wake of his anger, a heavy, cold weight that settled around him, smothering his heart. He had done this by trying to have something that was never his due. Something he'd lost the right to claim. He had brought this trouble to them, just as he'd known he would. He should have forced Alex's hand, made his brother hand him over to the authorities. But there was no time for regret or recrimination now. Now all he could do was try to protect everything he loved.

Chapter 32

"Wherein many things are broken, and much blood spilt."

"There." Lawrence felt his brother stiffen beside him, as he too saw the movement of someone closing in on the house.

"And there, look, three at least. What's that, twelve now?"

Lawrence followed Alex's gaze and cursed. That wasn't militia. Which meant they wouldn't give a damn about taking any innocent lives in their pursuit of him.

"Perhaps ..." he began, the inevitability of it sticking in his throat.

Alex snarled at him and grabbed him by the shirt, slamming him against the wall. "If you dare mention any fool notion about giving yourself up, I swear I'll kill you myself!"

Lawrence scowled at him and pushed Alex's hands away. "You know it's the sensible thing to do," he hissed back.

"I know no such thing," Alex raged as loud as was possible, considering they were trying to keep quiet. "I have no idea if they are pirates after you, or a rival smuggling gang after *me!*"

Lawrence blinked, momentarily stunned. "What?"

Alex returned his attention to watching the garden, but not before giving Lawrence a look of sheer exasperation. "I told you what I'd been doing didn't I, do you think the competition takes kindly to my dominance of the field?"

Frowning, Lawrence tried to piece the earlier conversation back together. "Yes, but ... I understood you'd been funding them. Damn it all, Alex! Do you mean to tell me you've actually been out, running contraband?"

"Well you needn't take that tone with me," Alex snapped. "As I doubt you're in any position to throw stones!"

Lawrence closed his mouth. It was a fair point. "If that's the case, why the devil aren't we better protected?"

At that moment both men looked up as Albert, one of the gardeners came in carrying a box, which he opened with care to reveal an array of pistols. "You were saying?" Alex remarked as he opened a cupboard to reveal an impressive range of daggers and swords.

"That's all well and good, but where are the men to wield them?" Lawrence asked, snatching up one of the pistols to add to his own and adding a pouch of powder and a quantity of shot. Checking the pistol was properly loaded he lodged it firmly in his belt and went to select a dagger and sword.

"Ah, you have me there." Alex turned to him with regret as he handed him a fine sword which Lawrence hefted in appreciation, admiring the craftsmanship. "As I was engaged in the pursuit of a target known to the militia, i.e. *you*, I brought The Revenge and the crew who are involved in my more legitimate legal business. Had I known how things would turn out ..." He gave a dignified shrug. "I have, as it happens, sent word to the crew back home, but of course it will be several days before they arrive." He nodded in reply to the look of astonishment Lawrence knew was on his face. "I figured a run would be an appropriate means by which to keep me from under your feet once ..." He waved his hand to encompass the situation with Henri. "Once you had come to your senses." He frowned at Lawrence who steeled himself for what was coming next. "You *have* come to your senses I take it?"

"Yes dammit! But that's hardly a topic for conversation now is it?" Lawrence hissed, peering back out the window. He half hoped the bloody men would attack, anything to keep his brother from continuing this conversation.

"Well thank heaven for small mercies," Alex muttered, pausing a moment before adding. "Though after seeing her last night, it really wouldn't be a hardship if you decided you want me to take her off your hands."

It took a moment before Lawrence's brain caught up and he realised he was holding a gun on his own brother. "You will forget what you saw last night," he said, his voice cool and even. "And you will never think of, speak about or look at her in a manner other than that of a brother, ever again. Do I make myself clear?"

"Perfectly," Alex replied, grinning at him, apparently unconcerned for his own well-being. "I'm only sorry it took such a lot of effort on my part to make you realise you were in love with the woman. Oh, and may I offer you my congratulations." He turned back to the window and scowled. "Now then, let's see what we can do about this lot, for I was rather hoping to attend a wedding, not my own funeral."

As if on cue, a voice called out from the gardens.

"Savage? We know yer in there. Come out quiet like an' there won't be no trouble. We don' want the rest o' them. Got no quarrel with 'is lordship."

Lawrence looked at his brother. "Still think they're after you?"

Alex shook his head, frowning. "No, but if you think they'd get this far and leave rich pickings such as could be found in a house like this, then you really are a fool. If you give yourself up, they'll just torture you in front of us until we let them in."

Grimacing, Lawrence accepted the truth of the argument.

A crash of noise had them rushing to the other window again.

"They're trying to break down the back door," Alex said, his voice grim. The two men looked at each other as an echo of the same noise came from the front of the house.

"You take the front," he instructed Lawrence who nodded and ran from the room in the direction of the sound of an axe splintering wood. He ran through to what had been his mother's room and opened a window as quietly as he could, before flinging back the shutter. Lawrence had only a moment to lean out and take aim before his position was seen but the scream that followed told him his shot had struck home. He ducked back, taking a moment to reload while curses flew at him from below.

"Savage! Yer a dead man."

Lawrence frowned as the voice became familiar. "Brant?"

"Aye, it's me," the voice returned with a spiteful laugh. "I've been lookin' for ye for nigh on a year, me old friend. There's a reward for ye' that will keep me in rum from now 'til the end o' my days an' I mean to claim it."

"Bastard," Lawrence muttered. He'd come across Brant before. He was more smuggler than pirate, but he would make money however it could be found, and he was well known for blackmail and stabbing men in the back. It wouldn't be the first time he'd profited from the reward money for bringing in one of his own. Lawrence pictured the wretch's face, and the thick black beard that covered the scars he bore. They said it was his best friend who'd done that, when he discovered Brant had betrayed him.

Swinging out of the window once more, Lawrence fired, throwing himself back into the room as a bullet smashed the window behind him, showering him with broken glass. He reloaded with quick, sure movements that testified to years of practise and grabbed the other pistol. The idea of a sick son of a bitch like Brant setting foot on the property while Henri was in the house ... Lawrence felt his guts turn. He couldn't let that happen.

The smashing began again, and Lawrence took his chance. Leaning forward he aimed true and fired both pistols. Two men fell, one dead, the other screaming from a wound in his thigh, neither one of them Brant. But Lawrence fell back, cursing as the fierce sting of a bullet burned against his flesh and splinters flew around him as bullets hit the window frame.

The Rogue

Muttering obscenities, Lawrence tore off a strip of his shirt and bound his arm. Thank God, just a flesh wound, though the blood was hot and ran freely down his arm as he tried to tie off the makeshift bandage. Lawrence wiped his hands clean of blood and reloaded both pistols. He could hear gunfire from the back of the house and prayed Alex was holding his own.

The sound of axes cutting into the doors continued and though he tried to access the window again, they were taking no chances and fired upon him at the first sight of movement. He waited until they'd discharged their weapons, hoping everyone had run out of powder, and leaned out once more, winging the bastard with the axe and throwing himself back into the room as a bullet thwacked into the wall a hair's breadth from his head.

"Damn me, that was close," he muttered, reloading. Getting to his feet he ran for the landing. The front door was thick and solid, made of good French oak but it wouldn't hold for much longer from what he could see, and he hurried down the stairs to find a position to hold them off. And not a moment too soon as the great door smashed to the floor, and five men ran into the house.

Taking his time, Lawrence stood his ground and fired, killing one man outright, the other crashing to the ground as a bullet tore through his upper shoulder. Dropping the pistols, he reached for his dagger and threw it, smiling in satisfaction at the dull thwack as it hit home, killing the blood thirsty-looking devil beside Brant as it struck square in his chest. But Brant and a giant of a man with tattoos over his bald head and gold in his ears were still coming, stepping over their fallen comrades without even a glance. Lawrence ducked down behind a dresser as two bullets hit the wood, smashing the glass-fronted windows.

"Devil take you," he muttered. With his pistols lost he drew the sword with his right hand and reached for the dagger he'd stowed in his boot and got to his feet. Brant grinned at him, showing a missing front tooth. He put away his own pistol, drawing a sword and advancing on Lawrence with the bald fellow following suit.

"An' why not settle this like gentlem'n," he chuckled. "As it appears you are one o' them fine fellows." Brant sneered, and Lawrence glared at him, moving to counter the coming attack.

"What on earth leads you to believe that?" he demanded. Only Mousy had known that the earl was his brother before he'd given himself over to The Revenge. Whilst he knew Mousy would have told his crew once they were safe away, he didn't understand how Brant could have come to hear of it. He remembered, though, that the militia had been out in force when he'd set foot on land back at home, and the crawling feeling he'd been betrayed returned all over again.

"Ye got a rat aboard, huh?" Brant chuckled. "Aye, see the money yer worth dead is a sore temptation, even to a loyal man."

"Who?" he demanded, as acid burned in his stomach. The men who had remained with him had been loyal and true, or at least he had believed they were. The idea that one of them had given him up ...

Brant shrugged. "It's o' no matter now, my lad. Ye'll have no cause to worry on it in a moment or two, nor on anythin' else neither."

Lawrence adjusted his grip on the sword and faced the two men. Maybe Brant was right, and his time was finally up, but either way, he was taking the two of them with him.

Chapter 33

"Wherein our heroine fights fire with fire and discovers a pirate is a very fine sight to behold."

By the time Henri had everyone crammed into the tower room, there was barely an inch in which to turn around. Which was a pity as she really needed to pace. This was the worst part of being born female, she raged internally. Why hadn't she got Lawrence to teach her how to fire a gun when she'd had the chance! So they were all supposed to cower here while the menfolk went off and got themselves killed. And yet she knew without skills with pistol or sword she was likely to be more of a distraction than a help. The knowledge rankled nonetheless, and she vowed that if they got out of this, it was a situation that would be remedied. *When* she got out of this, not if, she chided herself. They would all get out of this alive, there was no other option. She heard a man screaming in pain and closed her eyes, praying - with more fervour than she ever had for her own safety - that Lawrence would be spared.

Though the sounds were muted, shut away up here, each report of a gunshot made her heart leap and her blood run cold in her veins as she thought of Lawrence and Alex, fighting for their lives below. She felt like she was suffocating and as one of the maids began to cry, she squeezed through to the little slot of a window. She could see nothing of the fighting as it was all in and around the house but she scanned the surrounding countryside, praying that someone would have sounded the alarm. From below male voices drifted up.

"Go and help Brant, him and Tready 'ave got Savage cornered inside, but we need to move. We'll get the place cleared out and then light it up."

Henri felt pure fear slide down her back. Lawrence was cornered, trapped with two men after his blood, and once he was dead and the house looted, they would burn it down.

"No," she whispered. They wouldn't take Lawrence from her, not now, and they wouldn't burn this beautiful house or the innocent people within. She tugged on Annie's hand, pulling her maid to follow her down the stairs. "Annie," she whispered. "I have to do something, they're going to kill him and they mean to burn the house down." She squeezed Annie's hands as her eyes grew round as saucers. "I'm going to go and ... and do something," she exclaimed.

"But ..." Annie began but Henri covered her mouth with her hand to silence her.

"I love him, Annie, I won't let him die without even lifting a finger to help him. But these people need help too. You can't let them die up here. Keep them quiet for a long as you can but if the fire begins, you must try to get them out safely."

Annie's eyes filled with tears but she nodded and took a breath as Henri removed her hand. "Don't ye worry none, my little duck, I'll take care o' them. But ..." She sniffed as tears began to roll down her face. "Oh, Lawd, my sweet girl, please be careful!"

Henri pulled Annie into a swift hug and kissed her cheek. "I will, I promise, and you too, Annie. Good luck."

Henri scanned the corridor, and finding it empty, quickly slid out from behind the painting and closed it behind her. She needed a weapon, and she knew Lawrence had taken his, but Alex didn't strike her as the kind of man who took chances, and she knew he had enemies. He was bound to have weapons secreted close at hand. With that in mind she ran towards his room and flew through the door. She turned out drawers and rifled through the wardrobe. With a start she noticed a beautiful wooden box- she had seen that in his cabin on The Revenge. With a prayer on her lips she opened the lid and gasped with delight as her eyes fell upon two, beautiful duelling pistols. Thanking providence, she slid out the drawer secreted beneath the box to discover powder and shot.

Once, many years ago she had stayed one summer with her father's cousin. She had been little more than ten but they had an older boy and his father had been teaching him to shoot. Although they had banned her from the lessons, Henri had persisted in hanging around and watching as they poured in powder and rammed in the shot. It really hadn't looked very hard, so ...

Biting her lip with concentration and trying to steady her hands, Henri loaded first one pistol and then the other. The sounds of fighting and breaking furniture were becoming ever more desperate and it was with resolution that she grasped a pistol in each hand and headed for the stairs.

With her heart beating in her throat Henri stepped silently down the stairs, the clash of swords and the grunts of men immersed in a deadly battle coming from behind the staircase. Breathing hard she raised the pistols and looked around the bannister and saw two men and Lawrence, fighting for his life. The clash of blades rang out and she stifled a scream as she saw a crazed looking bald man lung towards him, but her man was too quick and clearly too skilled, turning the blade away and lashing out, dealing the brute a swift kick to his stomach that made him groan and stumble back. In terror she watched, praying for Lawrence to get clear of the shot for she feared killing him too if she tried now. Blood trickled from a wound on his arm and another at his side, and his shirt clung to him, dark and sticky red. In agony she saw that they were wearing him down, but he fought on and for a moment she thought he'd felled the dark-bearded fellow as he yelled out and stumbled, but to her desperate disappointment righted himself again. Then, with satisfaction she noted the man limping and a dark slash visible on his thigh, not killed then, but injured.

With frustration singing in her veins she watched as the fight became ever more brutal. All around them lay the debris of broken furniture, hindering their steps and tripping them up as Lawrence fought for survival. It was as if time stood still in some terrible nightmare as she was so desperate to help but knew if she called out at the wrong time, even the slightest distraction could get Lawrence killed. Suddenly he feinted right and then rolled, leaping to his feet and almost killing the bald lout as he lunged forward, but the fiend appeared surprisingly agile despite his bulk and leapt back, though he bore a deep slash across his chest for his trouble. The move however had put them facing her with Lawrence's back to her. Without another thought she yelled at him, the weight of the pistols making her hands tremble as she aimed.

"Lawrence, get down!"

The two men looked up and Lawrence's head whipped around, all three staring at her in astonishment. Lawrence gaped as he noted the guns in her hands and dived, hitting the floor. And she fired.

The noise was incredible and the power from the shots forced Henri to take a step back and she lost her footing, tumbling backwards down the stairs. Landing heavily, the air was forced from her lungs in a rush and pain exploded behind her eyes as her head hit a step, and then everything went dark.

She awoke to a world of pain. Her head was throbbing and she couldn't breathe. This last was quickly explained as she looked down and found a muscular arm wrapped tightly around her chest and the cold touch of a knife at her throat. She gasped, struggling to get free and then screaming for him to let her go, but the man just tightened his hold and pressed the knife closer to her throat.

"Shut ye mouth, bitch!" he commanded, as she came to her senses and looked around, seeing Lawrence advancing on them, a sword in one hand, a dagger in the other and murder in his eyes. Beyond him she could see the bearded man lying dead in a pool of blood on the floor. Had she done that? She very much hoped so. She screamed and struggled harder despite his curses as the man holding her dragged her unwilling form backwards towards the front door. No, no, no, she couldn't let him take her. She saw Lawrence's stricken face as he followed, unable to attack for fear the man would slit her throat.

He would never forgive himself. And then she realised she could smell the coppery tang of blood and that her right hand which was pinned to her side was sticky with it. She focused and realised with relief the blood was not her own, which meant ... She drew her elbow as far forward as she could within the man's iron grip and jammed it with all her might into his side. He bellowed with pain and momentarily lost his grip on her. But only for a moment, and Henri screamed as his hand shot out and struck her.

Dazed from the blow, her feet skidded in the blood that slicked a trail across the polished wood floor and she fell. Scrabbling in vain on the slippery surface she tried to get up but from the corner of her eye she saw the glint of a blade in the devil's hand. She cried out as Lawrence shouted, falling to his knees and pushing her flat, covering her as he countered the blade with his own, metal shrieking against metal in an agonising sound. Pushing Henri roughly out of the way Lawrence prepared to meet another blow, but his gigantic opponent was on the offensive and Lawrence in a vulnerable position on the floor as the blade smashed down on him from above. Sparks flew as the swords clashed and Lawrence was forced onto his back. The man drew back to strike again but Lawrence lashed out, kicking him hard in the knee and the big man fell to one leg, grunting as he righted himself again but not giving Lawrence quite enough time to find his own feet. Henri screamed as she saw the man's massive arms raise his sword and realised that Lawrence would not have time to deflect it before it struck him down.

Suddenly the man froze, his sword arm still raised as the sound of a gunshot exploded around them. As if in slow motion the blade clattered to the ground as the man dropped like a stone and Henri looked around in bewilderment to see the giant figure of Mousy standing in the doorway.

Chapter 34

"Wherein the brethren are reunited."

"Henri!" Lawrence was beside her in an instant, hands checking her over, panic in his eyes.

"I'm alright," she gasped, clutching at his arms. "I'm not hurt." She shook him, discounting the pounding in her head as trivial because he was *bleeding!*

"It's not my blood," she said, trying to reassure him so that she could look at what was most certainly his blood dripping steadily down his arm. "I'm fine, but you're injured."

He waved away her concern and looked up at Mousy who was stepping over a dead body, one he'd apparently supplied, in the doorway.

"Are the others here? My brother ..."

Mousy nodded and dragged the body from the doorway, dumping it in the garden. "Ye brother should be fine. This bastard 'ere was on 'is way to 'elp 'is mates finish ye off," he said grinning. "And aye, Cap'n, the crew's 'ere, alrigh'. I sent 'em round the back to get the earl clear, they'll jus' be moppin' up by now."

Henri sighed and saw her relief reflected in Lawrence's eyes as he turned back to her. "My God, Henri, when I saw you ... I believe my heart stopped."

She looked up at him and smiled, obliging him with a kiss as he pulled her closer still. They both watched as Mousy strode past them and kicked the body of Brant.

"Bastard," the big man cursed. "I always hated that double-dealing rat." He turned to Lawrence. "A good day's work that was," he grinned, gesturing at the corpse.

"Aye," Lawrence remarked, nodding. "I only wish I could take credit for it. Henri killed him."

Mousy looked down at her, scepticism clear in his eyes and she shrugged. "It's true, though I demand that one of you teaches me to shoot properly. The recoil knocked me backwards."

"Well she did fire two at once," Lawrence said, laughing at the look in Mousy's eyes and the indignation in hers. "Oh, ow," he gasped, clutching at the wound in his side, though it seemed to do little to diminish his amusement.

"Oh, Lawrence," she scolded. "We must see to that at once." But Lawrence was frowning at Mousy.

"What the devil are you doing here anyway? I mean, not that I'm ungrateful you understand."

Mousy grinned at him and sat on the stairs. "Been followin' ye. The crew didn't take kindly to their Cap'n bein' taken from 'em see. So, we figured we'd see where ye was off to, an' ifin ye was handed to the militia we'd see if we could grab ye."

Henri laid a hand over Lawrence's. He had said nothing, but she could see he was deeply touched by the loyalty of his men.

"Brant said we had a rat," Lawrence said in the end, looking up at Mousy as though he wanted to be told it was a lie, but Mousy's face darkened and he nodded.

"When we got 'ere the men hung about in Bordeaux while me an' a couple of the lads came after ye' to get the lie of the land. By the time I got back to tell 'em ye were safe with ye brother ..." He stopped, rubbing his jaw with one meaty fist. "Jay was flashin' the cash about like a bleedin' fool. Never did 'ave a bit o' sense that one."

"Jay?" Lawrence repeated, sounding disbelieving. "He sold me out?"

Mousy looked sorrowful but nodded. "Aye, an' not for the first time I reckon."

"Where is he?" he demanded, fury in his voice but Mousy raised his hand, shaking his head.

"'E's been dealt with, Cap'n. the lads, well ... when they found out." He shrugged, and Lawrence nodded.

"I've never been so glad to see you in my life," Lawrence said, smiling at him.

"Nor I," Henri added. "It was the finest, most wonderful sight, seeing you standing in the doorway with that gun in your hand. I will never forget it, and I will never be able to thank you enough. You saved his life."

To Henri's surprise and delight Mousy blushed and stared at his feet, rubbing the back of his neck and looking uncomfortable.

Lawrence chuckled. "Well I might have been moved to jealousy by that," he observed, grinning at Henri. "If it wasn't for the fact I agreed with every word. I owe you a great debt, Mousy."

The big man shook his head. "Nah," he said, his voice firm. "That' ye don't an' ye know it. I've had a debt to pay, fer ... well fer gettin' ye into this all those years ago, but now, maybe we're even."

"More than," Lawrence said, nodding. He reached out to shake Mousy's hand but then their attention was taken by a commotion at the end of the corridor, and more of Lawrence's men, that Henri recognised from The Wicked Wench, piled in from the kitchens with Alex between them, his hands bound in front of him.

"What ye wantin' doin' with thisun, Mousy?" One of the men demanded. He was an inch or two shorter than Alex and built like a barrel, with thick, hairy arms covered in tattoos. He poked Alex with the nose of a musket as he spoke. "There's a number o' corpses out back an' matey 'ere didna want to come quiet like. The bastard laid Nibs out cold and I reckon 'e broke Sharkie's arm, not to mention nearly breakin' me bleedin' jaw."

Mousy's eyes went wide with alarm. "Plague seize ye, let 'im go! I tol' ye that the Cap'n's brother was there, ye blitherin' idiot. I swear, Harry, ye got no more brain than a sea turtle."

"Tha's the earl?" Harry said in disbelief and looking him over Henri could see it was hard to believe. She had always thought he had a devilish appearance, what with those cold, flint grey eyes, but now, with his shirt filthy and in tatters, and the beginnings of an impressive black eye beginning to bloom, he looked thoroughly disreputable. "'E don' fight like no gentlem'n," Harry added, sounding very doubtful.

"Thank you," Alex said to the man with a grave expression before raising an eyebrow at Lawrence in amusement, apparently quite unperturbed by being held at gunpoint by pirates.

"I am glad to see you in one piece," Alex said, and then frowned as he took in Lawrence's bloody appearance. "You *are* in one piece?" he added, with a touch of anxiety.

"I'm fine, nothing serious." Lawrence said, getting up and then sliding back to the floor as all the colour drained from his face.

"Bed!" Henri cried. "Now. This instant! Mousy, help me get him up will you."

She glanced at Lawrence and could almost see the lewd remark gathering on his tongue. Scowling, she wagged a finger at him. "Don't you dare," she muttered. "We're not married yet."

Lawrence chuckled and submitted with very bad grace to allow Mousy to help him up the stairs as Harry released the earl.

"Sorry, ye lordship," Harry said, looking sheepish. "I didn't knows ye was 'is brother, like."

"No hard feelings I assure you," Alex replied, clapping the man on the back and making him wince. "I apologise for hitting you into the rose bed, but I had no idea you were on our side."

Harry rubbed at his jaw and glowered a little at the memory. "I guess we're even then?" he said, sounding a little worried, clearly not trusting the nobility to let such a thing go without causing trouble. But Alex just grinned at him and nodded affably before his face became disgusted as he took in the bloody corpse at his feet.

"Time to clear out the rubbish, I think. Lend a hand, there's a good chap."

Henri swallowed, feeling faintly ill as they both grabbed hold of Brant's body. She looked away and left them to it, hurrying up the stairs to Lawrence.

"My Lady!" Came a shriek across the landing and Annie ran at her, smothering her in a rib-crushing hug. "Oh, Henrietta!" the maid squealed, the use of her full name illustrating Annie's state of distress as the maid cast an eye over her bloody clothes. Before Henri could reassure her as to the fact the blood wasn't her own, Annie seemed to notice something behind Henri, and with a theatrical moan she clapped her hand to her forehead, her eyes rolled up and she fainted clean away.

"Oh, Annie!" Henri exclaimed, exasperated and wanting nothing more than to go and care for Lawrence. She looked up as Mousy appeared beside her, staring at the rumpled heap of her maid on the floor of the landing.

"She alright?" he asked, frowning.

"Oh, yes, I think so," Henri replied, eyeing her maid with suspicion. "She's just fainted. Can you help me get her up?"

Mousy nodded and reached down, lifting Annie into his arms with little effort and surprising care. Henri directed him to Annie's room where he laid her on her bed and then hovered, looking at her anxiously as Annie gave a voluptuous sigh.

"Should someone stay an' ... look after 'er?" he asked, watching the reclining figure with concern in his eyes.

Henri smothered a smile and cursed Annie, the shameless hussy. "I believe she will be well enough. Perhaps you could send one of the women with some smelling salts to revive her."

Mousy nodded but looked a little crestfallen and she felt bad spoiling Annie's fun, so she added, "But I am sure she would be grateful to know how you helped her, if you would call upon her later perhaps, when she has recovered."

"Aye," Mousy, nodded, looking pleased. "Aye, I'll send one o' the lasses an' pop roun' later. Jus' to see she's well, like," he added with haste.

"I think she would be most grateful for your kind attentions, Mousy."

She smiled at him and ushered him out of the room as fast as she could. The moment he'd gone Annie made a miraculous recovery and gave her a devilish wink. Henri rolled her eyes and ran back to Lawrence, finding him sitting on the edge of the bed with his shirt off and wadded into a bundle at his side. He looked up at her with a wounded air.

"Well at last, you're lucky I didn't bleed out the time you've taken!"

"Oh, Lawrence!" she cried, mortified and running to sit beside him. "I'm so sorry, only Annie would go and faint and then Mousy came, and do you know, I think he has a tendre for her!"

"Mousy? For Annie?" Lawrence said in alarm. "Well, I'll be damned."

Henri frowned as she removed the bloody shirt and inspected his wound. "Well," she added, before she thought the comment through. "Annie was unconscious."

Lawrence snorted with amusement. "Well that explains a lot."

"Odious creature," she scolded, smothering a laugh as she reassured herself that the wound was neither too deep nor grave. "Oh, thank goodness. We should get a doctor to look at it but the bleeding seems to have stopped. How's your arm?"

"Damn my arm," he growled, and she looked up to see an altogether different light in his eyes. He pulled her to him and tumbled her onto the bed, kissing her with desperation, and she clung to him only too willingly until he pulled back and regarded her, his blue eyes troubled.

"You see what life with me will entail, Henri? I can never guarantee that this won't happen again. I will always be a target while the price on my head is waving over me like a damned red flag."

She nodded and put her hand to his cheek. "Yes, I know, darling, and that's why you really must teach me to shoot properly."

"Henri!" he exclaimed. "That should not have to be the answer to our problems. I don't want you to have to kill men on a regular basis! Though you do seem to have an aptitude for it," he added, with a rueful sigh.

She smiled up at him and then grew still as an idea began to form in her mind.

"Oh, Lord, what the devil is going on in that tangled brain of yours now?" he demanded.

Henri blinked up at him, all innocence, and pouted. "Well, really, Lawrence, I don't know what you mean."

"Yes, you do," he grumbled, shaking his head. "That look means trouble. I have no doubt in my mind that was the exact same expression you wore when you decided to head out into the night alone and blackmail a pirate!" She flushed a little and he nodded. "I thought so. What are you plotting now, madam?"

The Rogue

Huffing at him she rolled her eyes. "That particular scheme worked out rather well didn't it?" she asked, one eyebrow raised.

He snorted and leaned down to kiss her again. "Well," he murmured against her lips. "I guess you have me there."

She wriggled underneath him and giggled. "I believe I have you everywhere," she said, biting her lip as his hands began to explore.

"Now hold on," he said, stopping abruptly. "Stop trying to distract me. You are far too good at it. What are you scheming and tell me the truth, or I shan't kiss you." He sat up, albeit with a wince of pain, and then crossed his arms.

Henri sighed.

"That is indeed a threat to be taken seriously," she replied with a grave expression. "So, I shall have to tell you everything."

She looked down and realised with disgust she was still wearing the blood-soaked dress, so she stood and began to wriggle out of it, enjoying the warmth in her pirate's eyes as he followed her every move.

"Well, Lawrence," she continued as the filthy dress fell to the floor. "It was only that I was thinking about our situation, and as you say, the dilemma of the price on your head and really, I think it would be best for everyone if Captain Savage … was dead."

Chapter 35

"Wherein the past must be consigned to Davy Jones."

Henri looked around the barn which had been chosen for the scene of this debate and found it hard to believe her eyes. There were more than a hundred men crammed into the space which had seemed quite vast before all of them had arrived.

At first there had been a good deal of sizing up and suspicious looks between the two groups which comprised Lawrence's men of The Wicked Wench and Alex's crews of the three cutters which made regular runs between France and the Cornish coast. But both Alex and Lawrence had spent some time moving between the men, making introductions and sharing stories, and there seemed to be the beginnings of an accord between them.

Henri had laughed when she had heard the names of the cutters, which were Bold Bessie, Jenny's Prize and The Flighty Susan. The names had bemused her rather and she wondered why the men insisted on calling their ships after women of questionable morals. She posed this query to Lawrence who chuckled and squeezed her waist.

"Because their wicked wiles cause us to stray into the dark, but even though they lead us into trouble and storms ... we love them just the same."

She snorted and rolled her eyes before frowning at Alex who had been listening in and nodding in accord.

"And what about The Revenge, sir, how do you account for that?"

Alex pursed his lips before answering. "I decided the men who forced the people of our coastline to break the laws by allowing them to starve were guilty for the death of my brother," he said. "And though the smaller ships are the ones who run between France and Cornwall, it is The Revenge who covers their tracks. My high-profile merchant trade takes the eyes of the militia from the smaller ships and holds their attention by sailing at times and with the kind of cargo that will help keep those men occupied. And as I am rather heavily involved with the militia myself," he added with a smug grin at Lawrence's scandalised expression. "I have rather a lot of inside knowledge as to who and what they suspect, and where exactly they will be searching for it."

"My God," Lawrence said, shaking his head, and Henri wasn't sure if it was admiration or despair at his brother's antics that shone in his eyes. "And they call me The Rogue."

"Ah, yes," Alex said with a characteristically cool smile. "But they call me *Le Loup de Mer.*"

Henri gasped and looked at him with astonishment. "You're the Sea Wolf?"

"Guilty as charged, Miss Morton," he replied with an amused glint in his eyes.

"Goodness, how stupid of me not to have realised. Why, my Lord Falmouth, you are famous," she said, wondering just what kind of future awaited her with a pirate for a husband and a brother-in-law who was a notorious smuggler.

Alex looked at Lawrence and shrugged, giving him a wry smile. "Yes, which is not always a good thing as we are discovering."

"Well we can't drown both of you at once!" Henri said, suddenly feeling rather flustered.

"Now, wait a moment, I still haven't agreed to this," Lawrence put in and Henri turned to scowl at him.

"Oh, Lawrence," she raged, fury boiling at her plan being pushed aside after rowing over it all the previous day. She raised her voice at him louder than she would usually have done in company. "You know it's the only way, Savage has to die so that you can come back and live! Don't you dare back out now, or I shall have something to say on the matter!"

She saw some of the men around them look to their captain as he was berated by the young woman who they had no doubt dismissed as a timid little thing up until that moment.

Lawrence held up his hands to her. "I didn't say that, love," he replied, shaking his head. "I don't disagree with you, it's only ..." He sighed and folded his arms looking mutinous. "I won't sink my ship."

Henri folded her arms in return, glaring at him. "You would choose your ship over me?" she demanded, a dangerous note in her voice she knew he couldn't possibly miss. Damn the man, he had better make the right decision here or she might shoot him herself.

Lawrence opened his mouth and then seemed to think better of it. He sighed and scowled at her. "Damn it, Henri," he began only to pause as Mousy stepped up to them.

"Beggin' ye pardon, Cap'n, Miss Morton." He nodded to Henri who smiled back at him. "But I couldn't help but overhear, an' well, his lordship ran me through the plan an' ..." He glanced at Henri, an anxious look in his eyes. "Well, miss, it's jus'. It don' sit right, scuttling a fine ship like The Wench."

Henri groaned and rolled her eyes at him and Mousy hurried on.

"But ... I think maybe I've an idea, how we migh' make people believe she's sunk an' the Cap'n drown'd but ... manage to keep 'er. I mean with a bit o' work an' a new name, no one w'uld be any the wiser."

Lawrence looked at Mousy with real affection. "My man, I am all ears, let's have it!"

Mousy grinned, looking pleased and Henri sighed and nodded. "Very well, let us hear your plan and see if we can't save his beloved ship."

Lawrence beamed at her and she smiled, shaking her head as he pulled her to him for a kiss.

***

By the time the plan had been thrashed out and all aspects of it considered, the men had other concerns, as Lawrence had known they would.

Harry was the first to step forward, carrying the word of some of his shipmates to their captain.

"Thing is, sir, some of us ain't as young as we once were, an' ye know the life we 'ad, well it's over to be blunt, an' some of us ..." He twisted his hat in his hands, frowning and clearly trying to find the right words, so Lawrence decided to help him out.

"You wish to retire, Harry?"

Harry sighed and nodded. "That be the long an' the short of it, aye. I mean I must work but ... I ain't got the heart for piracy no more, the fun's gone out o' it."

Lawrence looked to his brother and grinned. "Harry, I think you might want to listen to what his lordship has to say."

Harry looked at Alex who nodded and got to his feet.

"Gentlemen, I am very honoured to make your acquaintance. As you now know, I am Lawrence's brother, Alex Sinclair, the Earl of Falmouth. I am also a great believer in helping those who help themselves." His usually severe countenance showed a glimmer of humour as a chuckle rumbled around the room "It is possible you may have also figured out my other identity, or have heard tales of myself and my men ..."

"Aye, The Sea Wolf could take on The Rogue, I reckon," yelled one bright spark who was drowned out in a wave of indignation from the crew of The Wicked Wench while the cutter's men laughed and roared their approval.

Alex waited until everyone had quietened down once more.

"I would rather prefer it if we could work together this time. Killing each other really doesn't suit our purposes." He looked at his brother with a sardonic lift of one eyebrow and then turned to the crew of The Wench. "These are the crews of the Bold Bessie, Jenny's Prize and The Flighty Susan."

Those men who hadn't yet become acquainted moved around shaking hands and nodding, a little stiff and formal for the moment, but there was a good-natured air to the greetings that boded well for future relations.

"Now then," Alex continued, once the noise had died down. "As we are all aware, we are here to arrange for that fine fellow, The Rogue." He gestured to Lawrence who grinned and stood, making a leg and giving a sweeping bow that made him wince a little and clutch at his side as his men roared and cheered. "That is to say our good Captain Savage," Alex continued. "Is to be consigned to end his days with Davy Jones."

The cheers turned to boos and noises of disgust, though it was a good-hearted sound, full of regret rather than anger. "However, this means a great many fine and skilful men, out of a job. Which is something we simply cannot allow to happen. So ..."

Alex gave them a fierce and calculating look and Lawrence couldn't help but laugh. He wondered what their ancestors had been, Vikings perhaps, raiding and pillaging along the coast of England who had finally made their homes in the rugged land that was Cornwall. There had to be something of that nature in their blood as the piratical gleam in Alex's eyes was only too familiar.

"So," Alex continued. "I have work for those of you who would continue your trade, but this time free running, that is to say, smuggling contraband between here and Cornwall. I needn't tell you that this is dangerous work, the excise men are becoming ever

The Rogue

more resourceful and with the recent creation of the Preventative Water Guard, bringing the run home is harder than ever. It takes courage and skill and a great deal of cunning, so if any of you are interested, come and speak with me and my crews and we will see what can be done.

I know that Lawrence trusts each and every one of you with his life, and you have repaid that trust in being here today. For that you have my everlasting gratitude and I am happy to join my own fate with yours, and trust in you as he has done."

There was a cheer and a chorus of shouts of approval and Alex raised his hand for silence.

"However, for those of you who have a desire to keep your feet dry, I would also ask if you would stay with us. As you have seen our lives are dangerous ones and we need to take precautions to protect the ones we love and our livelihoods."

Alex glanced over at Lawrence who pulled Henri closer to him and planted a kiss upon the top of her head. He watched as the men around him nodded and murmured their approval, and saw Mousy cast an enquiring look towards Annie, who winked at him in return.

"That being the case we wish to create a guard to watch over us, both here at Longueville and at home at Tregothnan. In short, any man that wishes to remain with us will be found work to please him, we will consider each other as brothers, as the brethren of old, with a code of honour and friends who will always have our backs."

Lawrence stood and walked to stand beside his brother and addressed the men himself.

"Well, my old friends and comrades, we begin a new chapter, and any who choose to go their own way will always be welcome to return to us if life does not treat them kindly." He paused and reached for the bottle which Mousy held out to him with a grin.

"For whether we be rogue or wolf, pirate or smuggler, we are brothers, brethren and we look to the future."

He raised the bottle in a toast, and the men roared their approval.

Chapter 36

"Wherein the stage is set upon a sparkling sea, and the players take their places."

Henri walked beside her father and gathered the shawl a little closer about her shoulders. She was glad of her new *redingote a la hussard* as the heavy red velvet was certainly warm which was definitely a good thing today. There was a breathtaking view across the Cornish coast from here. All spread out before them, the sea glittered a bright blue against a cobalt sky, and a chill wind snapped at her skirts as they walked the rugged coastline.

The crash of the waves raged far below them as the icy water threw itself against the grey rocks, and the gulls wheeled far above, their raucous cries piercing through the sound of the sea roaring and the gusting winds. Her father shivered and looked at her in bewilderment as Henri suppressed a smile.

Never one to exert himself at the best of times, her father was rarely up before noon and certainly not up to anything further than tea, toast and perhaps a little undemanding conversation before late in the afternoon.

At least, she thought with satisfaction, he looked a little less shabby genteel now his debts had been cleared and he had money to buy some new clothes. She just prayed his promise to curtail his excesses would hold, at least for a while. Although she loved him dearly, she had no illusions about her only parent. He was a weak man and a selfish one, though he would never for one moment do anything to purposely make his daughter unhappy, she had come to realise he would do little to go out of his way to make her life easier.

In accepting this fact, she had resolved to feel no guilt for the use to which she was about to put him. It had in fact, taken all of hers and Annie's negotiating skills to winkle him out of the house and persuade him to take a walk with them - as it was such a very fine day.

They looked out to sea and Henri's heart began to thud. *Please God, please let everything go as it should.* She shared a glance with Annie and knew the woman was echoing her own thoughts.

"Look, papa," she said, pointing out to sea. "There's the earl's ship, The Revenge, he's due home today I believe."

Her father squinted out towards the horizon, his once deep brown eyes rather myopic and faded. "Is it, my dear? My eyes aren't what they once were you know."

"Oh yes, I'm quite sure, oh and look, here comes Lieutenant Bowcher." She tried her best to look surprised and smiled with a warm expression at the young man whom Alex had made a point of introducing her to, as he marched with his company of men towards them.

"Good afternoon, Lieutenant, a very fine day isn't it? Are you enjoying some fresh air?" she enquired, looking at the man and his assembled militia with as much innocence as she could muster when her heart was beating in her throat. She clutched her father's arm a little tighter, hoping any trembling would be put down to the icy wind whipping around them.

"No, Miss Morton, I should say not," the Lieutenant replied with a grave expression, not stopping to speak with her. "We've had a report, a sighting of The Wicked Wench at anchor. I've sent word to the Water Guard but we're off to check the coastline, see if they're bringing cargo in."

"Oh, The Wicked Wench, is that not Captain Savage's ship?" she asked.

But they were already marching away, and without another word the men strode past them, their excitement palpable.

"Good Lord," her father said, watching them go and then pausing as he was about to turn back as one of the men shouted and pointed out to sea.

"What is it?" Henri called out as the Lieutenant retraced his steps with clear disappointment.

"He's getting away," he cursed. "Someone must have warned him off!" And then he grew quiet as he watched the scene play out in front of him. "The earl's got a score to settle though," he said, brightening considerably as he saw The Revenge as she turned and set off in pursuit of the Wench. "After the devil got away from him in Bordeaux." He looked at Henri, his eyes alight with interest. "Is it true, Savage's men attacked the earl's house over there, to get their captain back?"

Henri nodded, her expression one of alarm and she clutched her throat to add to the drama, though the true memory of that day made it all too easy to play along.

"Yes, indeed. The earl fought valiantly by all accounts, with his brother Lawrence, but the Rogue had too many men and they got away, though they left many of their own dead there due to the Sinclair's efforts," she added, not having to embellish the pride she found in her voice.

"Well, every dog has his day," the Lieutenant said, turning to grin at her. "Look, The Revenge is gaining."

Henri hardly dared breathe as Annie grasped her hand and they watched The Wicked Wench disappear from view as it rounded the sharp outcrop of rock that was a natural feature of this rugged coastline. The Revenge was hot in pursuit and just as it too began to disappear, the almighty blast of cannon fire reverberated around the rocky cliffs. There was return fire and the guns boomed again. And then all was silent.

The Militia men whooped and began to run, but Henri knew by the time they had crossed the distant fields between here and the far shore and arrived down by the rocks, all they would find would be enough debris of a sunken ship. Just enough to clarify that The Wicked Wench was gone. It would appear to have been blown out of the water and sunk with all hands on deck. There would be enough barrels of fine French brandy washed ashore to make sure the militia were too busy fending off the locals to go looking too closely at the remains of what wasn't actually a Brigantine at all, but another smaller ship, rigged with enough explosive to spread its debris far and wide. The ruse would be clear enough if anyone took the trouble to investigate. Henri prayed they wouldn't.

Meanwhile the Wench slipped away, to a remote little cove to be reworked and reborn once again as The Redemption, a name that had seemed appropriate to Lawrence.

Henri walked with her father and Annie, back along the cliff, praying that all had gone just as it should, and that Lawrence and his men were free to start afresh. And so, the two women hastened their steps and chivvied along Lord Morton who was all excitement over the battle he had just witnessed. He was hard pressed to be swayed from his plan to follow in the militia's footsteps and see the wreck of The Wicked Wench going down.

By the time they reached the high-street, the village was abuzz about the death of The Rogue, thanks to the testimony from the men of the Flighty Susan, who just happened to be in a position to watch what had really happened and to ensure no one else could get close enough to call them liars.

Lord Morton quickly became something of a celebrity. Besides the militia who were still trying to wrestle barrels of brandy from the beach more quickly than the villagers could spirit them away, he was the only man to have seen the actual conflict. Something with which he was most helpful, embellishing with a little more colour than there had actually been to include seeing The Wench suffer and split apart under the weight of the bombardment that proved so fatal.

"Why, yes," he said for the twentieth time, as yet another man demanded if he'd really seen The Wicked Wench meet her end.

The Rogue

Henri laughed inwardly and shook her head as her father puffed himself up a little, smoothing one manicured white hand over the thick silk of his new embroidered waistcoat.

"Yes indeed, the earl got his man, blew the devil to pieces, what," he replied his eyes glittering with enjoyment at his new celebrity and brightening yet further as an attractive lady of a certain age, regarded him with interest.

When Alex finally set foot on land again, he was hailed a hero, along with his crew - who happened to be those men who usually served on the other two cutters. Henri and Annie watched with amusement as he was carried into the local tavern to be toasted with enthusiasm, by both those who thought he'd finished off The Rogue and The Wicked Wench, and those who knew that he had saved them.

As his retinue were so forceful in their desire to celebrate, Alex was unable to come and talk to them as he was borne away, but to Henri's relief he simply nodded to them in his cool way that all was well. With a sigh of relief, she felt she was finally able to breathe again. Lawrence was safe, and he would be back home again soon.

A special licence had been obtained - again - and they would be married and would return to Longueville to start a new life. This had inevitably set tongues wagging as Miss Morton was marrying a different brother. To hers and Lawrence's horror, they discovered that Alex had concocted some story to his own detriment to make it clear why an innocent young miss like Henri could never countenance such a wicked rake as her husband.

The fact that Alex was rather brazen in admitting to her that the story he'd spread was entirely true, so she had no right nor need to trouble him with a fit of the vapours, did little to alleviate her guilt. Lawrence was naturally furious, and Henri had been forced to intervene to calm things down, a role she suspected might become familiar.

The story did, however, serve the dual purpose of shining a very respectable light on Lawrence who had stepped into the breach and done the honourable thing. So once again, to Lawrence's chagrin, Alex had saved his younger sibling, and cast himself as the villain to do it. Henri was beginning to see, as Lawrence had predicted, just what kind of man Alex really was despite his rather forbidding and high-handed manner.

Chapter 37

"Wherein knots are tied, to everyone's satisfaction."

"What do you think?" Henri turned and looked at Annie. Her own nerves were all a flutter, dancing between excitement and anxiety but the teary fondness in her maid's expression put her mind at rest.

"Oh, ye do look a picture," Annie said, clutching a lacy hanky and sniffing. "I'm so proud of ye, Henri. T'is like yer my own girl."

"Oh, Annie." Henri ran to her and hugged her tight. "And are you sure you don't mind coming to France with us? I know it will be all new and strange, and there is the language to deal with but ... oh, dear, I don't think I can do it without you."

Annie yelped and waved her hanky. "Oh, stop, miss, ye'll 'ave me bawlin' if ye carry on. Course I'm goin' with ye. Keep me away - see if you can!" she said, dabbing at her eyes. "Besides," she added with a sly grin and a wink. "Mousy's goin' too."

Henri grinned as Annie laughed and did a comical little dance on the spot. "Oh, did he kiss you yet, Annie?"

Annie halted her little celebration and huffed with annoyance, shaking her head. "No! The great lummox is shy," she said, throwing her hands in the air. "But don't ye worry, I intend to take matter into me own 'ands tonight."

Giggling, Henri couldn't but help feel a little sorry for Mousy, who had no idea what he was in for. "What are you going to do?" she asked, wide-eyed.

Annie pursed her lips and then shook her head. "Ye not be married yet, lass. I'll tell ye in a week or two." And with another wink and a naughty smile on her lips, Annie went to fetch her veil.

Henri turned back to her reflection and sighed. She felt quite perfectly, deliriously happy. Smoothing down the heavy, dove grey satin, she turned this way and that. It was embroidered around the hem, the bodice and the cuffs with a flowery motif in silver thread that caught the light as she turned.

"E'll be struck dumb, ye look such a beauty," Annie said, smiling at her and pinning the fine lace veil in place. She took Henri's hand and gave it a squeeze. "Come on then, my little duck, best go an' marry that pirate, eh?"

***

In a beautiful little village, lost in the trees between the rivers Truro and Fal and at the gates of the vast Tregothnan estate, stood the ancient thirteenth century church of St Mawgan. And by the time Henri walked towards it on her father's arm she could hardly breathe, such was her excitement. Though she was not alone in this as she looked upon the people of the village who lined the streets now, smiling at her broadly and offering encouraging words, some of which might have put her to the blush if she hadn't heard far worse from Annie.

The wedding was to be a small affair, but because of the story put about by Alex, one that fascinated the locals.

The story of his Lordship's brother being found alive and well, after being captured by the French and losing his memory as a result of his injuries, was one that had been taken up, told, retold and embellished. This had been achieved with a little help from those of the brethren that had lived here all their lives, and some of the recent incomers who had decided to settle and find work on his lordship's estate.

Henri knew Lawrence had found his warm welcome hard to bear, knowing the truth of his history, but Alex had been steadfast in insisting this was how it must be done. The idea that the reward money that Alex had received upon bringing the Rogue to justice would be used to do good and help those families who needed it most was the only thing that had eased his conscience enough to allow him to show his face about before the wedding.

Indeed, Lawrence was not the only one with a guilty conscience. Upon returning home, Henri had begun to see she had wilfully believed much ill of the Earl of Falmouth, when indeed the poorest of the parish held him in the highest esteem. His womanising and rakish reputation may forever bar him from such hallowed ground as Almack's and make him a man mothers warned their daughters of, but it was of little interest to the parish. The good he did for those who had nothing, the endeavours he made to improve the life of those on his estate and beyond, all spoke far more of the man than any idle gossip in their eyes, which was how it ought to be.

Her father paused as they reached the little gates that led through the graveyard and onto the lovely old church.

"You're quite sure about this, my dear?"

For the first time since this affair began Henri detected the faintest glimmer of doubt in Lord Morton's eyes. Her father was still perplexed by everything that had gone on, but not being one to think on things too deeply if they did not concern his own comfort, he had accepted Henri's glib explanation of her rescue from the devilish Rogue by her then fiancé.

He had also taken to heart everyone's delight in her marrying said fiancé's younger brother with a benign, if slightly puzzled countenance. Happily, her father was not to be swayed against the earl, despite the tales of debauchery and vice that he'd heard had been the reason for Henri not wedding him.

With amusement Henri discovered that he had indeed been well aware of the earl's tarnished reputation, the stories of the man's many mistresses and scandalous love affairs being well known to him. On asking, out of curiosity, if he had been at all concerned about marrying her to such a man her father had simply looked puzzled.

"But he's an earl, my dear," was all the reply she was given, as if this would excuse the devil himself from any wrongdoing.

As far as her father was concerned, the earl had returned his daughter to him, and paid off all his debts and so could do no wrong. In her less charitable moments Henri wondered which one of those facts tilted the scales furthest in the earl's favour.

The tale of her abduction had thankfully been kept quiet and now no one else was any the wiser of anything but the fact that she was now marrying the earl's younger brother, rather than the earl.

Henri patted her father's hand and gave him a reassuring smile which quite chased away any inconvenient paternal concern he might belatedly be assailed by.

"Quite sure, papa," she said, replying to her father's question. "I do love him you see."

Her father sighed and smiled, quite happy to see his daughter wed a man she truly loved, especially as the earl had been so very generous as to keep to their original agreement and still pay him a generous stipend. Though when her father had remarked that it *"should keep the wolf from the door,"* he had been puzzled as to why Henri and Annie had been taken by a fit of hysteria and had been forced to leave the room and take some air before they could calm themselves.

Tales of the *Loup de Mer* were widespread, though, and despite their best efforts, he seemed to evade the militia's attempts to entrap him at every turn.

Henri entered the church and felt her heart lift as she looked to see Lawrence standing waiting for her. His eyes widened on seeing her, his expression one that made her heart swell, and then he smiled that charismatic, slightly piratical smile that made that excitable organ beat frenetically and Henri wanted to run, rather than walk demurely down the aisle towards him.

"Ready?" her father asked, smiling at her fondly.

"Yes. Absolutely, completely and without a doubt in my mind," she said, beaming in return and walking to stand beside the gorgeous figure of the man about to become her husband.

Any doubts she may have harboured, that Lawrence had wanted to stay simply to reclaim his old life, rather than for her, were forever dispelled by the look in his eyes as she came to stand next to him. The blue eyes were alight, dancing merrily with such love and happiness she felt a lump in her throat. Thank God, she thought, for that chance encounter, for the loss of a letter, and her foolish decision to blackmail The Rogue.

***

Lawrence looked about the room and couldn't help but smile. It was perhaps a rather unconventional wedding breakfast, but then the earl had long since been considered a rather wild and eccentric figure, so it was not so very extraordinary that his younger brother should likewise buck convention. He had to admit that some of the guests were a rum looking lot, and he noted with amusement the rather anxious and scandalised looks being cast by their disapproving Aunt Seymour and bewildered Aunt Dotty, as some of the more boisterous guests made their way through the Champagne.

He had expected to feel at least a slight sense of regret for the loss of his freedom but whenever he looked upon the dazzling face of his new wife, all he could feel was wonder. That life had somehow contrived to give him a second chance was beyond anything he had ever dared to hope for, and that he would be given that chance with Henri beside him made his chest grow tight with unexpected emotion.

In fact, he seemed quite unable to remove the ridiculous smile that had been on his face since the moment he'd laid eyes on the vision of his bride to be as she entered the church and had stolen his breath. So, he simply watched as his beautiful wife laughed and spoke animatedly with everyone around them and tried hard to rein in his impatient desire to grab her by the hand and get to what he considered the most important part of the wedding. Her dress might be lovely, and her hair exquisitely coiffed, but all he wanted was to divest her of every stitch with all haste and have her hair spilling freely over the pillows in a delightful disarray.

He was forced to put such happy thoughts aside for a moment, however, as his brother walked over to sit beside him.

"Congratulations," he said, a slight smile twisting his mouth as he raised his Champagne glass.

"Thank you, I feel quite worthy of such congratulations on behalf of my wife," he said. "Though I am sure I deserve none of it, I intend to take it all and enjoy it to the hilt."

"Spoken like a true Sinclair," Alex murmured sitting down beside him, his usually cold eyes alight with amusement.

"And what about you, Alex? I have stolen your intended it seems, so now you must be back on the market."

Alex raised one haughty eyebrow, looking faintly disgusted. "I was prepared to do my duty to continue the family name, but now ..." He raised his glass once more in a toast. "You have my blessing to take up that particular challenge as I feel no such urgency or desire to relinquish my freedom."

Lawrence frowned at him and wondered what Alex's life was really like. Was there truly no one he cared to share it with? Alex caught his expression and gave him a hard look in return.

"Don't you dare go getting any appalling notions about seeing me settling down. I am beyond happy to see you and Henri so well matched and content with each other, but I beg you to leave my own affairs well alone. I'd go as far to agree that your wife is a rather unique young lady and you are a lucky man but follow in your footsteps I will not." This last was said with no little force and

Lawrence knew he would be compelled to let the matter alone, but not until he'd added one last word.

Lawrence found himself seeking out his bride once more and knew his eyes gave him away. "Yes, I am a lucky man," he said, his voice quiet. "Which is why I would see you happy too, surely there is someone ..."

Alex cut him off sounding bored beyond belief. "Really, Lawrence, who do you think I could trust with the life I live? Any wife would be bound to discover what I was involved with eventually and I could never reveal it to someone I didn't fully trust. Besides that, the idea of having to forever explain myself to a woman or be forced to consider her comfort ..." He shook his head in apparent disgust at the idea. "No. I am quite content I assure you. I have enough willing bed warmers to keep me occupied, a full and busy life with my legitimate affairs, and adventure enough for any man with my less lawful endeavours." He patted his brother's shoulder with affection and got to his feet, effectively curtailing the conversation. "And now I would strongly suggest you stop meddling in my affairs and look to your own!"

Lawrence laughed and nodded. "I find I have no argument with that idea," he said, and went off in search of his wife.

***

Henri sighed with content and turned on her side to consider her sleeping husband. They had been married almost two weeks, and she still could not quite believe it had happened at all. It was such a short time ago she had been standing in the little haberdasher's shop with her heart in her throat as she gazed upon the dashing and rather terrifying figure of a pirate with bright blue eyes.

She reached over and pushed a lock of hair from his forehead, admiring the strong jaw line, and still a little regretful at the loss of his gold earrings. Last night, however, when she had complained about their absence, he had promised to wear them for her when they were alone, an idea which made her smile.

Henri trailed her fingers down a muscular arm and then pushed the covers back further to admire him as a whole. It was morning, and there was just enough light creeping around the curtains to allow her to enjoy the view. The new scar on his side was still pink and fresh but was healing well, and the older wounds did nothing to mar his perfection in her eyes. Broad shoulders and chest, with just a scattering of dark hair that led her fingers down a taut stomach to narrow hips and heavy thighs, and signs that her husband was possibly not as sleepy as he was making out.

Her smile widened and she trailed a finger over the hard length of him, biting her lip to stop herself laughing as goose bumps shivered over his skin. With a lazy and barely there touch, she continued, stroking one finger back and forth until there was a plaintive huff.

"Henri, it's cruel to tease."

Chuckling she bent her head and continued to tease him nonetheless, this time with her tongue, until he was writhing beneath her and cursing.

"Keep still," she scolded, trying to sound cross.

"I'm going to make you sorry for this," he growled, and she looked up to see his blue eyes gleaming with a wicked light that promised to make good on that threat.

"I should think so," she said, one eyebrow arched, before she returned to her work.

With diligent practise she had come to discover exactly what it was that made her pirate groan and buck his hips and she was only too willing to indulge him, finding her own pleasure in the harsh sounds of his breathing and the soft curses as she worked with mouth and tongue against his most sensitive flesh. But the sweet torment had clearly gone as far as he would allow and the next

The Rogue

moment, she found herself flipped onto her back and restrained against the mattress.

"And here I was," he said, his voice low and intimate. "Believing I had married such a sweet, warm-hearted creature, and now ..." He moved against her, sliding himself between her legs and making her gasp with pleasure. "And now I discover that she's a wicked temptress, determined to drive her poor husband out of his mind."

"Oh dear," she sighed, blinking up at him with as innocent an expression as could be found in the circumstances. "I suppose you will have to punish me, now that you've discovered my evil intent."

He nodded, his expression grave. "I am sorry to inform you, madam, that you will not be leaving this bed until I am satisfied that you are properly contrite."

Henri bit her lip. "That might take some time," she said, once she felt able to contain her laughter, though her voice still trembled with it.

She looked up to find her husband grinning at her. "I'm counting on it," he said, before joining them together with a sigh of pleasure.

Henri gasped and wound herself around him, sinking her hands into this thick hair, pulling his head down for a kiss.

"You may call your ship The Redemption," she said, laughing. "But you don't fool me, you're an irredeemable rogue!"

"Aye," he chuckled, biting her lip lightly and kissing her again, before adding with a smirk. "But I'm your rogue."

Enjoyed Lars' story? Keep reading to discover a sneak peek of Alex's!

The Earl's Temptation

Rogues & Gentlemen Book 2

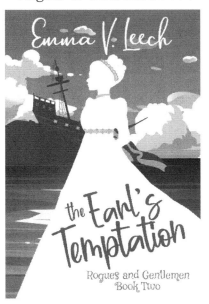

Alexander Sinclair, the Fourth Earl of Falmouth, has a reputation for revelling in vice. But his taste for wine, women and dice is only a fraction of the dangerous truth, for the earl is the force behind a powerful gang, smuggling contraband between France and Cornwall.

Never afraid to get his hands dirty and with an abiding love of living recklessly, Alex leads many of these runs himself, until one fateful night when the Revenue appear. Forced to sail into a violent storm, the ship is lost and Alex is washed ashore, barely alive, close to the French port of Roscoff.

Innocent beauty, Célestine Lavelle, has lost everything. The daughter of a noble French family forced to flee during the Revolution, she has been forced to work in the kitchens of the local whore house, where her future is shrouded in sin. Desperate and completely alone, the discovery of a half drowned English smuggler on the shore will lead her heart in directions she never dreamed of.

Determined to save his beguiling rescuer, Alex plans that her future should be full of everything that is good and honourable, but will the temptation to take her as his own be too hard to resist?

Read for free on Kindle Unlimited:

The Earl's Temptation

The Earl's Temptation

And on that cheek, and o'er that brow,
So soft, so calm, yet eloquent,
The smiles that win, the tints that glow,
But tell of days in goodness spent,
A mind at peace with all below,
A heart whose love is innocent!

She Walks in Beauty by Lord Byron.

Prologue

Roscoff. France. July. 1814

The old woman shifted her bird-frail bones on the thin pallet and coughed. The movement racked her fragile body, leaving her gasping and clutching at the ragged blanket that covered her. Her young charge ran to her and clutched at her hand, all wide blue eyes and desperation.

Old age was a curse and a blessing. Dying and leaving this God-forsaken place was no hardship, but leaving Céleste was hard indeed. The poor, sweet child. With both her parents gone, she had no one now and not a penny to her name. The last real money they'd had was spent years ago, on bribing the priest into giving her *Maman* a proper burial despite the fact she'd committed suicide. Since then their existence had consisted of grasping at life with frantic fingers, taking in washing and mending; the girl had even been driven to steal on occasion though the risks were dreadfully high. Marie knew her own bones would be consigned to a pauper's grave but couldn't find the will to care about that. Her worries were over, but Céleste ... God alone knew how she would survive.

"Now, Céleste, go to the chest over there, quickly," she rasped, her voice barely audible, her skeletal fingers pointing towards the girl's only hope. "There are papers. Get them out."

She watched the young woman move and wished, as she had wished every day since they had fled their old lives, that things had been different. The Revolution had changed many things. Supposedly it would bring a better life to the poor and the needy, though she had seen little sign of it yet, with the wars that had followed on its heels. A new world born of such bloodshed ... how could that ever be justified? And Napoleon seemed just as grasping and power hungry as any monarch had ever been.

"These, Marie?" The girl held up a thick roll of parchment and the old woman nodded. Céleste ran back to sit beside her, the papers clutched in her hand.

Marie reached out and touched the perfect face with a bony finger, the calloused and ugly digit looking obscene beside her sweet countenance. "The picture of your mother, such beauty." The words were not happy ones, though, for she well knew the kind of attentions the girl already attracted, a situation that would only get worse. She was eighteen now, almost nineteen, and did all she could to hide the gifts she'd been given, tucking her long hair under an ugly cap and wearing shapeless garments many sizes too big. But nothing could disguise those wide blue eyes framed with thick dark lashes, the porcelain skin, or the perfect bow of her pink lips.

"These papers," Marie said, dragging her tired mind back to the important matter she must deal with. "These you must guard and keep hidden until such time as you find someone you can trust, someone who can help you regain all you've lost."

Céleste shook her head and Marie felt a surge of anger. *"Oui!* You must and you will regain it. It is your duty, it belongs to you. You are Célestine de Lavelle, *La Comtesse de Valrey*. You are the last of your line. The title goes to you from your mother, and from her mother before her. You must ... *you must ...*" The old woman bent over as a cough shook her bones and chased away any remaining strength she had. "Promise me, Céleste," she whispered.

The girl looked up at her, eyes full of sorrow and fear, but she nodded. *"Je promets,"* she whispered and Marie sighed and laid her head down. She had done all she could, her time was up, and now the fates would take the girl where they would. She prayed they would be kind.

Chapter 1

"Wherein things go awry and the fates get tangled."

Just off the coast of Cornwall. 25 February. 1815

Alex Sinclair, fourth Earl of Falmouth, regarded his men with satisfaction. It had been another good night's work and once the last of the cargo was away, they could breathe again.

"Well, Mousy, how are you enjoying your first run?" he demanded of the big man as he shouldered a massive barrel of the finest French brandy onto the small boat drawn up beside the larger hulk of The Bold Bessie. An Earl he may be, but he got his hands just as dirty as the rest of the men.

"I liked it fine, m'lord," Mousy replied with a grin, reaching up to take the barrel from him. "'Specially as it kept me out o' harm's way for a day or two."

"You can't hide from her forever," Alex said, not bothering to hide his grin. "She's going to want you to ask her on your return."

Mousy went quiet and looked a little queasy. "Aye, well. Maybe I'll jus' lie low for a day or two. 'Till it blows over. "

Alex chuckled. His sister-in-law's maid, Annie, had set her eyes firmly on Mousy and had made no secret of the fact she wanted them to get married. She was a formidable woman and Alex very much doubted the likelihood of the situation *blowing over*. She expected Mousy to return with a ring and a question for her and heaven help the poor blighter if he didn't.

"Right, thisun' is full, 'ow much left?"

Alex turned to regard the remaining haul. Boxes of tea and bolts of the finest French silk, all wrapped in oil cloth to protect them from the elements and the salt spray, and over a dozen or more half anker tubs of brandy remained. Alex could see the beach in the moonlight, a hive of activity with maybe two hundred tubmen running back and forth with barrels on a harness over their shoulders, loading the ponies and getting the shore cleared as fast as they may. The crew of his brother Lawrence's old ship, The Wicked Wench, had switched from pirates to smugglers like the proverbial ducks to water the moment Lawrence had given up his dangerous lifestyle. The extra hands that had come Alex's way made light work of the offloading. Mousy had stood as spotsman, guiding the ship to its location from a signal offshore to one of various landing points. The more hard-headed and ruthless volunteered as batmen and patrolled the cliffs, eyes on alert for the Revenue.

"One more and we're done."

"Righty' ho." Mousy nodded and then looked up, frowning. "Wha's ..."

He didn't have time to finish the question as the boom of canon fire exploded overhead and shouts bellowed from all round the beach as the men saw the boat approaching.

"Hell and damnation!" Alex cursed, untying the line. "The Revenue are upon us, lads, get moving!"

All hell broke loose as he pushed the small boat with Mousy in away from his ship, The Bold Bessie, with force. "Get back to shore, get everyone safe away," he yelled.

"You'd bes' come n' all, ye Lordship," Mousy exclaimed as Alex shook his head.

"No, I stay with Bessie, get away ... *now!*"

The sails unfurled with a snap as the wind caught the single-masted cutter, pulling them away from shore. In the distance Alex could see the men scurrying back and forth but the Revenue were not on the beach at least. The greater part of the cargo had been unloaded, now all that mattered was getting free. He looked up at the skies, frowning as the moon disappeared. Disappearing in the dark was not a bad thing with Water Guard sticking to his arse like a burr, but the approaching storm would do nobody any good. He prayed that they'd ride it out.

"What now?" called his man from the helm and then threw himself to the deck as cannon shot screamed overhead.

Alex flinched as the cannon overshot and hit the waves on his far side, dousing him with icy water. "Back to Roscoff," he yelled, his face grim as thunder cracked overhead. "And pray we make it."

***

Céleste reached down and grabbed another piece of driftwood, barely feeling the smooth, worn surface between her numb fingers. *Merde* but it was cold. Mimi wandered behind her, humming a little tune that had begun to irritate her over an hour ago. Barely more than three notes, he repeated it over and over. His voice was surprisingly childlike, considering his bulk and the ugly, craggy face. But Mimi was a gentle giant. His mind was gone, lost somewhere on a battlefield thanks to a stray bullet that almost took his life. Instead it let him live and simply took all the meanness and pessimism that seemed to thrive in all other men and left him sweet but stupid. He had become her shadow, her protector, and she was thankful for that. He had saved her more than once now, and she would happily endure the irritation of his annoying little habits and endless silly songs in gratitude for that.

She straightened as Mimi grunted and gestured further down the beach. Céleste looked up, blinking as the frigid wind made her eyes water.

"I don't know?" she replied, looking at the large dark shapes laid out on the shingle. They walked a little closer until the image arranged itself into shapes her mind could recognise. *"Mon Dieu!* They are men," she cried and moved to run towards them. Mimi stopped, dropping his clutch of drift wood and it clattered to the ground. His large hand grasped her arm and he shook his head, his eyes fierce.

"Let me go!" she said, her voice firm. "I won't let men die if I can help them." She had seen enough death in her short life. Death from war, from violence, from poverty, from filth, illness, starvation and old age. No matter how many times she saw it, it was ugly and to be fought at all costs. She shook her arm from his grasp and ran to them. Turning the first, her heart grew heavy. Certainly dead, drowned last night, and by the stillness of the three others they were all beyond saving. She looked around and saw other shapes among the corpses. Barrels and boxes wrapped in oil cloth. A wreck. They must have run afoul of the storm last night, the poor bastards. Smugglers most likely, the English were always here, stocking their boats with brandy and gin, tea and silk and lace. All of it a fraction of the price without the heavy taxes the English Prince Regent levied. Well, it would do them no good now but ... It was an ill wind.

"Mimi, see all the boxes and barrels?"

Mimi nodded, his slow eyes scanning the beach.

"They're ours now, our secret. We must get them hidden as fast as we may. Can you do that? Can you be clever and fast, *mon brave?*"

Mimi beamed at her and nodded.

"Alors, off you go then."

With a heavy but practical heart, Céleste began to search each of the bodies in turn, checking pockets for money or gold. She left anything personal but took what she could that might keep the cold out and her belly full for a little longer. They'd be robbed soon enough of boots and anything else when the scavengers found them. She'd been lucky to get here first.

She was methodical, checking each body in turn with quick fingers. The farthest away was a fair distance up the beach and she ran, her feet slipping on the shale, aware that they could be discovered at any time and their plunder taken from them. Turning, she noted with satisfaction that Mimi had done well clearing the beach and disguising their haul under the hull of a ruined boat. It would do for now. They'd have to come back when it was dark and find a better hiding place until it could be sold.

Turning her attention to the last body she struggled to turn him over. He'd been a huge man. Heavy broad shoulders and long, long legs, he would have towered over her. She gasped as he finally rolled onto his back and looked in sorrow at the still face. My, he'd been a handsome one, she'd bet he'd been a scoundrel with the women in life with a face like that. Carefully she pushed the thick dark hair from his face and leapt back with a squeal as he murmured and his eyelids flickered.

"Mon Dieu," she whispered. "You do have the luck of the devil, smuggler." She looked up to see Mimi walking back towards her and gestured for him to hurry. "He's alive!" she called. "Quick, we must get him indoors and out of the cold before he freezes to death."

This was easier said than done. Big as he was, Mimi struggled with the dead weight, dragging him by increments, and it was a blessing when the man came around, though he seemed not to know what had happened.

"Bessie?" he mumbled as Céleste patted his hand. *"Non,* not Bessie," she said with care, her English was excellent, or so she'd been told, but she hadn't practised it since her mother died. "I am Céleste, and you are very 'eavy. Please, you must help us and walk."

The man did his best to oblige and leaned on Mimi, putting one foot in front of the other with effort until they reached the door of Madame Maxime's. At least the whores would all be abed at this early hour of the morning. They might just make it up to the attic if they took care. She turned to the man and his eyes flickered open, trying to focus on her. Flinty grey, they spoke of a determined soul and for that she was glad. He was half drowned and frozen, his teeth chattering fiercely now. He'd have a fight to recover his strength.

"You must be quiet. *Silence,*" she whispered, putting her finger to her lips.

He nodded his understanding and they began the arduous journey up the stairs to the cramped attic where she slept.

Mimi had just pushed him through the door to her room when Madame Maxime herself stuck her head out of the door on the landing below.

"What the devil are you doing, you stupid girl? Some of us have been working all night. Have you lit the fires?"

"Oui, Madame, I have. I'm sorry to have disturbed you. I tripped on the stair."

The door slammed shut without another word and Céleste breathed a sigh of relief. Up all night working, *bah,* she thought to herself, scowling. The other girls had been working perhaps, for work it indeed seemed to be with some of the disgusting characters that passed through Maxime's door. But the Madame herself would simply *arrange* and swallow enough brandy to keep her sour temper sweetened for the benefit of her paying customers.

Céleste scurried up the narrow, curving stairway to her attic room, where Mimi had laid the smuggler down on her pallet bed. Everything seemed even more cramped than usual with the two big men taking up all the available space, and she squeezed past Mimi and ducked the rafters as she moved around to the thin, straw-filled *palliasse* that served as her bed.

"We must get these wet clothes off him," she said, reaching forward to get started and yelping as Mimi smacked her hand away. *"Merde!"* she exclaimed, rubbing her stinging knuckles, and then began to laugh at the mutinous look on Mimi's face. "Oh, Mimi." She giggled. "I've lived in a brothel for the last six months. I promise he has nothing I haven't seen before."

Though she began to rethink that particular statement once Mimi relented and they began to peel away his sodden clothes. She had seen plenty of men, and women, in various states of undress, and a bewildering array of positions, some that seemed undignified. It was hard to miss such sights in a house like this one, no matter how hard she'd tried, to begin with at least. By now she believed she was unshockable; there was nothing left in the world that could possibly surprise her. And yet her curiosity was piqued as the layers were stripped away to reveal a hard, muscular body, quite unlike those she'd seen up to this point.

His large frame on the mattress shivered, his skin puckered with goose-flesh and she reached for the dry scrap of coarse linen that served her as a towel.

"*Alors*, you go, Mimi," she said, rubbing the linen hard over the man's heavy arm, both to dry him and to warm him. "You need to fetch the bread from the *boulangerie* and get some water on to boil. If they don't get their breakfast, there'll be hell to pay. You must cover for me."

Mimi glowered at the unconscious figure and Céleste huffed. "Oh be reasonable, he's in no position to do me any harm, now is he?"

Mimi left, though clearly unhappy about it, and Céleste returned to the job at hand, relieved to be able to look her fill without an audience. She rubbed dry one muscular arm before moving onto this chest. His skin was smooth but marked in places with scars that spoke of a violent life. One was perhaps a bullet wound, high on his left shoulder. She paused for a moment to place her hand flat on his chest, feeling the reassuring thud of his heart, strong and steady under the heavy muscle and coarse hair on his chest. Forcing her attention back to the job at hand she moved to his feet and dried them, rubbing them with vigour to get the blood moving and carrying on up his legs. She ground to a halt as she came upon the sodden under drawers which clung to his massive frame. They would have to come off. With difficulty and much cursing, she finally managed to wrestle the damned things off and then swallowed as she turned back and looked at the naked man, sprawled on her bed.

"Mon Dieu," she whispered. He was perfection in masculine form and she couldn't help but take a moment to admire him, from this thick dark hair, square jaw, full mouth and the slight cleft in his chin. Her gaze drifted lower. She took in the impressive width of chest and shoulders, the sculpted belly and the intriguing trail of dark hair that led to his manhood. This she lingered on with interest, for she had been truthful in her words to Mimi, but she had never had the opportunity to see a man in repose, and so close. She bit her lip considering the things she had seen with the whores if he was this size before he was roused ...

He shivered again and she scolded herself forcefully, the poor devil would die of cold while she sat there staring at him like a fool. Chastened, she covered him as best she could with her only blanket and piled every scrap of clothing she possessed on top of that. Then she lit the tiny stove with what remained of her driftwood. Maxime allowed her the room and a meagre supply of food in return for working her fingers to the bone from dawn till late at night. But she had to provide her own fuel, and so collecting driftwood from the beach was always an early morning chore if she didn't want to shiver all night.

She coughed as the tiny space filled with smoke until the fire caught and the little chimney drew. With one last look at the handsome smuggler she sent a prayer to whatever cruel God seemed to look down on her and begged that he let the man live. She would work twice as hard, she would be very, very good, if only he would live.

Want more Emma?

If you enjoyed this book, please support this indie author and take a moment to leave a few words in a review. *Thank you!*

To be kept informed of special offers and free deals (which I do regularly) follow me on *https://www.bookbub.com/authors/emma-v-leech*

To find out more and to get news and sneak peeks of the first chapter of upcoming works, go to my website and sign up for the newsletter.
http://www.emmavleech.com/

Come and join the fans in my Facebook group for news, info and exciting discussion...

Emmas Book Club

Or Follow me here......

http://viewauthor.at/EmmaVLeechAmazon
Facebook
Instagram
Emma's Twitter page
TikTok

About Me!

I started this incredible journey way back in 2010 with The Key to Erebus but didn't summon the courage to hit publish until October 2012. For anyone who's done it, you'll know publishing your first title is a terribly scary thing! I still get butterflies on the morning a new title releases, but the terror has subsided at least. Now I just live in dread of the day my daughters are old enough to read them.

The horror! (On both sides I suspect.)

2017 marked the year that I made my first foray into Historical Romance and the world of the Regency Romance, and my word what a year! I was delighted by the response to this series and can't wait to add more titles. Paranormal Romance readers need not despair however as there is much more to come there too. Writing has become an addiction and as soon as one book is over I'm hugely excited to start the next so you can expect plenty more in the future.

As many of my works reflect I am greatly influenced by the beautiful French countryside in which I live. I've been here in the South West for the past twenty years though I was born and raised in

England. My three gorgeous girls are all bilingual and the youngest who is only six, is showing signs of following in my footsteps after producing *The Lonely Princess* all by herself.

I'm told book two is coming soon ...

She's keeping me on my toes, so I'd better get cracking!

KEEP READING TO DISCOVER MY OTHER BOOKS!

Other Works by Emma V. Leech

(For those of you who have read The French Fae Legend series, please remember that chronologically The Heart of Arima precedes The Dark Prince)

Rogues & Gentlemen

Rogues & Gentlemen Series

Girls Who Dare

Girls Who Dare Series

Daring Daughters

Daring Daughters Series

The Regency Romance Mysteries

The Regency Romance Mysteries Series

The French Vampire Legend

The French Vampire Legend Series

The French Fae Legend

The French Fae Legend Series

Stand Alone
The Book Lover (a paranormal novella)
The Girl is Not for Christmas (Regency Romance)

Audio Books

Don't have time to read but still need your romance fix? The wait is over…

By popular demand, get many of your favourite Emma V Leech Regency Romance books on audio as performed by the incomparable Philip Battley and Gerard Marzilli. Several titles available and more added each month!

Find them at your favourite audiobook retailer!

Girls Who Dare– The exciting new series from Emma V Leech, the multi-award-winning, Amazon Top 10 romance writer behind the Rogues & Gentlemen series.

Inside every wallflower is the beating heart of a lioness, a passionate individual willing to risk all for their dream, if only they can find the courage to begin. When these overlooked girls make a pact to change their lives, anything can happen.

Ten girls – Ten dares in a hat. Who will dare to risk it all?

To Dare a Duke

Girls Who Dare Book 1

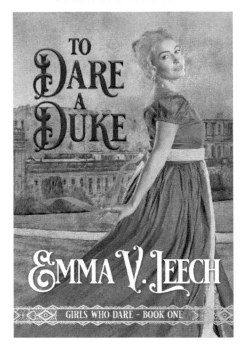

Dreams of true love and happy ever afters

Dreams of love are all well and good, but all Prunella Chuffington-Smythe wants is to publish her novel. Marriage at the price of her independence is something she will not consider. Having tasted success writing under a false name in The Lady's Weekly Review, her alter ego is attaining notoriety and fame and Prue rather likes it.

A Duty that must be endured

Robert Adolphus, The Duke of Bedwin, is in no hurry to marry, he's done it once and repeating that disaster is the last thing he desires. Yet, an heir is a necessary evil for a duke and one he cannot shirk. A dark reputation precedes him though, his first wife may have died young, but the scandals the beautiful, vivacious and spiteful creature supplied the ton have not. A wife must be found. A wife who is neither beautiful or vivacious but sweet and dull, and certain to stay out of trouble.

Dared to do something drastic

The sudden interest of a certain dastardly duke is as bewildering as it is unwelcome. She'll not throw her ambitions aside to marry a scoundrel just as her plans for self-sufficiency and freedom are coming to fruition. Surely showing the man she's not actually the meek little wallflower he is looking for should be enough to put paid to his intentions? When Prue is dared by her friends to do something drastic, it seems the perfect opportunity to kill two birds.

However, Prue cannot help being intrigued by the rogue who has inspired so many of her romances. Ordinarily, he plays the part of handsome rake, set on destroying her plucky heroine. But is he really the villain of the piece this time, or could he be the hero?

Finding out will be dangerous, but it just might inspire her greatest story yet.

To Dare a Duke

From the author of the bestselling Girls Who Dare Series – An exciting new series featuring the children of the Girls Who Dare...

The stories of the **Peculiar Ladies Book Club** and their hatful of dares has become legend among their children. When the hat is rediscovered, dusty and forlorn, the remaining dares spark a series of events that will echo through all the families... and their

Daring Daughters

Dare to be Wicked
Daring Daughters Book One

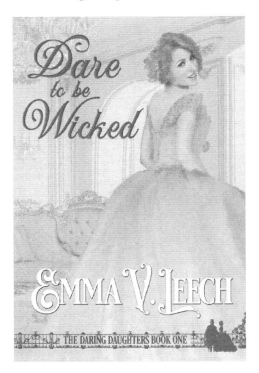

Two daring daughters ...

Lady Elizabeth and Lady Charlotte are the daughters of the Duke and Duchess of Bedwin. Raised by an unconventional mother and an indulgent, if overprotective father, they both strain against the rigid morality of the era.

The fashionable image of a meek, weak young lady, prone to swooning at the least provocation, is one that makes them seethe with frustration.

Their handsome childhood friend ...

Cassius Cadogen, Viscount Oakley, is the only child of the Earl and Countess St Clair. Beloved and indulged, he is popular, gloriously handsome, and a talented artist.

Returning from two years of study in France, his friendship with both sisters becomes strained as jealousy raises its head. A situation not helped by the two mysterious Frenchmen who have accompanied him home.

And simmering sibling rivalry ...

Passion, art, and secrets prove to be a combustible combination, and someone will undoubtedly get burned.

Order your copy here [Dare to be Wicked](#)

Interested in a Regency Romance with a twist?

Dying for a Duke

The Regency Romance Mysteries Book 1

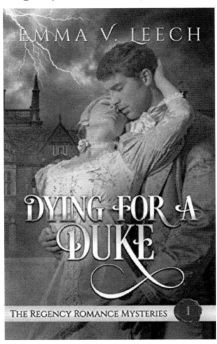

Straight-laced, imperious and morally rigid, Benedict Rutland - the darkly handsome Earl of Rothay - gained his title too young. Responsible for a large family of younger siblings that his frivolous parents have brought to bankruptcy, his youth was spent clawing back the family fortunes.

Now a man in his prime and financially secure he is betrothed to a strict, sensible and cool-headed woman who will never upset the balance of his life or disturb his emotions ...

But then Miss Skeffington-Fox arrives.

Brought up solely by her rake of a step-father, Benedict is scandalised by everything about the dashing Miss.

But as family members in line for the dukedom begin to die at an alarming rate, all fingers point at Benedict, and Miss Skeffington-Fox may be the only one who can save him.

FREE to read on Amazon Kindle Unlimited.. Dying for a Duke

Lose yourself in Emma's paranormal world with The French Vampire Legend series.

The Key to Erebus

The French Vampire Legend Book 1

The truth can kill you.

Taken away as a small child, from a life where vampires, the Fae, and other mythical creatures are real and treacherous, the beautiful young witch, Jéhenne Corbeaux is totally unprepared when she returns to rural France to live with her eccentric Grandmother.

Thrown headlong into a world she knows nothing about she seeks to learn the truth about herself, uncovering secrets more shocking than anything she could ever have imagined and finding that she is by no means powerless to protect the ones she loves.

Despite her Gran's dire warnings, she is inexorably drawn to the dark and terrifying figure of Corvus, an ancient vampire and master of the vast Albinus family.

Jéhenne is about to find her answers and discover that, not only is Corvus far more dangerous than she could ever imagine, but that he holds much more than the key to her heart ...

Now available at your favourite retailer

The Key to Erebus

Check out Emma's exciting fantasy series with hailed by Kirkus Reviews as "An enchanting fantasy with a likable heroine, romantic intrigue, and clever narrative flourishes."

The Dark Prince

The French Fae Legend Book 1

*Two Fae Princes
One Human Woman
And a world ready to tear them all apart*

Laen Braed is Prince of the Dark fae, with a temper and reputation to match his black eyes, and a heart that despises the human race. When he is sent back through the forbidden gates between realms to retrieve an ancient fae artifact, he returns home with far more than he bargained for.

Corin Albrecht, the most powerful Elven Prince ever born. His golden eyes are rumoured to be a gift from the gods, and destiny is calling him. With a love for the human world that runs deep, his friendship with Laen is being torn apart by his prejudices.

Océane DeBeauvoir is an artist and bookbinder who has always relied on her lively imagination to get her through an unhappy and uneventful life. A jewelled dagger put on display at a nearby museum hits the headlines with speculation of another race, the Fae. But the discovery also inspires Océane to create an extraordinary piece of art that cannot be confined to the pages of a book.

With two powerful men vying for her attention and their friendship stretched to the breaking point, the only question that remains...who is truly The Dark Prince.

The man of your dreams is coming...or is it your nightmares he visits? Find out in Book One of The French Fae Legend.

Available now at your favourite retailer

The Dark Prince

Acknowledgements

Thanks as always to my wonderful editor for being patient and loving my characters as much as I do. Gemma you're the best!

To Victoria Cooper for all your hard work, amazing artwork and above all your unending patience!!! Thank you so much. You are amazing!

To my BFF, PA, personal cheerleader and bringer of chocolate, Varsi Appel, for moral support, confidence boosting and for reading my work more times than I have. I love you loads!

A huge thank you to all of Emma's Book Club members! You guys are the best!

I'm always so happy to hear from you so do email or message me :)

emmavleech@orange.fr

To my husband Pat and my family ... For always being proud of me.

Can't get your fill of Historical Romance? Do you crave stories with passion and red hot chemistry?

If the answer is yes, have I got the group for you!

Come join myself and other awesome authors in our Facebook group

Historical Harlots

Be the first to know about exclusive giveaways, chat with amazing HistRom authors, lots of raunchy shenanigans and more!

Historical Harlots Facebook Group

Printed in Poland
by Amazon Fulfillment
Poland Sp. z o.o., Wrocław

34283259R00163